Yours,
Eventually

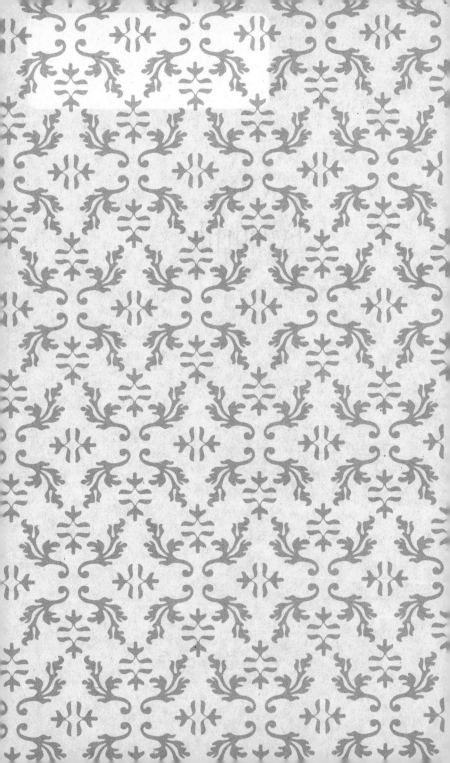

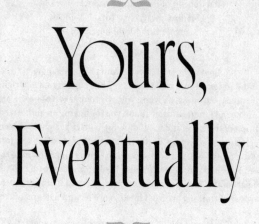

Yours, Eventually

A Novel

NURA MAZNAVI

DUTTON

DUTTON

An imprint of Penguin Random House LLC
1745 Broadway, New York, NY 10019
penguinrandomhouse.com

Copyright © 2025 by Fathima Nura Maznavi
Penguin Random House values and supports copyright. Copyright fuels
creativity, encourages diverse voices, promotes free speech, and
creates a vibrant culture. Thank you for buying an authorized
edition of this book and for complying with copyright laws by not
reproducing, scanning, or distributing any part of it in any form
without permission. You are supporting writers and allowing Penguin
Random House to continue to publish books for every reader. Please note
that no part of this book may be used or reproduced in any manner for the
purpose of training artificial intelligence technologies or systems.

DUTTON and the D colophon are registered trademarks
of Penguin Random House LLC.

Book design by Ashley Tucker

LIBRARY OF CONGRESS CATALOGING-IN-PUBLICATION DATA

Names: Maznavi, Nura, author.
Title: Yours, eventually: a novel / Nura Maznavi.
Description: New York: Dutton, 2025.
Identifiers: LCCN 2024030817 (print) | LCCN 2024030818 (ebook) |
ISBN 9780593475812 (paperback) | ISBN 9780593475829 (ebook)
Subjects: LCGFT: Romance fiction. | Novels.
Classification: LCC PS3613.A976 Y68 2025 (print) |
LCC PS3613.A976 (ebook) | DDC 813/.6—dc23/eng/20240806
LC record available at https://lccn.loc.gov/2024030817
LC ebook record available at https://lccn.loc.gov/2024030818

Printed in the United States of America

2 4 6 8 10 9 7 5 3 1

The authorized representative in the EU for product safety and compliance
is Penguin Random House Ireland, Morrison Chambers, 32 Nassau Street,
Dublin D02 YH68, Ireland, https://eu-contact.penguin.ie.

For Layla, Maliha, and Idris

Yours,
Eventually

ONE

The Qawwali singer hit the note, then held it. He sang for so long that the audience stopped breathing. Finally, he inhaled. Murmurs rose from the crowd, murmurs that turned into cheers as he started up again, this time accompanied by the twelve-piece ensemble sitting on the floor around him on a stage adorned with swaths of silver and gold fabric. On cue—or perhaps because of the enthusiasm of the musicians and the vibrato of the singer—the tiny white lights inside the lanterns strung from one end of the stage to the other began to flicker.

Asma barely noticed the lights. Or how the guests packed into the backyard of her family's Palo Alto Mc-Mansion had already lost interest in the musicians. They had turned their attention back to their plates piled high with fried appetizers swimming in pools of green and red chutney. Aunties gossiped about the latest engagements and other people's children while uncles debated foreign policy and conspiracy theories.

Asma couldn't take her eyes off her phone. Her older sister, Iman, had scheduled this party without checking the dates with her first, and Asma was on call for the hospital tonight. But instead of being an inconvenience, the prospect of being called away to work was a potential relief. Though she had grown up surrounded by this kind of money, and all the glitz, drama, and gossip that came with it, a night of accidental injuries and belligerent drunks in the emergency room was definitely more Asma's scene. She was bracing herself for intrusive questions from their guests. About her outfit, appearance, marital status—or lack thereof— and praying that she could escape to work before the onslaught.

Asma glanced up and saw her father's good friend and long-suffering accountant, Mr. Shafiq, weaving through the crowd toward her. He was dodging guests and buffet tables crowded with silver chafing dishes of meat. Lamb, beef, chicken, goat, fish—was that duck? There was much more food than they had agreed on in their meetings with the caterer. Iman must have gone back and increased the order.

"Qawwali singers? This is a retirement party, not a wedding!" Mr. Shafiq's usually slick and careful comb-over was tousled, and there was a deep crease between his eyebrows. He passed a crumpled napkin between his hands.

"Uncle, I had no idea this would be so over-the-top."

"Asma! You said you'd handle it!"

"I said I'd try! But have you ever known anyone who can rein in my father and Iman when they get going?"

"This won't do, this just won't do." The napkin in Mr. Shafiq's hand was in damp tatters. Asma gently pried it from his clenched fist and put her hand on his arm.

"Uncle, please go and eat. There's nothing more we can do about it tonight."

Asma pushed Mr. Shafiq in the direction of the buffet. She understood his low-simmering panic about her family's finances; she shared it, in fact. Her father, Muhammad Ibrahim, was in denial and still behaving as if his rug import business were at the height of its success, when really the family was teetering on the edge of financial ruin. It had recently come to light that Mr. Ibrahim had put most of the family's money in an investment fund that turned out to be a Ponzi scheme. He'd lost nearly everything, and his only recourse now was to shut down his business and sell off its remaining assets, a move he was trying to cover with his supposed "early retirement." Now, however, it seemed his lavish retirement party might bankrupt them yet.

"*What* are you wearing?"

Asma turned at the sound of her younger sister's voice. Maryam was standing behind her, arms crossed, a pointed look on her face.

Asma had been so convinced that she'd be called into work that she hadn't bothered to figure out an outfit until just minutes before the first guest arrived.

"What's wrong with what I'm wearing?"

Asma smoothed down the fabric of her beige salwar kameez. It had seemed fine when she put it on: it was the kind of understated outfit that demonstrated her lack of interest in the latest trends, because Asma had more important things to care about. But now, standing next to her younger sister, who was wearing a bright turquoise number custom-fit to her petite frame, Asma felt dowdy and decidedly out of fashion.

Maryam responded with an eye roll.

"Where's Iman?" Asma asked, glancing around the yard. "This is not what we discussed at all."

"I don't think it's too bad," Maryam said. "Except that cow Aunty Uzma was just asking me when I'm going to have more kids. I swear, if another aunty asks me if I have good news . . ." Maryam trailed off with a threatening shake of her head, her hair, recently cut into a sharp A-line bob, catching in her gold hoop earrings. "I don't know why she's bugging me when you and Iman aren't even married."

"She hasn't found me yet." Asma checked her phone again. Nothing. Could the ER really be that slow, tonight of all nights? "Or maybe she thinks I'm a lost cause."

"Especially in that outfit," Maryam said, attention already elsewhere. "*What* is Hassan wearing?"

Asma was relieved that Maryam's husband was now the focus of her fashion policing. Hassan stood across the yard, deep in conversation with a group of men. He wore a well-tailored charcoal suit, his hair covered in so much gel it looked as though he had just stepped out of the shower.

"Is that a trick question?" asked Asma.

"That's not the suit I laid out for him on the bed."

"You lay his clothes out for him?"

"I told him to wear his navy suit today because he needs to wear *this* suit tomorrow for his new headshots."

"He can just wear it again tomorrow."

Maryam looked at Asma like she'd suggested Hassan pose nude for the portrait. "You're joking, right?"

Maryam stalked off toward her husband, narrowly missing the caterer rolling an ice sculpture of their father toward the stage. The sculpture had already started to melt, water dripping down the nose as though it were running. Perhaps for the best, Asma thought—her father was terribly self-conscious about the size of his nose. Iman trailed the caterer, clutching the pallu of her silver chiffon sari, which had once belonged to their mother. Iman looked elegant and perfectly put together, as she always did. Her long hair was pulled back into a soft chignon at the nape of her neck and her sari draped perfectly, accentuating her figure, kept in shape thanks to hours upon hours of hot yoga. Though Maryam had been the first Ibrahim daughter to marry and have children, Iman was still the clear favorite for a good match, despite her being a year shy of the dreaded thirty. She'd nearly been engaged to the son of Mr. Ibrahim's financial advisor before the Ponzi scheme revelation had severed their relationship, and she was now a prime—if somewhat aged—marriage prospect for the men of their community.

"Have you seen Rehana Aunty? I'm so pissed." Iman searched the backyard for their aunt, her thick, meticulously shaped eyebrows narrowed into a frown.

"Iman," Asma said, ignoring her question. "Did you increase the catering order? I thought we agreed you'd stick to the budget."

"You worry too much," Iman replied. "It'll pay off in exposure. Like a business expense." In the past few years, Iman had become the premier event planner in their community, and their family functions were always her signature events. But now, Asma was beginning to fear that, like their father, neither of her sisters really believed the gravity of the family's financial situation, despite the accounting books and spreadsheets that Asma and Mr. Shafiq had gone over with them several times.

"Uncle Shafiq was very concerned," Asma said, but Iman was distracted, wrapped up in some kind of drama that was unfolding in their midst.

"You know how Rehana Aunty insisted I invite Aunty Saira because we were inviting Aunty Shaheen?" She didn't wait for a response. "Well, I said fine because I just could not deal with the drama, but I was very careful to make sure they knew that Aunty Saira's daughter wasn't invited. And yet . . . here she is."

Iman motioned to a group of young women a few

yards away, though Asma wasn't sure which woman was the specific target of Iman's ire. It was difficult for her to keep track of who was in or out of Iman's good graces, or the ever-evolving social dynamics that governed events like this.

"Does it matter?" Asma asked. "We have plenty of food and more than enough room."

"Of course it matters! That trick didn't invite me to her graduation party."

"That was five years ago, you need to let it go," Asma suggested, though she knew it was probably futile. As usual, the guest list for this event was less about gathering their closest family and friends than it was about payback: rewarding the loyalty of those who had invited the Ibrahims to their special occasions over the years and exacting revenge on those who hadn't.

"The nerve of her, standing there in the middle of all those aunties with her stupid fake smile—she's totally here to get rishtas, but nobody's going to marry her, she's such a skank." Iman glared at the women. "Remember that fat white guy she was hooking up with in college? I should ask her if they're still in touch!"

"Iman!" Asma admonished, but it was too late— Iman was already headed in their direction.

Asma wondered how much damage control she'd have to do with their guests after the party. Perhaps packing up what was sure to be tons of leftover meat for any offended parties would be a sufficient peace offering.

Asma felt her phone, tucked into her pocket, vibrate. Finally! A text from the hospital.

She read the message eagerly, hoping she was being summoned so she could leave. But, to her disappointment, it was just a question about a patient's medicine dosage that only required a text reply.

"Excuse me, excuse me, dear friends."

Mr. Ibrahim was standing on the stage, tapping the microphone. He was wearing a spotless cream sherwani that contrasted spectacularly with the mop of hair on his head, an unsubtle jet black that could only come from a box. He beamed at the guests and pulled his glasses down on his nose in a way Asma knew he thought looked professorial and made his nose look smaller. At the sound of his voice, the crowd filtered out from the house and across the backyard to congregate near the stage. Mr. Ibrahim waited until he held their undivided attention.

"My dear, honored guests. Thank you so much for joining me on this auspicious occasion." Mr. Ibrahim loved the limelight, the captive audience of all the important need-to-know people of the community. "I hope you've all had enough to eat."

Mr. Ibrahim gestured to the buffet stations and paused—a beat too long, thought Asma—until the guests had turned to admire the spread.

"When I started my company, I had no idea that it would grow to be such an esteemed, respected, and profitable enterprise. I have enjoyed the hard work of bringing our beautiful Pakistani carpets into the homes of so many."

Asma, who knew the truth, suppressed an eye roll: her father hated to work.

Mr. Ibrahim was used to a life of luxury and ample wealth. Born into a rich Pakistani family, he had immigrated to the United States almost thirty years earlier, bringing with him the capital to start an American branch of his family's rug export business. The company's wild success, and sterling reputation as an ethical business whose gorgeous, intricately designed, and handcrafted rugs were made from naturally sourced materials, had little to do with Mr. Ibrahim. It had all been thanks to the shrewd fiscal management and innate business instincts of the company's behind-the-scenes CFO, Mrs. Ibrahim.

Asma suppressed a grimace as Mr. Ibrahim took the credit for her mother's success in front of all these people. After Mrs. Ibrahim's death, when Asma was just fourteen, the company had coasted by for years on its early gains—that is, until Mr. Ibrahim decided to take its financial matters into his own hands. And all it took was one terrible investment, supported by a man he trusted like family, to bring it all down around them. But their guests knew nothing of the family's financial situation, or the fact that they were about to rent out this very McMansion to stay afloat; the crowd looked adoringly at Mr. Ibrahim as he gave his "retirement" speech.

"I'm looking forward to starting this new chapter of my life and spending more time with my family," Mr. Ibrahim continued. "But it's on occasions such as these that the absence of my beloved wife is felt most greatly." His voice broke slightly. "May Allah continue to shower his blessings on her."

Asma flinched at the mention of her mother while the crowd whispered ameens and InshAllahs. In the chaos of figuring out the details of the company's loss and decisions related to their finances, Asma had been careful to avoid thinking too much about her mother. What she would have thought about this premature retirement, renting out the house, moving—Asma's inability to keep things together. Asma saw her father's sister, Rehana, just offstage, draw the edge of her dupatta to her eye. Aunty must be thinking about her mother too. Rehana had moved to the U.S. over two decades earlier after the death of her husband, and she and Asma's mother had quickly become inseparable. Asma felt a kinship with Rehana at moments like these, when it seemed that Rehana still felt Mrs. Ibrahim's loss just as acutely as Asma did.

"She would've been so grateful. There are so many of you to thank. I start first with my dear sister, Rehana."

Rehana nodded with a strained smile.

"And my beautiful daughters. My eldest, Iman. She put this wonderful party together. Such taste, such vision. No expense spared."

Iman waved to the crowd like a beauty pageant contestant perched atop a convertible in a small-town parade.

"And of course Asma and Maryam. I think you all know my youngest, Maryam, is married to *Doctor* Hassan Qureishi." Mr. Ibrahim lingered on the word *doctor* for so long that no one would have guessed that Hassan was only a dentist. "Maryam's given me the best retirement present any man could ask for: two grandsons!"

The audience laughed. Maryam beamed at her father. Next to her, Hassan looked embarrassed. Their sons, at Iman's insistence, were out of sight, parked in the guest room with pizza and iPads.

"Thank you so much for coming!"

Mr. Ibrahim raised his water glass as if to toast. Rehana looked across the backyard at Asma, alarmed.

"Asma! Say something about Asma," Rehana hissed under her breath. What was supposed to be a whisper was picked up by the microphone and amplified across the backyard.

Asma felt herself flush, mortified. It wasn't unusual for her to feel invisible next to her sisters: Iman, the beauty, and Maryam, already married and a mother of two. She knew her father would have preferred her to be more like them, instead of studious and professionally driven. But it was another thing entirely to have it pointed out to her, especially in the middle of a party.

Part of her wanted to remind her father that she could have been married years before Maryam, if it weren't for his disapproval. She had to focus for a moment to swallow that old bitterness back.

"Oh, yes, Asma. My middle one," Mr. Ibrahim said with a big smile and a flourish of his hand in Asma's direction. "She's a doctor too!"

The guests looked around as Asma emerged from the shadows and forced a smile, the shreds of Mr. Shafiq's napkin falling to the ground from her hands.

ASMA WOLFED DOWN THE CAKE, A MINIATURE replica of a Persian rug. According to Iman, communal sheet cakes were *so out* and individual miniature sheet cakes were *so in*. Asma had protested the cost of the cakes and vowed that she wouldn't try any on principle, but now she was eating to hide her embarrassment. In the minutes after her father's gaffe, he had paraded her around the backyard, personally introducing her to all the guests.

"She works so hard, we never see her! You know she's always taken her studies so seriously!"

Asma needed no introduction to their friends. She was widely known as the glue that held the Ibrahim family together. The one who made sure the vendors were paid after Iman's lavish functions and the one who kept everything running smoothly during periods of transition, like Maryam's marriage and the birth of her twins. And while normally a family such as theirs—a wealthy, silly patriarch with two unmarried adult daughters— would be the subject of much derision in their social circles, the Ibrahims were largely immune. Asma knew it was because Mr. Ibrahim refused to remarry, despite the best attempts of family and friends. His loyalty to his dead wife earned him high respect from the aunties, who all lived with the suspicion that their own husbands, if given the opportunity, would remarry within days of their passing. And likely to much younger women.

Asma had managed to escape her father and tuck herself into a corner of the backyard to text her best friend, Fatima, and plot her exit. She'd fake a call from work and sit in the hospital parking lot all night if she had to. She was so focused on her phone that she hadn't noticed Rehana come up beside her.

"Asma beti, have you spoken to Uzma Aunty yet?"

"No, thank God," Asma replied, already wary of where this conversation might be leading.

"She wants to introduce you to her nephew—he's a doctor, a dermatologist. Strange specialty for a man." Rehana lowered her voice. "He went to medical school in the Caribbean so, you know . . ." Her aunt made a face like she smelled something unpleasant, the kind of expression Asma recognized from her father. While Mr. Ibrahim had grown somewhat stout in his advancing age, and sported deep shadows under his eyes, the family resemblance the siblings shared was always un-canny. Rehana, on the other hand, was aging gracefully, with only the barest strands of silver threading through her dark hair and a perfectly unlined forehead. Asma suspected Botox.

"Uzma, Uzma!" Rehana called out to a squat lady hovering around the buffet, before Asma could stop her. The only thing Aunty Uzma enjoyed more than talking about single women behind their backs was badgering them to their faces about their marital prospects.

Call now! Asma texted Fatima, then turned up her ringer.

"Aunty, it's the hospital," she said, waving her phone in the air when it rang less than a few seconds later. "I have to take this."

Asma grabbed another miniature cake off the tray of a passing waiter and took a bite before answering. She would never admit it to Iman, but these cakes were delicious.

"You're still at the party," Fatima said, because she and Asma never bothered with the formalities of hello.

"I'm stress eating," said Asma, her mouth full. "Just had a near miss with Aunty Uzma."

"She's the worst," said Fatima. "She told me that I should watch what I'm eating because it's making my face break out."

"How's the wedding?" Asma asked. "I can barely hear you." Fatima's voice was faint over the din of music and people talking loudly on both ends of the phone.

"Boring. Please stop me the next time I agree to go anywhere with my parents when Salman is working late."

"I can't believe I haven't been called into work yet," Asma replied. "If I'd known I'd actually have to stay here and make small talk, I would have dragged you here instead to keep me company."

"I've been following the hashtags on Instagram," said Fatima. "Iman did not come to play."

"I'll grab you a swag bag on my way out. In case you run out of gold-flecked lavender bath salts."

"So listen, before you go. I need to tell you something," said Fatima. "I just overheard some interesting information."

"Gossip?"

"Information. Gossip. Whatever." Fatima's voice dropped so low that Asma had to press her phone closer to her head and stick a finger in her open ear. "Don't freak out."

"I'm not going to freak out," said Asma. "When have I ever freaked out about goss—"

"It's about Farooq."

Asma swallowed hard, the cake she'd eaten forming into a rock in her stomach at the sound of her ex-fiancé's name.

"What? Farooq?" she repeated. It was the first time she'd said his name aloud in years, and it caught in her throat. She broke out into a sweat and wiped a damp palm on the side of her outfit, inadvertently smearing a blob of icing onto her clothes.

"These aunties were talking about him. They were saying that— Ammi, I'm on the phone."

Fatima interrupted herself before she could finish.

"They were saying what, Fatima?" Asma asked urgently.

"Asma, give me a second." Asma heard the phone muffle and Fatima greeting someone. "Salaam, Aunty. No, InshAllah soon. Please pray for us."

Asma felt like she might throw up. News about Farooq could only mean one thing. After all these years, the worst had finally happened. He was getting married.

Asma's phone beeped. The hospital, of course, right when she was in the middle of something else.

"Fatima, hold on," she said, though her friend was still talking to someone else on the other end of the line.

Asma could barely focus on what the nurse was saying but gathered that she needed to go in. But instead of relief at the out she'd been waiting for all evening, Asma only felt cold dread as she switched back to the other line.

"Fatima—I have to go. Quickly! Tell me what you were going to say about Far—" But she caught herself from saying his name out loud as Rehana and Uzma appeared next to her.

"Never mind, just text me!"

"What are you wearing?" Uzma took a critical look at Asma as she hung up the phone, her eyes resting on the icing stain on the side of Asma's outfit. Uzma turned to Rehana. "I told you that my sister sells the latest fashions at her shop in Fremont, she didn't have to wear such an old, stained suit."

"You know these girls," Rehana replied. "They all have their own styles."

"This isn't a style," Uzma said, wagging her finger at Asma's clothes.

"I'm sorry, Aunty, I've just been called into the hospital," Asma said. "Emergencies, you know?"

Asma mumbled goodbye salaams before either of the women could protest, then sprinted toward the house, too distracted to even be all that offended by Aunty Uzma.

The kitchen, ground zero for the party, was a disaster. Platters spilled out of the ovens lining the wall, chafing dishes were piled up on top of one another in the sink, and the doors of the fridge protruded open from the food stuffed in it. A pink liquid was oozing out of a foil container and dripping down the side of the island, forming a puddle and matching shoe prints on the kitchen floor. Asma cringed inwardly at the prospect of making sure the place was spotless before the real estate agent began showing it to potential renters.

Asma weaved through the tumult and slipped out the front door only to be greeted by an equally chaotic sight. Cars were parked every which way on their front lawn and in their driveway, which wound down the hill and around a huge marble fountain shooting water once again after years of drought-time disuse. She craned her neck and saw her reliable, beat-up black Camry parked near the garage door, pinned in by a row of cars.

"Excuse me." She waved over the young man working at the valet station. "That's mine."

As Asma waited for the valet to extricate her car, she pulled out her phone. No text yet from Fatima.

HELLO?!!! Asma typed.

Sorry! Aunties were hovering, Fatima replied a minute later.

So??? Asma stared impatiently at the typing bubble in Fatima's text window.

Farooq's startup just sold for half a BILLION dollars!

Fatima's text popped up on Asma's screen as she heard a huge, cracking explosion behind her. Asma yelled and grabbed her head, the sound so loud and close that she was convinced she had been hit by whatever exploded. More blasts followed, this time in rapid succession as bright flashes cut across the lawn. Asma dropped to the ground, her heart pounding in her ears along with the deafening bang of another, larger explosion.

After a moment, she peered up from the ground to see the sky above their house lit up with fireworks. Disoriented, she needed a moment for things to register. She vaguely remembered her father saying that he wanted a party with "all the fireworks." At the time, she had been amused at his misuse of the phrase *the works*. Clearly Iman had taken the request seriously.

TWO

The gash was on Mr. Shepard's chin but the blood was all over his face.

"I know it hurts, but keep applying pressure," Asma said.

Mr. Shepard's hand shook as he pressed the gauze to his chin, his pale blue eyes watering from the pain. "I'm trying."

Asma pulled the thin white curtain around Mr. Shepard's bed to cordon him off from the patient stretched out on the gurney in the adjacent examining room. She put her hand on his shoulder and carefully checked the rest of his face to make sure there were no more cuts.

Mr. Shepard, a widower who lived in Green Meadows, the retirement home next door to the hospital, had slipped in his bathroom and split open his chin.

Asma gently moved his hand and lifted up the gauze. The bleeding had stopped. As a nurse cleaned the blood off the rest of his face, Asma rolled a stool up to his bed, pulling open the suture kit the nurse had set up beside it.

"You'll feel a pinch, but squeeze my arm if it gets unbearable," said Asma, reaching for his face.

Mr. Shepard closed his eyes, grimacing as Asma began stitching.

"Do you have grandkids?" Asma asked to take his mind off the pain.

"One. Olivia." Mr. Shepard's eyes fluttered open as he said his granddaughter's name. "She wants to be a doctor."

"So she's smart?"

"Smarter than me," he replied.

Asma smiled. If her grandfathers had been alive, they'd be around his age, she thought. She had never known them. She had only warm, faded memories of her grandmothers from her childhood summer trips to Pakistan—the smell of perfumed powder lingering on her clothes after enveloping hugs with murmured duas, hands clutching sandalwood tasbeehs with green tassels. The trips slowed after her grandmothers' deaths, then ended completely after her mother died. But she thought of them often, especially now that Maryam had children of her own. Her father had come fully alive again after her nephews were born, almost a decade after his wife's death. Asma sometimes felt a dull pain when she saw her father with them—a stark reminder of the one who was missing, the grandmother her nephews would never know.

The intercom in the exam room buzzed.

"Dr. Ibrahim, Mrs. Martin is still complaining of pain." Asma could hear the early-nineties rock music the ER night nurses liked to listen to floating through the intercom.

"Double her dosage of acetaminophen and call in Dr. Marjan for a neuro consult."

"And the lab results for Mr. Nichols?"

"They should be in by now." Asma continued to talk to the nurse on the other end of the intercom without taking her eyes off Mr. Shepard's chin. "I'll review them when I wrap up here."

Asma leaned back in her stool and admired her handiwork. Five clean stitches so close together that they would likely not leave a noticeable scar.

"All done, Mr. Shepard. You did great."

Asma pulled off her gloves and glanced at her watch. It was after midnight. The few hours she'd been at the hospital had been so chaotic that sitting down to stitch up Mr. Shepard's face had been a welcome respite. Two car accidents, a five-year-old with an asthma attack, and a wedding ring stuck on the finger of a waterlogged pregnant woman. It was a typical, hectic night at the ER—the kind of environment in which she thrived. No time to think, only time to act. She had been about to return Fatima's call when Mr. Shepard arrived. Of course, now that the ER was finally quiet, it was too late.

She accompanied Mr. Shepard to discharge, then

slumped in a chair at an empty nurse's station. She pulled her phone out of her lab coat pocket. There were four missed calls from Maryam and two from Iman— no voicemail or texts, of course. Her sisters never left messages for her. They just called and called until she picked up, claiming she never answered their texts. "It's not email," Iman had complained. "You can't wait two days to respond!" They were probably calling to whine about something related to the party, the last thing Asma wanted to hear about now. Instead of calling either of them back, Asma reread Fatima's texts.

Farooq's tech company had been acquired for a staggering amount of money. According to Fatima, all of the aunties agreed—he was now the hottest bachelor on the market.

Asma let out a strangled sound, unsure whether she was on the verge of laughter or tears. Eight years. It had been eight years since Asma's family had persuaded her to break off her engagement to Farooq. And in those years, it seemed, everything had changed. Everything, except for Asma. Farooq had gone from a college dropout to a tech scion, and Asma was the same as she'd always been. Studious, driven, and still single, despite her family's wishes to have it otherwise.

"Someone die?" Jackson Wong, Asma's co-resident, removed his lab coat and plopped into the chair next to her. "You look like you're about to cry."

Asma slipped her phone back into her coat. "I'm tired, it's been a long night."

"Go home, dude. I'll cover for you."

"I can't do that."

"Come on, why don't you let someone else have a chance of being Dr. S's favorite, for a change?"

"I'm not her favorite," Asma replied, though she couldn't help the twitch of a smile at the corner of her mouth. Her attending physician, Dr. Saucedo, was brilliant, compassionate, and one of the most highly regarded doctors at the hospital. Asma was never sure what drew Dr. Saucedo to her. She hoped it was her attending's desire to mentor a promising student, or at least lower a ladder to another woman of color in a challenging field. Sometimes when she was feeling particularly self-conscious, Asma wondered if Dr. Saucedo had looked at her and seen to her core: a lonely, broken-hearted young woman in desperate need of a mother. But, whatever the reason, Dr. Saucedo had taken Asma under her wing during her intern year and now served as Asma's mentor and professional role model.

"Well, if you're not going anywhere, then cover for me." Jackson jumped to his feet and grabbed his coat. "I'm going to get a burger."

Asma waved him off, then pulled out her phone once he had disappeared down the hall. She glanced around to confirm that no one was watching before she googled Farooq. Asma had internet-stalked him for years after their breakup, but for a man working in tech, he'd done a remarkably good job of keeping himself off the internet—her searches had always turned up empty. Until now.

Farooq, it turned out, had been hard at work.

Asma's search was greeted with pages and pages of articles detailing Farooq's success. She skimmed the details of his company's product—a technology platform that would reshape delivery of medical services to rural populations. She felt herself choke up. He had done it. He had created what he had envisioned so many years ago. She scrolled quickly past his picture; even the quick glimpse of his eyes and smile set off a riot of competing feelings within her, though none louder than her regret. Regret that she'd been the good daughter and broken off their engagement. That she hadn't fought harder to make her family see Farooq's potential. Now everyone understood what she alone had seen back then. That he was brilliant, that any woman would be lucky to marry him.

She knew better than anyone that beneath the wealth and the success, there was kindness and compassion. The kind of person who had understood the deep pain she suffered in her life and would bring her flowers on her mother's birthday. He had a character that she hadn't been able to find in anyone before or since then. Not that she had tried. What would be the point? She had already met the love of her life, and he hadn't met her family's exceedingly high expectations. She couldn't risk that kind of heartbreak again.

Asma was reading an article about Farooq in the *Wall Street Journal* when she heard shouting and running in the hallway.

So much for the few minutes of quiet. She dried her eyes and straightened out her lab coat, heading—as she always did—toward whatever crisis was unfolding.

ASMA LAY ON HER BED IN THE FAMILY HOME, staring at the framed picture on her nightstand. It was of Asma and her mother, taken Halloween morning when Asma was in the third grade. She was wearing a white doctor's coat that skimmed the ground, the sleeves rolled up to her wrists covered in plastic friendship bracelets. Her mother had borrowed the coat and a stethoscope from a friend when Asma insisted that she wanted to dress up as a doctor.

It was one of the few pictures Asma had of her and her mom alone. The curse of the middle child—in all other family pictures she was either the baby in the shot or had a baby positioned next to her. Her mom's hand lay gently on the side of Asma's face, as Asma leaned into her, one arm wrapped around her leg. When she was growing up, everyone had always said that Asma resembled her father, likely because of their similar, darker complexion. But Asma knew that she looked like her mother. She had the same high cheekbones, strong sharp nose with a slight bump on the bridge, and wide-set eyes with faint bags underneath that were only accentuated with the sleeplessness of residency. She also had her mother's temperament. Calm and sensible, the rock to her more dramatic and flamboyant husband.

Asma always came back to this picture when she felt confused or lonely. How would her mother have helped her through this moment? She was the only one who would have understood. Her mother had also wanted to be a doctor, though she'd never spoken of it when she was alive. After her mother's death, Asma found out from Rehana that her grandparents had refused to send her mother to medical school, convinced that her economic salvation lay not in education but in marriage. And her marriage had been a happy one—full of affection and sometimes PDA, to the great embarrassment of their three daughters—in sharp contrast to the marriages Asma saw within their community. Mr. Ibrahim adored his wife and doted on her, and in return, she was his most loyal and devoted partner. It was only now, as a doctor herself, that Asma realized what a sacrifice her mother had made in forgoing a medical career to care for her family.

Her mother was still one of the smartest people Asma had ever known, as evidenced by her successful running of the family business from her husband's shadow. Asma's own success had always felt like a vindication of her mother's secret desire to be a doctor. She'd worked hard during medical school and residency, determined to live her life in a way that defied the decision foisted on her mother: to pursue a family over a career. That was the only way Asma had been able to justify breaking up with Farooq.

Asma heard a soft knock at the door, before it opened slightly and Rehana poked her head in.

"Are you packing?" she asked, glancing at the still-empty moving boxes that were stacked in the corner of the room.

"I'm going to get it all done this weekend," Asma said to her aunt, propping herself up on her elbow. Now that her father's retirement party was behind them, the real work of salvaging the family's finances had begun. And the first order of business was to rent out their Palo Alto house and move Mr. Ibrahim, Rehana, and Iman to Sacramento. It had been where the Ibrahims first moved upon their arrival in the United States and where Mrs. Ibrahim had insisted they purchase a home. They had lived there for a couple of years before moving to the Bay. They'd rented out the modest house in the nearby city for years—it was ironic that it would now become a haven for their little family, while their grand Palo Alto family home would become a much more lucrative rental property.

"The house has to be fit for showing by next week, Asma," Rehana chided, sitting down on Asma's bed. "I know this is difficult. But we all need to make sacrifices."

"Easy for you to say, you're not the one being forced to move in with Maryam," Asma countered, still resentful that Mr. Ibrahim had deemed it unacceptable for Asma to remain in the Bay if she didn't live with family. "Especially when I can afford to get an apartment of my own. At least until the end of residency."

"You cannot live on your own," Rehana replied, adopting the same tone as Asma's father, like her words were a grand edict that could not be argued. But Asma was an adult now, not a teenager asking to be allowed to go to a movie with her friends. Asma was long familiar with the faults in Rehana's judgment and no longer took her word as law.

"Why not?" Asma replied. "I lived away for four years at Berkeley."

"You were in school. This is different. It's not done."

"You mean, it hasn't been done. That doesn't mean I can't."

Asma knew as the words left her mouth that this was the wrong approach. Her aunt had no admiration for pioneers or trailblazers. Theirs was a family that honored the status quo, that held in highest regard those who fell in line without complaint.

Rehana shook her head. "You know how people talk."

As soon as Rehana uttered those words, Asma knew there was no way to win the argument. What people might say was her aunt's trump card, based on her belief that the wrong type of gossip would cause irreparable damage to their family's reputation and their social standing. More specifically, it would ruin the prospect of marriage for both Asma and Iman. As much as Iman's haughty materialism grated on Asma, she did not want to be responsible for her sister's spinsterhood. That was the problem: in a community that deemed marriage the ultimate goal for a young woman, what people said actually mattered. Couples were introduced to each other based on status rather than compatibility, and weddings were the marriage of families, not just individuals. Everyone in their community was kept in check by a social code, shackled by the fear of what people would say if they broke it. Everyone, including Asma.

"It's like it doesn't matter at all that I'm a doctor. As long as I'm not married, that's all anyone will care about."

"We're proud of you for becoming a doctor. But, beta, you're twenty-seven."

"I never said I didn't want to marry, Aunty. I just want to establish myself first," said Asma. "You and I both know, it's what Ammi would've wanted."

"I know nothing of the sort," Rehana replied.

Asma did a double take and felt a sharp sting of anger, so taken by surprise that she could only shake her head. Her aunt had said as much to her. At the end of Asma's sophomore year in college, when Farooq proposed.

Asma knew her father would be difficult to convince when it came to Farooq. After all, everyone knew the story of her cousin's fiancée, who had given up a Fulbright in music to join her cousin in dental school just so he would be considered a suitable match. Everyone

in their community knew that doctors married doctors, and dentists married dentists, and a man who had
dropped out of college after his freshman year was completely unsuitable for anyone. But Asma had counted
on Rehana to take her side, as she imagined her mother
would have, if she were still alive.

So it hit her like icy water when Rehana had joined
in Mr. Ibrahim's objections to the match.

"Not in college?" Rehana had asked, incredulous.

"He completed his first year," Asma had responded.
"But he doesn't need a degree for the type of work he's
doing." She told her father and aunt about Farooq's
business plan, convinced they would be impressed by his
innovation and how he'd so intentionally thought about
how he would support himself—and her—through his
job at the campus computer lab. Taking the steps necessary to turn his dream into a reality.

"Does he think he's Bill Gates?" Asma could still hear
her father's and Rehana's laughter. She regretted then
that she hadn't allowed Farooq to come and present his
case to her family himself, as he had wished. He would've
done a better job. Maybe then they would've seen what
she had.

Although perhaps she feared what she encountered.
That her family wouldn't think he was good enough.
That they would laugh in his face.

They could not be swayed, despite Asma's tears and
pleas. Farooq came from a no-name family. He had no
money, no education, and Asma would be forced to

support the two of them if they were married. What would people say, if they allowed Asma to marry someone like that?

"Your mother didn't have a choice when she married, Asma," Rehana had said, the memory so clear in Asma's mind it might have been a recording. "This is not what she would've wanted for you."

Those words were the primary reason Asma had finally broken things off with Farooq, even though she was also breaking her own heart at the same time. She couldn't stomach the idea that she might be marrying against her mother's wishes, and that weighed more heavily than any objections her father might have made. So Asma couldn't imagine how Rehana had possibly forgotten those words now.

"You told me," Asma said now, trying to keep her voice from shaking. "You told me that Ammi would have wanted me to choose my career."

But Rehana only shook her head.

"I meant, your mother would've wanted to see you settled," continued Rehana. "A suitable match."

"But that's not what you said," Asma replied, her eyes pricking with angry tears. "You told me that Ammi didn't have a choice, and that I did. And that she wouldn't have wanted me to choose marriage."

Asma felt the creep of panic, that she'd been stupid enough to listen all those years ago.

"You know," Rehana said, as if she hadn't heard

Asma, "Uzma said you never responded to her nephew's email."

Asma gritted her teeth. Unsure of everything now. Asma thought her mother wanted her to be a doctor instead of marrying young and potentially being thrown off course by the demands of a family. But now, if her aunt was admitting that those were not her mother's wishes after all, it would change everything.

"Asma?" Rehana said, clearly noting the change in Asma's disposition.

"Her nephew didn't email," Asma heard her voice rising. "He sent me a text that said 'hey.'"

"Well, that's something, isn't it? You've refused to meet anyone."

"Because of—" Asma stopped herself. There was no use, her aunt would never understand. "I was in college, then med school, and now I'm a resident," she said. "I haven't had time."

"And then you finish residency and join us in Sacramento and then what? There will always be something. Asma, beta, it will not get easier as you get older."

Asma knew that Rehana assumed her silence implied agreement. But as Rehana left the room and Asma settled back into her bed, anger made her resolve harden. Rehana had invoked Asma's dead mother once before to get her to do what she wanted, and it had cost Asma the love of her young life. She wasn't going to let it happen again.

THREE

A sma examined the box in front of her and mulled her options. A shriveled old-fashioned donut, a chocolate glazed marked with the fingerprints of someone who had changed their mind, and half a cherry-filled donut, the insides oozing out from either side of the knife used to cut it in half. None of them looked particularly appetizing, but Asma hadn't had the stomach for breakfast after her discussion with Rehana the previous evening, and she needed something to get her through this resident meeting.

Asma grabbed the old-fashioned, then pushed the box just out of reach. Her fellow residents were scattered around a large table in the hospital's executive conference room in various stages of attentiveness. A few fiddled with their phones and one appeared to be napping. Dr. Saucedo, sitting at the head of the table, was busy speaking to a nurse who had come in for a patient consult. No one except Asma seemed to be listening to Jackson drone on about a patient's stomach pains.

Asma swallowed a yawn and caught the eye of the resident sitting next to Jackson. The resident tilted her head subtly toward Jackson while mouthing *blah blah blah*.

Asma stifled a laugh with a huge bite of her donut. It was stale.

"He was in last week, too, with a high fever, which we know can be particularly dangerous in geriatric patients," Jackson continued with his patient summary. "He lives in a local nursing home, so I contacted his family, who live on the East Coast."

Despite her years in the ER, Asma was still struck each time an elderly patient came in unaccompanied by family. It was one of the times Asma felt most keenly the cultural divide between how she was raised and the reality for many of her patients. Asma couldn't imagine her father, or any of the aunties or uncles in her community, alone in a hospital. Mr. Ibrahim's every health issue was monitored by Asma, and that's how it would be for the rest of his life.

Mr. Ibrahim had sprained his foot playing tennis during Asma's freshman year in college and was under strict orders to not drive for the month it would take to heal. Asma had moved home—over Iman's protestations that she could handle things herself—to coordinate his care and make sure the rest of the household continued to function. If not for her, she was sure her father would've been late for all his physical therapy appointments, and Maryam late to school every morning, while Iman finished putting on her face.

Asma felt a pang of regret as she remembered her father hobbling around on his crutches, but it was soon overtaken by anger, rekindled after the recent news about Farooq. Not only had her father squandered her mother's success and their family's finances, but he'd forced her—with her aunt's help—to end her relationship with Farooq. As difficult as it was for her family to relocate to Sacramento under these circumstances, Asma was actually looking forward to having some distance from her father. And her aunt. Even if it meant living with Maryam and her theatrics until the end of her residency.

As the meeting came to a close and the residents gathered their things and began to leave, Asma turned to find Dr. Saucedo beside her.

"Mind if I talk to you for a moment?" the older woman asked, nodding toward the opposite end of the conference room, which was now empty of residents.

"Of course not," Asma said, following Dr. Saucedo until they were out of earshot of the stragglers.

"How's your job search going?" Dr. Saucedo asked, her voice slightly hushed.

"It's on pause. My family is moving to Sacramento— I'm staying with my sister until graduation but then it looks like I'll be moving there too," Asma replied. Dr.

Saucedo's mouth turned down at the corners, a small twitch of disappointment.

"That's a shame. I just got word that there might be an opening here, and I wanted to encourage you to apply. I could give you a hell of a recommendation."

Asma felt a simultaneous thrill and the deep pull of regret. She wanted nothing more than to keep working for Dr. Saucedo in the ER that had begun to feel like a second home to her. And to be singled out and mentored by someone as discerning as Dr. Saucedo was an honor. But as angry as Asma was with her family, she couldn't defy her father's edict that it was inappropriate for her to remain in the Bay without them. She felt guilty even thinking about it. Her father had supported her through college and med school; she wasn't sure she would have come this far without him.

But then she thought back to her conversation with Rehana. What about what Asma wanted? Did that ever matter? Did her father's financial support come with a lifetime of obligation? Hadn't she already sacrificed enough?

"Well, nothing's decided for sure yet." Asma shook her head to stop the memory from surging back and to stifle the anger and regret rising within her. "If there's an opportunity here, it would be silly for me not to at least apply."

"That's what I wanted to hear," Dr. Saucedo said, squeezing Asma's shoulder before following the rest of the residents out of the conference room.

ASMA WAS RUNNING TWENTY MINUTES LATE for her lunch with Fatima. They were attempting, once again, to find the new halal Mexican food truck. By the time they tracked it down through its Instagram stories the previous week, the truck had run out of carne asada. But when Asma arrived at Fatima's house to pick her up, she found her sitting at her dining room table, stacks of paper almost entirely covering the glass top.

"Fatima! Tacos!"

"I know, I know, I need ten minutes—I shouldn't have assigned a final paper."

Asma took a seat across from Fatima and glanced at the first paper in front of her.

"'I'd like to be an investigative reporter for ProPublica so I can expose how the government's war on terror hindered freedom of speech for American Muslims,'" she read, her eyes widening in admiration. "Intense! What was the writing prompt?"

"Write about your dream job," Fatima replied. "Mainly journalists and astrophysicists with a healthy dose of celebrity stylists and brand ambassadors."

"All noble professions."

"I got only one essay about wanting to be a doctor."

"At an Islamic school full of Desi and Arab kids?"

"I know, right? And that was so he could work in refugee camps."

"What a generational shift. Every kid I knew growing up wanted to be a doctor."

"Almost every kid," said Fatima with a rueful smile. Fatima had wanted to be an architect when she and Asma met in college, but instead had followed her mother into teaching.

"It's never too late," Asma said.

"Ha! Right," said Fatima.

"Actually, I wanted to ask you about something," Asma said, and then waited the requisite minute for Fatima to realize it was important and look up from the paper she was grading.

"Okay," Fatima said, folding her hands on the table in front of her. An armchair life coach, open for business.

"Do you think I made a mistake breaking up with Farooq back in college?" Asma asked.

Fatima had never met Farooq. She and Asma met at the beginning of their junior year, the summer after Asma had broken off the engagement. Asma had been sobbing in the bathroom outside the lecture hall where her first class of the semester was starting in minutes.

"You okay in there?" A gentle question accompanied by a gentle knock at the stall door.

"I just dumped my fiancé," Asma blurted out, mortified when she opened the door to find a girl with similar height and complexion, a lavender hijab wrapped around her head. *Just what I need*, Asma had thought, *a Desi Muslim woman to judge me.*

But Fatima turned out to be divinely sent. She was a compassionate and understanding confidante. She had blown off that first lecture to sit in the quad and listen as Asma narrated the past two years—to a stranger, the first and only person she had spoken to at length about her relationship with Farooq.

"Did you make a mistake because it turns out he's absolutely, insanely loaded now?" Fatima asked with a quick, inquiring smile. Trying to see if Asma was serious.

"No, not that," Asma said. "I mean, I always knew he'd do something brilliant. It's just, maybe I should have fought harder to convince my family that it was only a matter of time before he'd make something of himself. I believed in him, I really did. I was just so young and got turned around by my family."

Fatima sat back in her chair, crossing her arms, considering. She had a look on her face that said *This is serious business*.

"But it was about more than that, wasn't it? I thought you broke up with him because you knew your mother would have wanted you to focus on medical school, instead of getting sidetracked with marriage and kids, and all that?"

"That's what my aunt said my mom would have wanted."

"So that's a good reason," Fatima said. "And you've done it. You're a doctor, and you're amazing at it. Why are you second-guessing that now?"

"Because, it turns out, Rehana just told me that to convince me to break up with him," Asma said, feeling tears prick her eyes. "I don't even know if there was any truth to it. I have no idea what Ammi would have wanted for me. And now it's too late to change any of it."

"Oh, Asma," Fatima said, reaching forward and taking Asma's hand. "I didn't know you still thought about him."

"I don't think about him that often. Only every time I hear a sad song, or a love song, or see someone who looks like him, or someone mentions Berkeley, or—"

She stopped herself, feeling foolish for thinking so much about a heartbreak that was nearly a decade old. Fatima shook her head with a look of pity.

"Well, what if it's not too late after all?" Fatima said. "What if you talk to Farooq? Call him and explain."

"And say what? 'Hey, remember me, the chick who dumped you because my family thought you were a broke college dropout? They heard you're rich now, so never mind! Let's get back together!'"

"Or, 'I saw you in the news and realized I made a mistake all those years ago,'" Fatima countered.

"Fatima, his last words to me were literally 'I never want to see you again.'"

Asma could still feel the anger radiating off him as he sat next to her in her car. It was the second-worst moment of her life, and it had occurred in the parking lot of her dorm. She remembered thinking how awful it was even then, to have such an important conversation while drunk students stumbled by on the sidewalk across from them.

"I love you, Farooq. And I believe in you," she had cried, reaching out to hold his hand. "But my family can't get over that you're not in college. And I can't go against them."

He had yanked his hand back, out of her reach. "This is how you believe in me?" Asma could still hear the pain in his voice and see the betrayal on his face all these years later.

She winced remembering how he'd slammed the door when he got out of the car, how she'd jumped from the force of it, the sudden loud noise in the silence of the car's interior. And he'd made good on his promise to rid her from his life. After her explanatory emails and calls went unanswered, she had camped out at the computer lab to see if she could catch him before or after a shift. It was only then that she found out, from another student worker, that he had quit the job and moved home to Stockton to live with his parents.

"I'm the one who dumped him," Asma said. "I sat there and told him that my family didn't think he was good enough for me. Can you imagine how much that must have hurt him?"

Fatima drew back in sympathy, though Asma suspected the sympathy was more for Farooq than her.

"Still," Fatima said, "it's been eight years. That's a lot of time and distance. He could have realized that marrying young might not have been the best thing for either of you."

"If I reach out to him now, he's going to think I'm only interested in him now because he has money."

"I'll be happy to testify to the fact that you've regretted it since it happened and have been pining away for him ever since."

"I wouldn't say pining." Asma was indignant.

Fatima cocked an eyebrow. "You haven't had a single romantic interest since Farooq."

"I've been busy."

"You don't make time for a personal life."

It was the first time Fatima had ever called out Asma about this—and Asma didn't like it. "You sound like an aunty," she said.

Fatima mouthed *Wow.* "You're my best friend, so I'm going to let that one slide."

Fatima had come too close to the truth. Which was that Asma couldn't imagine letting someone else in, after the twin losses of her mother and Farooq. She couldn't imagine finding anyone who measured up to that first love, a relationship where she'd felt fully safe and seen. It was easier to close off her heart and to focus on her career. To throw her life and energy into something she could control.

"You made a mistake, Asma! Everyone should get a second chance." Fatima leaned across the table toward Asma. "Do you still love him?"

It was a question Asma had been avoiding for years

but had been mulling over since she first heard the news about Farooq.

"Honestly, I don't know. I did, so much. But then I spent so much time trying to move on with my life that I got good at being alone."

"You have to figure this out. At least for your own peace of mind. I mean, reach out to him—what's the worst that can happen?"

"It always makes me nervous when people say that," replied Asma. "That's the part in the movie where they cut to my mangled corpse in an alley."

Fatima rolled her eyes and air-stabbed Asma with her pen. Asma laughed and swatted Fatima with the essay she'd been reading about government surveillance just as she heard someone coming down the stairs.

It was Salman, Fatima's husband. The world's dullest man, who didn't deserve her best friend.

"Salman!" Asma called out, the guilt from her true thoughts about him making her greeting come out extra enthusiastically.

Salman flinched and dropped the box he was carrying.

"Sorry, didn't mean to startle you." Asma jumped to her feet as papers fluttered out of the box and through the railings of the staircase. "Haven't seen you for a while!"

Salman responded as he always did—politely. He nodded, then hurried down the stairs to bend awkwardly and help Asma pick up the papers.

Salman was short, bald, and chronically disheveled, the opposite of what Asma had always imagined a big law firm partner looked like. But he was brilliant and had risen through the ranks of his firm with lightning speed because of his technical background. He'd made partner in just six years, his firm doing everything they could to keep him from going to another.

"Big case, huh?" Asma asked as he shoved the papers back in his box.

"Yes."

"Anything you can talk about?"

Salman responded with an ambiguous grunt.

"What's that? Then you'll have to kill me?" Asma joked.

When Salman didn't respond, Asma gave up trying to make conversation. Despite her attempts, she had never been good at engaging Salman and was disappointed that, even after years of knowing him, she wasn't getting any better.

Asma looked at Fatima, who was ignoring them both, scribbling notes on a paper, her long curly hair spilling onto the table in front of her. Asma marveled at the mismatch of their relationship. Fatima, full of life and light, married to Salman, an old soul growing even more curmudgeonly as he aged. Fatima and Salman had been introduced by their families during Fatima's senior year in college and got engaged after a two-month courtship. Asma was convinced Fatima was settling and could do better—at least someone with some semblance of a personality. After one too many times of Asma asking, "Are you sure?" Fatima had responded with her characteristic good sense tinged with uncharacteristic irritation: "He's decent, has a stable job, and comes from a good family. I don't need to be swept off my feet, this isn't a movie." Asma had backed off. Fatima seemed content. And this was, in fact, how many of the young women in their community were married, although Asma's view of relationships had been forever altered by her romance with Farooq.

But Fatima had compromised a lot for Salman over the years, beginning when Fatima had wanted to pursue a career in architecture after college. Salman had been encouraging at first, promising they could relocate so she could pursue graduate school. And it seemed to work out perfectly when Fatima was accepted into Columbia—her first choice—as he could easily transfer to his firm's New York office. But when it came time for her to enroll, Salman was in the middle of a huge case and didn't want to bring up a transfer with his partners. Fatima deferred her enrollment for a year, but again, the timing wasn't right for Salman's career. It was then that Fatima realized the timing would never be right. She shelved the dream and accepted a position at her mother's school. Asma was outraged on her behalf but Fatima refused to talk about it. She was wary, Asma realized with dismay only much later, of Asma's judgment.

"I'll be home late, eating dinner at the office," Salman said, on his way out.

"Sorry," said Fatima as the garage door slammed closed behind him. "He's been in a mood. We went to see the fertility specialist last week and he's been acting weird ever since."

Weirder, thought Asma.

"How was the consultation?"

"The doctor seemed pretty optimistic about our chances."

Fatima and Salman had decided to start a family shortly after Salman made partner. After years of batting away questions from family and friends about when they would have a baby—*InshAllah* was an answer that appeased no one—Fatima now had to answer the prying questions with the knowledge that it wouldn't happen on its own. They had been trying for two years and it appeared as though their only option was IVF.

"She said we'll start everything during my spring break. I just have to get through these papers."

"Well then, let's get a move on," said Asma, rejoining Fatima at the table. She picked up another essay. "'When I grow up, I want to be a professional gamer.'" She looked at Fatima in confusion. "A professional gamer? Like sports?"

"No, like video games."

"Is that a thing?"

"Everything is a thing."

———

MARYAM, IMAN, AND REHANA WERE SITTING around the kitchen table gupshupping over tea when Asma got home. Around them, the kitchen was in chaos, with moving boxes sitting open and partially filled on every inch of counter space. Asma wasn't sure how they'd be ready to move out so soon, especially if her sisters and aunt took such frequent tea-and-gossip breaks.

"They are completely out of control," Maryam was saying as Asma walked in.

"Bushra lets them run wild," Rehana agreed, meeting Asma's eyes. Asma glanced away, pointedly. There had been palpable tension between her and her aunt since their conversation the previous night. Asma was angry and not ready to address any of the complicated feelings that the conversation, or her debrief with Fatima at lunch, had brought up.

"The boys?" Asma asked, taking the empty seat at the table.

"You think my boys are out of control?" asked Maryam, a mixture of surprise and indignation. While the answer was a resounding yes—Iman was still grumbling about how Maryam's sons had escaped from the guest room during their father's party and jumped into the pool—Iman shot Asma a look that had her backtracking immediately.

"Of course not!" Asma replied.

"We're talking about Lubna and Saba," said Iman, helpfully, if a moment too late.

Hassan's sisters had been favorite targets of gossip for the Ibrahim women ever since Hassan and Maryam were married. Maryam didn't approve of how late they stayed out with their friends, particularly when it left them unable to help her with early-morning babysitting. Rehana thought their total disregard for how they were perceived reflected badly on the entire extended family, including the Ibrahims. And Asma was pretty sure that Iman was just jealous that they were at the beginning—rather than the latter end—of their twenties.

But Asma found Hassan's sisters refreshing. At nineteen and twenty, they were confident and passionate—so completely unlike how Asma had been at that age. She couldn't imagine either of them allowing their family's objections to stop them from marrying a boy they were in love with.

"They are really developing a reputation. It won't be good when it comes time for them to marry," said Rehana. "Uzma said that Saba was seen in a bar a few weeks ago!"

"What was Uzma Aunty doing in a bar?" Asma asked, still avoiding Rehana's gaze but unable to avoid the subtle dig at Uzma.

Rehana wasn't amused. "It's not a joke, Asma."

"Saba was in a bar for her stand-up comedy, she's not drinking," Asma replied.

"Well, she shouldn't be in that environment at all. It's not appropriate," said Maryam.

"Especially because she wears hijab," Rehana added.

"What does that have to do with anything?" Asma asked.

"The optics are weird," Iman said. "But if you *are* going to hang out in a bar, do it on the DL. You don't have to share *everything*."

"Like Lubna, constantly taking pictures of herself and posting them online," added Maryam.

"Lubna is the worst kind of influencer," Iman said. "Selfies, outfits of the day—what is she promoting, other than herself?"

"Harsh words from someone who has benefited from her two hundred thousand followers," said Asma. "You didn't seem to mind when she gave you a shout-out for planning her friend's bridal shower last year."

"Which is why I won't call her out publicly," Iman said.

"How generous of you," said Asma. "I think it's great that they're doing what they want and aren't bothered by what any of you have to say."

"All you ambitious ladies," Maryam said in a tone that made it clear this was not a compliment. "You're in fearless pursuit of being the world's best ER doctor and they're on a ruthless path to achieve the most Instagram followers."

Iman snickered.

"It's a mutual lovefest," Maryam continued, buoyed by Iman's reaction.

"Ohhhh, Asma's so nice!" Iman said, imitating Lubna in a fake singsong voice.

"At least they like one of us," Asma retorted.

"Girls, enough!" Rehana said with a sharp look at Asma. "Asma, Bushra Aunty sent us some haleem, it's in the fridge."

Asma knew she was being dismissed but followed her aunt's instructions anyway—she always had room for Maryam's mother-in-law's cooking. She helped herself to a bowl of haleem and ignored Maryam and Iman, who were listing all things they'd done for Saba and Lubna, as though it were evidence that they, too, were well-liked by the girls.

Asma had finished her first bowl of haleem and was midway through her second when Mr. Ibrahim and Mr. Shafiq entered the kitchen with broad smiles.

Mr. Ibrahim announced the news. "Shafiq has found us a tenant!"

"He's famous," offered Mr. Shafiq.

"Yes, he's a well-known writer," added Mr. Ibrahim. "So they say. I've never heard of him. And I'm quite well-read." He pulled his glasses down his nose.

"I was introduced to him at a dawat last week," said Mr. Shafiq. "He's starting a teaching fellowship at Stanford next month and he and his wife are looking for a home nearby."

"A writer who is also a teacher," Mr. Ibrahim said with a shake of his head. "Who would have thought that someone like *that* would be able to afford a house like *this*?"

"Well, his last book *was* made into a big Hollywood movie," said Mr. Shafiq. "His name is Yusef Abdullah."

Asma felt the blood drain from her face at the sound of the name. Her spoon clattered onto the table.

Rehana looked at her with alarm. "Beti, are you okay? What's wrong?"

"I'm full." In fact, Asma suddenly felt nauseated.

"He's an African American. And Muslim," continued Mr. Shafiq. "His wife is Pakistani. Actually, I think her brother used to live around here."

"Can't be," said Mr. Ibrahim, "we've been in this neighborhood for years and I don't remember any other Pakistanis nearby."

"No, I'm sure he did. I used to run into him at jumma. Dr. . . . Dr. . . . umm, Dr. . . . ." Mr. Shafiq tapped his pen to his teeth, thinking. "I can see his face, I am just forgetting his name . . . Dr.—"

"Waheed." Asma could barely say the name.

"Ah yes, Dr. Waheed. He was an Islamic studies professor at Stanford."

"Oh. Yes, I think I remember him. You confused me by calling him a doctor," said Mr. Ibrahim. "A professor should be called a professor."

"And there was a younger brother too." Mr. Shafiq looked at Asma, who was staring down at her hands, willing herself to keep down the haleem. Why had she eaten two bowls? "Asma, do you remember his name?"

"Farooq," whispered Asma. Saying her ex's name in front of her entire family made her feel faint.

Rehana's head snapped up with recognition.

"Yes! Farooq. Farooq Waheed." Mr. Shafiq nodded enthusiastically.

"Why does that name sound so familiar?" asked Mr. Ibrahim.

"That's true, I've heard that name somewhere recently. From where?" asked Maryam.

Iman abandoned the group text on her phone, in pursuit of this much more interesting conversation occurring in real time. She looked at her father, then at Asma, then at her father again.

"Remember, Abu? Asma went to school with him," she said, her eyebrows raised in curiosity.

Asma felt her cheeks grow hot. Asma had kept her relationship with Farooq a secret from her family, which hadn't been such a difficult feat, considering they'd been at Berkeley. She had never spoken to her sisters about him—not even after the fact. Iman had been so wrapped up in her life, and they didn't have the type of relationship where they confided in each other about anything so intimate as romantic relationships. Maryam had been in high school at the time, too young. Asma didn't want to set a bad example, make her think that it was okay to date. And then when he proposed, it had been over so quickly with her father and Rehana that she'd never spoken of Farooq again. But it was clear Iman knew something based on her interest in this piece of news.

"Hmm, I don't remember that," said Mr. Ibrahim. "No, it's something else." Asma wasn't sure if she was surprised or not by the fact that her father didn't remember the name. Farooq had just been a gnat to swat away, an unfit suitor to be dismissed and then forgotten completely in pursuit of a worthier match.

It was Mr. Shafiq who piped in to supply the missing information.

"He was in the news recently. His startup was bought by Google. He's worth hundreds of millions."

"Oh, right!" Maryam said. "Lubna and Saba won't stop talking about him!"

Asma stood up and grabbed her bag where she'd dropped it by the door. She couldn't take another minute of this conversation. She left the kitchen, calling over her shoulder, "Don't wait for me for dinner. I'm going to bed soon. I have an early shift tomorrow."

As she darted up the stairs to her room, Asma could barely see straight. It had been years since she'd last seen or spoken to Farooq. And now, in the span of just a few weeks, the man who hadn't been good enough for her family had come crashing back into her life in the most unexpected ways. And his sister would soon be living in their house.

FOUR

⚜

The rolling green hills off the 280 freeway in San Mateo were a welcome, soothing respite from the mass of gray buildings that flanked the 101. Crystal Springs, a serene human-made reservoir, was tucked away at the bottom of the hills, a not-so-secret refuge for joggers and hikers eager to escape the bustle of city living. And for Asma, who'd decided that the only way to clear her head of the previous night's news was to exhaust herself in nature.

But still, even after an hour of hiking, Asma couldn't believe that Farooq's sister would be her family's new tenant. What were the chances?

Asma took a gulp from her water bottle as she reached the end of the trail. She made her way to a nearby bench and plopped down, out of breath from the hike and the gorgeous view of the reservoir.

The view made her think about the summer before her freshman year at Berkeley. She'd lied to her father so he would let her go on an orientation trip to Yosemite, telling him the trip was only for women on the premed track. She'd justified it at the time by reminding herself that she was about to be living on her own at school, away from her home and the rest of her family. She was about to be making all of her decisions on her own, without her father's permission. So what was the harm in diving into that world a bit early?

She'd noticed Farooq immediately when she arrived, loaded down with a backpack full of camping gear and flush with the idea of a fresh start. Brown, skinny, and tall—wearing a Berkeley sweatshirt, jeans, and sneakers—Farooq had a bright, lopsided grin that lit up his entire face as he introduced himself to the group. His eyes crinkled up at the sides when he and Asma made eye contact, his smile growing wider as she felt something pass between them. But she did her best to avoid him at first, wary that the aunty network might catch wind of her deception about the trip through this unknown boy. And also because a part of her wanted to blend in with the other teenagers, to not be set apart by immediately buddying up with the only other Muslim kid on the trip.

But on the first night, as their group sat around the campfire roasting hot dogs for dinner—Asma despairing at the sad hockey puck of a veggie burger that was the alternative option for the evening—she felt a tap on her shoulder. She turned to find the cute Muslim boy, still with a smile on his face. Without a word, he held up a pack of halal hot dogs.

It was a simple gesture. But in that moment, away from home for the first time, in the middle of the woods, with the light disappearing and a chill in the air and a bunch of strange teenagers for company, the sight of those hot dogs was so comforting she wanted to cry. And Farooq—that was his name, she learned, as they sat shoulder to shoulder, spearing their hot dogs with sticks and holding them over the campfire—felt like finding home, in that strange place. From then on, being with Farooq always felt to her like coming home.

Asma pulled out her phone, trying to shake off the memory. It wasn't yet six a.m.—too early to call anyone for a chat to clear her head. She considered hiking back—this wasn't the distraction she'd hoped it would be, not when all she could think about was him. But working at the hospital had taken it out of her, and even the thought of getting up to start the hike back was exhausting. She almost laughed at herself, now that she was nearly on the other side of residency. When she was in college, part of her never imagined she'd actually get here.

He did, though. Farooq seemed to never doubt it for a second.

They danced around each other that first semester, gravitating toward each other when they arrived on campus, simply because it was nice to already have a friend. They made up excuses to see each other—sharing books they thought the other would like and snacks pilfered from student group meetings—though they didn't have any of the same classes and lived in different dorms. They'd take trips to the halal restaurants near campus and drive out to the various state parks around the Bay Area, their hands brushing against each other as they explored new hiking trails. When his roommate insisted on practicing his trumpet in their dorm room, Asma was happy to have Farooq hang out in her room until they got the *all clear* text from his neighbor across the hall. He'd go with her to the indie and foreign movies her friends didn't want to see, sitting close to her, attentive, never complaining that most of them were romances.

And then there was the morning her organic chem grade was posted. Asma had been obsessed about the final for a month, unable to keep from fixating on it as the "make-or-break premed class," as she explained to Farooq over and over again. When he failed to coax her out of the library or her dorm for weeks at a time, Farooq started bringing her meals between his shifts at the computer lab. The day after the test, he'd driven her out to a remote hiking trail in the Santa Cruz Mountains and stood in the middle of nowhere with her, demanding she yell as loud as she could.

"I promise, it'll make you feel better," he said, when she laughed at the suggestion.

"I'm not going to just yell," she'd replied. "That's crazy. Someone will think you're trying to hurt me."

"There's nobody for miles," Farooq said, and then laughed when Asma gave him a horrified look. "Okay, so look, you've been under so much stress lately that your body thinks you're being chased by a wild animal or something. You have to find a way to let all that stress out."

"You're going to make fun of me," Asma said.

"I promise you," Farooq replied. "I will never make fun of you for this. Other things, sure. But the next thirty seconds, whatever you do, I'm not going to make fun of you for it."

"Thirty seconds?" Asma asked.

"I'll time you," Farooq said, pushing a button on his digital watch. The one Asma teased him made him look like a computer nerd, which was exactly what he was. "Go!"

Asma took a deep breath, then let out a little noise that immediately dissolved into laughter.

"You have to do better than that!" Farooq said.

"Okay, okay," Asma replied. She took another breath and looked up to the slice of sky between the trees above them. She closed her eyes, feeling the light breeze on her face and Farooq beside her. She thought about all the hours she'd studied for that final, all the sleepless nights, all the effort that was compressed down into that one hour-long test. She thought about her mother, who had also wanted to be a doctor, whose dreams were cut short—first by marriage and then by illness. And then Asma let out a yell so loud she was surprised she couldn't hear it echo off the nearby mountains.

"Excellent!" Farooq shouted, clapping. "Do you feel better?"

Asma considered. She felt a little dizzy, but lighter. Elated even.

"I do!" she replied, feeling a rush of relief. The test was over. Her future, whatever it would be, was momentarily out of her control. It felt great, actually.

"Well, you still have eight seconds if you want to do it again," Farooq replied.

But she didn't.

Instead, she stepped forward and kissed Farooq. He went still as she did, as if both of them knew she was crossing a line, and neither was sure if it was the right move. And then, as soon as he started to kiss her back, her body relaxing into the comfort of his and her face tingling where his hand touched her cheek, his digital watch began to beep. She stepped away, blushing furiously at what she'd just done.

"Okay, well, you're not allowed to make fun of me for that," Asma said, as he glanced down to silence the alarm.

Farooq looked at her with such tenderness that she grew warm from head to toe. "Never," he said, taking her hand and drawing her close. "I've wanted to do that since the day we first met." Asma understood immediately from the look on his face the depths of his feelings toward her; he didn't have to say anything else at all.

They didn't talk about the kiss after that, but the

next week, when the organic chem grade was posted, she found that she couldn't look at it. She made him finally click the link, sitting in her dorm in her pajamas, because she couldn't even get dressed until she knew how she'd done.

"Why aren't you saying anything?" she said, her hands over her face. "Because it's bad, right? Oh God, I knew I should've taken more practice exams. I just thought at the end that maybe I should get more sleep." Asma babbled on until she felt Farooq's arms around her. A startling feeling, at first, in the way she'd startled him with the kiss.

"You got a ninety-seven," he had said into her hair.

"What?" she said, feeling the tension in her go slack, until all her weight was resting against him. "Really?"

"I'm so proud of you," he said, his lips brushing against her ear.

It was the first time anyone other than her mother had said that to her.

Asma had told Fatima that she was unsure if she still loved Farooq. But his return had brought her feelings to the surface from where she had buried them all those years ago.

Of course she still loved him. She wasn't sure she could ever stop.

ASMA FLIPPED THROUGH AN OLD ISSUE OF A GOSSIP magazine, its well-worn pages ripped and dog-eared.

She was pretty sure the celebrities who were just like her—eating pizza! pumping gas!—didn't spend their only afternoon off work sitting in the waiting room of a doctor's office. She put the magazine down and checked her phone. It had been thirty minutes, much longer than it usually took for Mr. Ibrahim's exam. She couldn't help but worry.

Mr. Ibrahim had never been good about taking care of his health. When Asma was young, her mother had gently coaxed him to eat less and exercise more, his love for her the only motivation he had to take a walk each night after dinner. He had lost his appetite when she passed, dismissing his daughters' concerns over the years that he was losing weight and seemed depressed. His spirit had improved considerably when Rehana moved in with the family, although not his diet. Neither Mr. Ibrahim nor Rehana could understand the harm of eating fried food and meat for breakfast, lunch, and dinner. After all, they said, that was how generations of their family had eaten—ignoring that generations of their family had passed away from complications related to heart disease.

"Dr. Ibrahim?" The receptionist was holding open the waiting room door. "They're ready for you."

Asma had been taking her father to his doctors' appointments since she could drive—it was the only way he'd ever go. It had become a ritual of sorts but took on a new level of importance once she started medical school. Her father had almost entirely delegated his medical care to Asma, depending on her to schedule his appointments, order his medications, and review his test results.

"Dr. Ibrahim," said her father's physician, Dr. Razfar, rising to greet her with a firm handshake. "So nice to see you again."

Dr. Razfar was an internationally renowned cardiologist, whom Asma had tracked down at a medical conference after deciding that her father could do better than his general practitioner, an old friend of his who Asma believed should've retired at least a decade earlier. Dr. Razfar hadn't been accepting new patients, but Asma had managed to convince him to make an exception as a professional courtesy.

"The good news is that your father's cholesterol is responding well to the new statin. But I would like to see his blood pressure a bit lower. Have you been under any extra stress lately, Mr. Ibrahim?"

"Well . . ." Mr. Ibrahim began, but then he looked to Asma to step in.

"We're in the middle of moving to Sacramento," Asma replied, deciding this wasn't the time to mention the ruination of the family finances. "Getting the house ready to be rented. It's been a lot."

"Mitigating stress is very important, especially at your age," Dr. Razfar said to Mr. Ibrahim. "Make sure you don't overexert yourself. And I want you to get a blood pressure cuff and use it every day. Let your daughter here know what the numbers are. If they go up any higher, we'll adjust this new medication."

Dr. Razfar directed his comments at Mr. Ibrahim, who again looked at him blankly before turning to Asma. She nodded.

"I'm happy to continue seeing your father even after your move to Sacramento, or I can refer you to a colleague there. Whatever you prefer."

"Thank you, we'll find a way to make it work," Asma replied.

Mr. Ibrahim was unusually quiet on the walk to the car, brushing off Asma's concerned inquiries. "I'm just a bit tired today."

As Mr. Ibrahim slid into the passenger seat, Asma was startled to see gray hair near his temples. He must really not be feeling well if he'd neglected to do his roots.

Her worry only increased when he nodded off during the ride home. It wasn't like him to take an afternoon nap.

"I know you'll take good care of your father and your sisters."

Asma's mother's words came to her so suddenly and clearly that she whipped her head around to the back seat, half expecting to find her sitting there. She straightened around and took a deep breath, remembering the evening after the doctor told them that her mother's cancer was terminal. Asma had gone into her mother's room to check on her before going to bed. Her mother had clutched Asma's hand and whispered those words to her. Asma had taken them to heart, vowing to herself that she wouldn't let her down.

It was an enormous burden to put on a teenager. But who else was there? Her father had broken down at the diagnosis, unbridled emotion that made it impossible for him to even think about life without his beloved wife. Maryam had been a child, not yet a teen. And Iman? Asma had tried to talk to her, to see if they could handle things together. But Iman had shut her down—she was in denial and kept repeating that everything was going to be fine, that their mom would pull through. It was only Asma, just fourteen years old, who seemed to understand what was waiting for them. So Asma swallowed her fear and stepped up as her mother had hoped, her mission to keep her family upright the only thing that got her through those difficult years after her mother's passing, even if it was to the detriment of her own grief.

What would things have been like if her mother had never died? Asma thought about it often, unable to envision the trajectory of her life with someone else for them to all lean on. Would she be spending what little free time she had worrying about her family's finances and father's health? Or would she have had the peace of mind to focus solely on her career? Would she and Farooq be married, without Rehana's dictate that it was against her mother's wishes?

Asma's anger simmered into guilt. Her mother had never asked anyone for much. How afraid she must have been to leave her dependent husband alone. And how devastated she must have felt that she would not live to see her daughters grow into women.

Asma knew now that her mother had sought comfort the only way she knew how—to rely on the one person she thought could handle the responsibility of taking care of their family the way that she had. And for years Asma had tried to live up to that expectation.

But she was reaching the end of her rope.

FIVE

Asma wasn't planning on being home the day that Farooq's sister, Sophia, and her husband, Yusef, came by for a walk-through of their house. She still didn't know how she'd conduct herself around this woman who could've become her older sister through marriage. But despite her reminders to her father and Iman that the house needed to be cleaned—or at least presentable—before the showing, it was a wreck when she came home from work that morning. Everything was still partially packed, with moving boxes stacked in every corner and cabinets half emptied onto countertops. And, of course, Iman was nowhere to be found. Asma felt an old embarrassment—about her family, their garishness, their sloppiness, the ways in which they'd all coarsened since her mother died—at the thought of Farooq's family seeing the Ibrahims' carelessness.

There wasn't much she could do in the kitchen

besides clearing off the counters and shoving the stack of boxes into the farthest corner she could. She did her best to straighten up the dining and living rooms before heading upstairs. Asma particularly resented cleaning up after Iman in their former guest room turned Iman's home office, for which Iman had hired an outrageously expensive interior decorating firm. The room, filled with custom-built furniture and overpriced, mass-produced art, ended up just being a fancy storage space. Asma gathered dozens of gold tiaras strewn around the floor into a box with an equal number of small glass slippers. She then went to work on her father's office, piles of unopened magazines that he had subscribed to and never read covering the big mahogany desk she'd never seen him use. She was wiping down the counter in the upstairs hallway bathroom when she heard the doorbell ring.

"They're here!" Mr. Ibrahim called out.

Asma slipped down the stairs at the back of the house and out the patio door, shoving her bare feet into an old pair of sneakers that lived outside. Her father's booming salaam echoed through the house. Asma was intent on escaping before anyone saw her. But when she tried opening the side gate, it wouldn't budge. She shoved once, twice, to no avail. The garbage cans were blocking her exit, even after she'd told Iman and her father a million times that the gate swings out!

Asma took her frustration with her family out on the gate, pushing with all her might, managing to pry it open a few inches, just wide enough to squeeze one leg through. She kicked at the garbage can closest to her, but it was of no use—it wasn't budging.

"Asma?"

Mr. Ibrahim was standing by the side of the house accompanied by a young couple who could only be Sophia and Yusef.

Sophia's face was framed by a brilliant blue hijab that made her look regal, even though she was wearing jeans and a T-shirt. She had big brown eyes that crinkled at the side as she smiled at Asma—just like Farooq. The resemblance struck her immediately, a pang in her chest that made her draw in a quick breath.

Yusef was a handsome man with glasses and a huge grin that showed off his dimples. Asma thought he was better-looking in real life than he was on the YouTube clips she'd watched. Sophia's expression seemed pleased, perhaps a bit curious, to be meeting their new landlord's middle daughter. But her smile betrayed no hint of recognition, even though part of Asma was desperate for it. Asma had insisted that Farooq keep their relationship a secret from his family, as she had from hers. The Desi community was well connected and she didn't want their relationship to be fodder for gossip or—worse—to get back to Mr. Ibrahim.

Asma knew Farooq's family was different, which was why he had found it so difficult to understand hers. His parents had immigrated to the Central Valley from Pakistan shortly before Sophia was born. And while they were deeply religious, they exhibited an open-mindedness that was foreign to most of the families in Asma's upper-middle-class Pakistani community. Farooq's parents encouraged all their children to get an education, starting with their only daughter, Sophia, their eldest—even allowing her to move to the Bay Area for college. And when she brought home Yusef, a Black Muslim man born and raised in Chicago, whom she met in a freshman seminar, their blessing of the relationship made them outliers in their community. Such an interracial marriage—between a Pakistani woman and a Black man—was virtually unheard of at the time given that many Desi families harbored deep racial prejudices that they were perfectly comfortable revealing publicly when it came time for their children to marry.

Asma wanted to meet Sophia when she and Farooq were together, but they couldn't risk it. In Sophia she imagined an older sister who would have been more compassionate and attentive than Iman. Someone who might have noticed—and offered—some of the comforts Asma so missed from her mother. Or, at the very least, a friend. An ally in her relationship with Farooq. Asma never imagined she'd meet Sophia for the first time halfway stuck in the side gate of her yard by the trash cans.

"What are you doing?" Mr. Ibrahim asked Asma as she gave her salaams with an awkward wave.

"Taking out the trash."

"Trash day isn't until Wednesday." Mr. Ibrahim looked confused. "It's only Saturday."

"I didn't want it stacking up." Asma dislodged her leg from the gate as she spoke, losing a shoe in the process.

Asma stuck out her hand to Sophia, who, God bless her, pretended not to notice that Asma was standing before her with one bare foot.

"We can't wait to see the house," Sophia said. "The pictures Uncle Shafiq showed us were beautiful."

Asma had worried that their gaudy home with its intricate columns, excessive use of marble, and mirrors in inappropriate places would be a turnoff, but apparently it photographed well.

"We're so lucky we met him," said Yusef. "This rental market is absurdly tight."

"No thanks to all the tech bros." Sophia smiled warmly at Asma. "Asma, your dad told us you're a doctor. And that you went to school with my brother!"

"I did, yeah." Asma kept her expression neutral, using the poker face she had perfected over years of giving patients difficult diagnoses.

"It's too bad you two won't have time to do any catching up. It turns out he's moving back east with his fiancée. We'd been hoping that they would settle here after the wedding, but it looks like it wasn't meant to be."

"I didn't realize he was engaged." Asma surprised herself by how measured her voice sounded. Of course, the minute Asma admitted to herself that she still had feelings for Farooq, she'd find out he was getting married. She swallowed hard, her mouth going dry. She felt like her legs might be shaking.

"Just this past year. Her name is Seema. She's so lovely. A doctor, like you!"

A doctor. Farooq was marrying a doctor. Asma leaned on the gate to steady herself.

"A doctor! MashAllah!" said Mr. Ibrahim. Mr. Ibrahim had apparently forgotten the insurmountable impropriety of a college dropout marrying a doctor. Fame- and wealth-induced amnesia, Asma assumed.

Mr. Ibrahim checked his watch. "Shafiq will be here any minute, let me show you the house."

"I'll catch you all inside," Asma said.

Asma collapsed against the gate the minute they were out of sight. Her eyes filled with tears that she angrily brushed away. It felt like a cruel joke, like everything that had happened in the past few weeks—Farooq's company being in the news, her conversation with Rehana, the fact that Farooq's sister was renting their house—had conspired to make this news even more difficult to bear. Now, after spending days thinking about Farooq, replaying their relationship in her mind, second-guessing her decision to break off their engagement . . . now it brought with it a wave of pain and regret that made her think of all the time she'd spent mourning their breakup.

But no. Asma refused to go back to that kind of desolation. She straightened up and wiped her eyes, sniffling. She was a doctor now too. She had a life that anyone would be proud of. And she'd been the one to break off her engagement to Farooq. It was childish of her to expect him to stay single forever. All she could do now was move forward.

Except she couldn't. Not until she found her damn shoe.

Asma peered through the gate and saw the sneaker on the grass next to the trash can. She stretched her leg back through the opening, but it was too far out of reach. She looked around to see if there was a rake or other garden tool she could use to drag it closer, but seeing none, she got down on her stomach and stretched out her hand. Her fingers managed to grab hold of one of the laces and she dragged the shoe back through the gate, scraping her arm in the process.

"Ow!" she yelled, struggling to her feet.

For a tiny scratch there was a surprising amount of blood. Asma hopped on one foot and threw her arm in her mouth to stem the bleeding. So much for her plan to escape unnoticed. She would have to go back inside to clean up her arm.

She turned, still on one leg, and froze.

There, standing just a few feet away and staring straight at her, was Farooq.

At first, she thought she might be hallucinating. There were cases, weren't there? Hallucinations brought on by stress? After all, it wasn't possible that she'd spent the past few days thinking of little but him and had somehow conjured him as a result.

But then his eyes met hers. And time stopped—along with Asma's breathing. There it was, that electric recognition that had existed between them from the moment their eyes met during that freshman orientation trip in college. Like kindred spirits, he once said. It was a feeling she hadn't experienced since the last time she saw him, and it was that feeling that made her recognize that this was, indeed, reality. Her body went numb. How long had he been watching her?

"I had to get my shoe."

It was the first thing that popped into her head, as she struggled to catch her breath. Then she watched as her hand, seemingly of its own volition, held out the shoe to him as evidence.

Farooq looked from Asma to the shoe. There was blood on the toe.

"I should go get cleaned up," Asma said when she couldn't take the silence any longer. She bent to try to get her shoe back on, but the rush of adrenaline that accompanied Farooq's presence in her backyard left her so shaky that she couldn't manage it.

"Asma—" He stepped forward when she nearly toppled over, as if preparing to grab her if she fell. And she jerked away from him, a reflex so quick it seemed to startle them both.

Their eyes locked once more. He looked almost the same as he had in college: the same deep brown skin, large expressive eyes, and strong cheekbones, now with a shadow of stubble. He was wearing a black T-shirt just fitted enough for Asma to notice how he'd filled out—the outline of his shoulders, his chest, those biceps—she glanced away quickly, hit with a wave of heat that made her empathize with her menopausal patients experiencing hot flashes. Farooq, memorialized in Asma's mind as a scrawny college boy dressed in jeans, a Cal hoodie, and scruffy Chucks, had morphed into an exceptionally fit and handsome man.

God, she'd missed him. And then she remembered. The fiancée. The doctor.

"Congratulations, by the way," she said, before turning and rushing toward the house. Walking on her one bare foot, too embarrassed to remain in Farooq's presence for one more second in this state.

She nearly crashed through the back door into the kitchen and went right to the sink, turning the water on full blast and splashing some on her face before she rinsed the blood off her arm. She was just stanching the bleeding with a paper towel when she heard a voice behind her.

"There you are!" It was Sophia, coming into the kitchen from the dining room. But Sophia wasn't talking to her. When Asma turned, she found Farooq standing just inside the back door. In her house.

"I was worried you got lost," Sophia continued.

"Nope, my phone has GPS too, Soph," Farooq replied, and his voice, although deeper and more confident than Asma remembered, sent a shudder of recognition through her.

"Asma," Sophia said, turning toward her, "this is my brother Farooq."

"Right, yeah. We went to college together," Asma said, her voice sounding far away. Hadn't she and Sophia just had this conversation? Maybe this was all just a terrible dream.

"Oh! I thought you meant my brother Haroon!" Sophia said. "It all makes sense now. Of course, you'd be too young to be in Haroon's class, how silly of me. So you know our tech bro—the reason we have to rent in the first place."

Farooq flushed, looking everywhere but at Asma.

"So have you two been catching up?" Sophia asked.

"No," Farooq said, quickly. "To be honest, it's been so long, I didn't even recognize her."

Ouch. Asma couldn't slow down the whirlwind of thoughts that were rushing through her. And with them, a small bit of hope. At least Sophia's misunderstanding meant there was no fiancée. No other doctor.

"So I guess I shouldn't have congratulated you on your engagement," Asma said, fishing, though Farooq still wouldn't look at her.

"Right, right," Sophia said, stepping in. "Sorry, it's Haroon who's engaged. This one is just dating an Arab supermodel."

And just like that, the hope rushed right back out of Asma.

"Sophia!" Farooq hissed at his sister, appalled.

"I'm kidding, I'm kidding," Sophia said. "I like to tease him about this hilarious internet rumor that a Desi startup guy is dating an Arab supermodel. Everyone thinks it's him!" Sophia gave Farooq a friendly jab to the shoulder. "Although maybe dating a supermodel would help you relax a bit."

"Seriously?" Farooq reddened even more as Sophia laughed. Asma tried to smile but her mouth wouldn't widen past what she could only imagine was a grimace. Still, the playfulness between the siblings and the fact that Farooq wasn't engaged had brought some of the feeling back into Asma's body.

"Now that I'm done embarrassing you, would you mind coming with me?" Sophia asked. "I want to show you the room that could work as my art studio." Sophi grabbed Farooq's arm. "We'll see you in a bit, Asm

"Sure thing."

Asma caught Farooq's eye once more and her breath. He turned abruptly. She slipped her not on, considering running out the back d arooq stopping until she hit New York, as Soph disappeared farther into the house.

SIX

A bu, I'm ready!"

Asma stood outside her father's bedroom, jangling her keys. Iman and her dad were moving at the end of the week, now that Sophia and Yusef had signed the lease on their house, but there was still so much to do. Asma relished the frenetic pace, adding things with pleasure to her to-do list. She would much rather label boxes than dwell on her cringeworthy run-in with oq.

ey had run out of empty moving boxes the previ-
ing, and Mr. Ibrahim and Iman's packing had
grinding halt.

Iman again why we didn't hire people for this,"
"B s a question than a complaint.
"Ne can pack ourselves," said Asma.
"We ar wing we *can't*, Asma," Iman retorted.
"I thi don't want to."
"We ca ll find someone," said Mr. Ibrahim.
ne," Asma replied, with a pointed

look at Iman. "But we're not going to. Movers are expensive, and unnecessary expenses are what got us into this mess in the first place."

Under normal circumstances, Asma would've roped in Aunty Rehana to help with packing or at least to wrangle her father and sister. But Rehana had left that morning for an extended trip to Pakistan, one she had announced to the family at the very last minute. Asma wondered if her sudden departure had anything to do with the tension between the two of them since their conversation in Asma's room. Asma couldn't quell the anger she'd been feeling toward her aunt since Farooq's reappearance and had been doing her best to avoid her. Or perhaps Rehana simply wanted to escape the chaos of the Ibrahim relocation. If it was that, Asma couldn't blame her.

"Come in, beta!" Mr. Ibrahim called from inside, voice muffled. "I need a few minutes."

Asma followed her father's voice into his room. "Abu, we don't have time, I am working tonight, we have to leave—"

Asma stopped at the sight of her father, sitting on the floor of his palatial walk-in closet with an open box in front of him—the box of her mother's old saris. Asma recognized the box immediately. The last time she'd seen it had been well into her mother's treatment, the afternoon when Rehana and Mrs. Ibrahim had carefully folded and packed up her clothes, unaware that Asma was sitting on the floor outside the room and watching through a crack in the door. Rehana had urged Mrs. Ibrahim to rest, but Mrs. Ibrahim—the little hair she had remaining covered by a soft cotton dupatta—would not take a nap until her saris were put away. "I don't want the girls to have to do any of this when I'm gone," she had said. Asma had taken the gesture at face value—it was only now, seeing the look on her father's face and feeling a lump grow in her throat, that Asma understood her mother's wisdom in removing the things that would remind them of her.

"I thought this box had my old ties, but instead I found some of your mother's clothes. She wore this one to the grand opening of our showroom." Mr. Ibrahim held up a red silk sari. "It was a beautiful afternoon, such a classy affair. She didn't want to have a big gathering, but I insisted. And she supported me. She always supported me. I had such great success because of her."

Asma's frustration with her father dissipated. She felt taken off guard by his tenderness. He had never acknowledged her mother's business contributions before.

"Abu, are you okay?" Asma remembered her father's nap in the car on the way back from the doctor. Was this nostalgia motivated by a premonition?

"Moving is hard. Especially from a place with so many memories."

Asma felt growing compassion for her father as she saw him carefully fold the sari and place it back in the box. Her father rarely spoke about her mother. There was much she didn't know about their relationship and so much she had forgotten over the years. Asma never knew how to bring her up with him, so she hadn't.

But their moment was over.

"Abu! Abu!" Iman stuck her head into the closet and looked from her father to Asma. "What are you guys talking about?"

"Nothing," said Asma, her tone betraying her irritation at being interrupted. Besides the car rides to and from her father's doctors' appointments, it was rare for Asma to find herself alone with him, and she was surprised by how much their conversation had meant.

"We're packing up your mother's old saris," Mr. Ibrahim said.

Iman looked from Mr. Ibrahim to Asma again. A look crossed her face that Asma couldn't read before Iman glanced down at the box. "Oh good, you have it out—I was just coming to return this."

Iman tossed the sari she had worn at their father's retirement party into the open box. "Can't wear that again."

"Why, what did you do to it?" asked Asma.

"Nothing! But I was wearing it in the picture I gave to Aunty Uzma. It's a good picture, my hair looks perfect."

"Picture as in a rishta picture? You *gave* one to Aunty Uzma?"

"It's for her book."

"What book?"

"Her matchmaking book! The one of the most

eligible people in the area. I can't imagine what the men are like in Sacramento . . . and I don't want to miss out on any chance of finding someone in the Bay."

Asma was surprised to hear Iman speak so openly about meeting someone. There had been a number of serious contenders for Iman over the years, but no one had come close to fulfilling the high standards that Mr. Ibrahim—and Iman—had for Iman. That is, save for one: Omar Khan, the son of Mr. Ibrahim's former financial advisor. Asma suspected that Mr. Ibrahim had long taken for granted that Omar would one day be his son-in-law. A handsome, well-educated Muslim man from a good Pakistani family. Iman liked him. He checked all the boxes. But it was Omar's father, embroiled in secret financial struggles of his own due to a clandestine gambling habit, who had convinced Mr. Ibrahim to invest his money in the Ponzi scheme. By the time the scheme was uncovered, Omar's father had absconded from the country, along with Mr. Ibrahim's money. The girls had been furious, betrayed by a man they thought would one day be family. And then came the second betrayal—Omar had cut off all communication with Iman, presumably to disentangle himself from his father's mess.

At first, in the aftermath of the family's financial ruin and Iman's breakup, Asma wondered if she and her sister might grow closer. After all, both knew what it was to be all-but-spinsters in the eyes of their community, both had built successful—if very different—

careers for themselves, and both had experienced a failed engagement. But whereas Asma had spent months after her breakup with Farooq nearly inconsolable, Iman's cool callousness when it came to Omar took her by surprise. So Asma never brought up her breakup with Farooq to Iman, and the sisters remained as they always had, each focused on her own set of distinct priorities, rarely overlapping.

Asma glanced at Mr. Ibrahim, but he wasn't paying attention, still preoccupied by the saris.

"So you won't go online to meet someone, but you'll let Aunty Uzma put your picture in some yearbook for single people?" Asma asked Iman.

"Anyone can go online. Matchmakers are making a comeback. To get into Aunty's book you have to be asked and have a certain income, family, and look. I mean, no offense, but has anyone asked *you* to be in the book?"

"Good thing they haven't," said Asma. "I don't have time to take a rishta picture. I'm too busy with residency."

THAT NIGHT, AS ASMA PACKED UP THE LAST OF her room, she faced her own box of memories: a shoebox at the back of her closet full of mementos from her time with Farooq—letters and cards, movie ticket stubs, photos.

She pulled out her favorite—a photo booth strip

featuring her and Farooq. They were making silly faces in the first two pictures, and he had his arm around her in the third. Asma was wearing a Santa hat.

The picture was taken freshman year, the weekend before they were both headed home for winter break. They would be just ninety minutes apart—Farooq in Stockton, Asma in Palo Alto—but they knew they wouldn't see each other for a month. Asma had been determined to hide her relationship with Farooq while at Berkeley, but she wasn't the kind of girl to sneak away while living at home to meet up with her secret boyfriend. On their last day of finals, Farooq had planned an outing to San Francisco, which he didn't realize coincided with the city's Christmas tree lighting. They pushed their way from BART to Union Square, weaving through throngs of tourists and shoppers, and into a branded promotional photo booth. Farooq slipped the Santa hat onto Asma's head just before the camera started clicking. They then sat on a bench while the sun set and the Christmas lights went on. Between the lights, the peppermint mocha Asma was sipping, and Farooq's warm fingers laced through hers, the evening felt magical—enough warmth to carry her through the coming month without Farooq.

With Farooq, Asma could just be. No worrying, no explaining, no caretaking—there was a peace she didn't have in any of the other relationships in her life at the time. Or since.

Asma hadn't gone through this box in years but had never been able to bring herself to throw it away either. She found she still couldn't.

"I DIDN'T KNOW THIS WAS GOING TO BE AT A bar." Fatima rummaged through her purse for her ID, the bouncer waiting patiently as she pulled out a wad of crumpled tissues, a ChapStick, and finally her wallet.

"It's not a bar," Asma replied, "it's a club."

"That makes me feel better," Fatima deadpanned.

The hostess guided Asma and Fatima to an empty small round table on the side of the room. Asma looked around. They were twenty minutes early, but the club was nearly full.

"Two-drink minimum." Fatima pushed the table tent over to Asma as she took her seat. "I don't think two Diet Cokes is what they had in mind."

"Maybe they'll think we're recovering alcoholics," Asma replied.

"Couldn't you just have asked Farooq for his number like a normal person?"

"Oh sure, in front of my dad and his sister, covered in mud with my arm bleeding like I was just bitten by a dog. Not to mention the fact that he told his sister he didn't even recognize me." Asma shook her head. When Sophia and Yusef were leaving their house, Sophia had invited Asma to the launch party for Yusef's new book.

"I'm pretty sure he's still pissed about the breakup. He didn't say a word to me the whole time we were together."

"So what are we doing here, then?" Fatima asked. "If he's pissed, do you really think showing up to his brother-in-law's book launch is going to be enough to smooth things over?"

In truth, Asma wasn't sure how she was going to navigate her next interaction with Farooq. All she knew was, if they were ever going to clear the air between them, being in the same place at the same time would be a start. And this time she was ready—freshly showered and even wearing mascara.

"There's Sophia!" Asma waved to Sophia, peeking out of a door near the stage. She grinned at Asma and headed over to their table.

"I'm so glad you were able to make it!" Sophia leaned down to give Asma a hug.

"Me too! I have the night off," Asma said. "This is my best friend, Fatima. We went to Berkeley together."

"So nice to meet you, Fatima!" Sophia greeted Fatima with a hug too. "So you also know Farooq?"

"Not personally, only by reputation." Fatima glanced around the room. "Is he here?"

"Not yet," said Sophia. "My parents are remodeling so he's been in Stockton, dealing with the contractors. Then he was taking my mom to her physical therapy appointment. She just had knee replacement surgery. Then—"

"—he's rescuing some feral kittens?" Fatima asked with a laugh.

"I know, right?" Sophia smiled. "The good son. He's always made Haroon and me look bad."

Sophia turned to look at the door she had just emerged from, enough time for Asma to tilt her head toward Fatima with a look that said *See?*

"It looks like Yusef's calling me." Sophia waved to Yusef, who was standing at the door. "I think they're about to start. I'll come find you guys later."

"Is Farooq for real?" asked Fatima when Sophia was out of earshot. "Nice *and* super rich?"

Asma remembered Farooq's relationship with his family—respectful, patient, and genuine. What other freshman guy willingly called his parents, just to check in and hear their voices?

Asma sighed. "He was nice before he was super rich."

FAROOQ STILL HADN'T ARRIVED BY THE TIME the MC took to the stage. Asma had been trying to look around the club discreetly, turning her head every time anyone entered. Fatima's eyes were glued to her phone, which was unusual for her.

"Everything okay?" Asma asked.

"I just wanted to check in on Salman."

"I thought you said he's working late."

"That's what he said. But I don't think that's true. He's not answering my texts."

"What do you mean?"

"I think he's cheating on me." Fatima's words tumbled out almost involuntarily. She clapped her hand over her mouth.

"What?" Asma said it so loud that the waiter passing next to their table jumped, the glasses on his tray rattling. He gave Asma a look, which she returned with her hand up to say sorry.

"Salman? Cheating?" Asma lowered her voice as she twisted around to stare at Fatima.

Salman had been so awkward when she ran into him at their house. She supposed that for another man it might have seemed suspicious, but for him it seemed to be par for the course. Asma was certain that Salman lacked the basic social skills she imagined one needed in order to cheat—or even talk to a woman other than his wife.

"He's been spending more and more time at work."

"But he's always working, it's nothing new."

"It feels different. He didn't come to my last appointment with the fertility doctor—he told me he had a last-minute business trip. But all his clients are here. Where could he be going?" Fatima asked. "And last week, I was looking for a number in his phone and I found a text from an unknown number that said, 'Thanks for dinner.'"

"He had dinner with someone?" Asma asked, feigning alarm. "No!"

"I called the number and a woman answered."

"She's probably a client, or another lawyer at the firm."

"Maybe."

"Sweetie, you're going through a stressful time. I'm sure there's a perfectly logical explanation for it."

Fatima didn't look as convinced as Asma felt. Asma reached across the table and took her hand.

Salman, cheating? Please, thought Asma, as the house lights dimmed and a jazz trio began to play. Nerdy Desi men didn't cheat.

FAROOQ NEVER SHOWED. ASMA COULDN'T HELP but suspect that he had avoided the event specifically because he knew Asma was invited. By the time she accepted that he wasn't coming it was late. Much later than Asma ever stayed up when she wasn't working. The anticipation—then disappointment—of waiting for Farooq coupled with Fatima's anxiety about Salman left Asma more tired than if she had spent the night tending to patients.

And it showed the next day at work.

"The hell you yawning so much?" Jackson shoved a coffee under Asma's nose, then waved it around as though the aroma would be enough to wake her up. "You were off last night."

"I went out."

"No way!"

"Don't look so surprised," Asma said. "I go out."

"Spending time with your family at family parties is not 'going out,'" Jackson said with exaggerated air quotes.

Something in Asma's face must have given her away. Jackson peered at her with special interest. "Did you go out with a guy?"

"No," Asma said quickly. Then, after a pause, she added, "He didn't show. Are you going to answer that?"

Jackson silenced his pager, which had been beeping for several seconds. "Not until we're done with this." He pulled out the nearest chair and plopped into it, turning his full attention to Asma. "Who is he?"

"An old friend."

"You mean an ex?"

"Kind of."

"I thought you didn't date," said Jackson. "Because of your religion."

"It wasn't like that." Asma could never stomach the word *dating*, even though she knew that was a shorthand way of describing her relationship with Farooq. Dating implied physical contact, forbidden before marriage. But she felt the term denigrated her relationship with Farooq—they were not just boyfriend and girlfriend, they were meant for each other and would one day be husband and wife. Until they weren't.

"Ohhh, I get it." Jackson wiggled his eyebrows. "Go on, Asma."

"It wasn't like that, either," said Asma.

"Sure, it wasn't." Jackson bit his bottom lip as he made a strange, suggestive movement with his hips.

"What's wrong with you?" Asma laughed.

"What's his name?" Jackson swiveled his chair around to grab his phone. "I'm going to Google him."

"Farooq," Asma said. "Farooq Waheed."

Jackson was quiet for a second, then let out a low whistle. "Daaang, Asma. He's cute." Then, after another second: "Damn, Asma!" Jackson looked up from his phone, his eyes nearly bugging out of his head. "Five hundred million bucks?"

Asma waved him off. "Use that phone to answer your page, someone could be dying."

Jackson continued to gape at his phone.

"Jackson!"

"Okay, okay," Jackson said. "But we need to talk more about this later."

Asma grabbed the coffee from where Jackson had set it down on the table and took a sip. But it was unnecessary. Their conversation had perked Asma up in a way that the caffeine couldn't. Jackson was right—it was unlike her to go to Yusef's book launch, without a plan, determined to speak to Farooq.

Farooq's reappearance couldn't just be coincidental—especially at this stage in her life. It had to be a sign that they were meant to reconnect.

SEVEN

Maryam and Hassan lived twenty minutes south of the Ibrahims in San Jose, on a tree-lined street of cookie-cutter suburban sprawl. As Asma pulled into the driveway of Maryam's house—a two-story wood-shingle-roofed home in the middle of a row of almost a dozen identical others—she saw Maryam peek out of the upstairs window. She'd disappeared by the time Asma got out to open the trunk, but Asma knew she wasn't on her way down to help.

It wasn't lost on Asma how pitiable it was for her to have to crash with her younger sister's family because she herself was unwed. It was as if she still needed supervision, despite being a doctor and Maryam's older sister. In fact, the whole situation created a strange sense of vertigo for Asma, a glimpse of the life that might have been hers, if Farooq and medicine had not found her first.

It was an old family not-so-secret that Hassan and Maryam were together because Hassan and Asma weren't. A matchmaking aunty had brought Hassan's rishta to the Ibrahim family intended for Asma, but she had turned it down immediately. It was more than two years after her breakup with Farooq, but Asma was focused on finishing school and had no intention of marrying anyone else. Maryam, however, had seen his picture and sought him out on Facebook afterward. She'd become the first Ibrahim girl to marry, despite being the youngest.

Asma had been amused, and impressed, by Maryam's gumption. And self-awareness. She'd instinctively known what she needed in a partner—an easygoing, good-humored man who would take care of her and be more charmed than irritated by her theatrics. Asma's affection for Hassan had only grown over the years. He was a welcome addition to their family, the brother she didn't realize she needed. His marriage to Maryam felt like a godsend—another person to look after her little sister, to lighten the weight of Asma's responsibilities.

Asma let herself into the house and dumped her bags by the front door. She looked around the cozy and cluttered home. Toys were everywhere, shoes were piled by the front door, and a basket of unfolded laundry sat by the stairs. The house was outfitted with the Ibrahims' old furniture cast off over the years from Iman and Mr. Ibrahim's frequent, frivolous remodeling. Asma's eyes narrowed at the sight of the couch: a completely impractical, ridiculously overpriced mahogany chesterfield that Iman had purchased on Mr. Ibrahim's credit card over Asma's strenuous objections. Iman had lost interest in it just a few months after its arrival and passed it on to Maryam.

"Maryam? Boys?"

No answer. Asma sighed. It was so like Maryam to pretend as though she couldn't hear. Asma trudged up the stairs and knocked lightly on Maryam's bedroom door. Nothing. She knocked again. Still, no answer.

Asma pushed open the door slightly, "Maryam?"

The shades were drawn and the lights were off. It took Asma a second to adjust to the darkness. When she did, she saw her sister sprawled out on the bed, hand flung over her forehead.

"Asma? Is that you?" Maryam whispered.

"You know it's me, Maryam. You just saw me from the window."

Maryam ignored the comment. "I'm so sick."

"You are? You sounded fine an hour ago." Asma tried to hide the annoyed skepticism in her voice. Maryam had a storied history of coming down with vague, chronic ailments any time she felt she wasn't getting enough attention from her family. It had begun in the years after their mother died, and while Asma had been willing to coddle her sister, then just a preteen, her patience with this particular act had run thinner and thinner the older Maryam got.

"Yeah, well, I wasn't. I've been sick since Thursday. But I didn't want to make a big deal out of it. I swear, I'm just getting worse."

Asma walked to the window and threw open the curtains. "Where is everyone?"

"Hassan took the boys out. Can't believe he left me alone while I'm this sick," Maryam said. "Although he did bring me those flowers." Maryam gestured to a bouquet of deep orange tulips on the nightstand.

Asma smiled at the sight of them. Hassan knew just the formula for handling her sister. He'd acknowledged Maryam's feelings, then deftly removed himself so as not to indulge her. Devotion without pandering.

"Do you think I might have croup?" Maryam asked.

"You don't have croup. You're not coughing."

"Well, not right at this moment, but I do have a cough." Maryam coughed feebly.

Asma looked out the window at the house across the street. Maryam was in one of her moods. As with a child, it was best to redirect.

"Are the Qureishis home?"

Maryam had been less than thrilled when Hassan had announced excitedly just months after their wedding that there was a house for sale across the street from his parents'. Asma felt for her. Who wanted to live that close to their in-laws? But when Maryam became pregnant with the twins, Asma realized that Maryam couldn't have had it any better. Aunty Bushra, Maryam's mother-in-law, was indispensable when it came to helping take care of the boys.

"I wouldn't know. I haven't seen any of them today. I'm sure it didn't even cross Hassan's mind to tell them

I'm sick. Can you feel my glands? I think they're en-
larged."

Asma humored her sister, lightly touching Maryam's neck. "Nope, totally normal. And I'm sure they'll
stop by. It's still early."

"Well, I don't really want them to. The house is a
mess and you know how Aunty is so judgmental. And
Saba and Lubna—they make me so tired. Nonstop
talking and laughing."

Maryam paused, then coughed for effect.

Asma knew Maryam wanted her sympathy, but she
didn't have the patience to give it to her. She attempted
to change the subject, again.

"I would've come sooner but I had so much to do."

"Like *what*?"

"Well, I basically packed up the entire house by myself in between shifts at the hospital because Iman and
Abu are useless and spent their time complaining that
we didn't hire anyone. I was counting on Aunty to help,
but then she bailed for Pakistan last week. It's a wonder
I pulled it off."

Asma had thought she'd be more emotional about
the move, but she'd felt nothing but relief as the last of
the moving trucks pulled away from their house that
morning, her father and sister close behind. One chapter closed, a new one beginning—with a pit stop at
Maryam's.

"Okay, I get it. You were busy," Maryam said. "I've
been busy too."

"Oh yeah?" Asma was actually curious. The twins were in preschool for most of the day, Maryam had a housekeeper who came by once a week, and her mother-in-law cooked for them almost daily.

"Just because I don't have a job doesn't mean I'm not busy. Hello, I am the room mom for the boys' preschool class. I'm in charge of coordinating their big field trip to the zoo and the gift for Teacher Appreciation Week. And I have to work with all these other moms who are not pulling their weight."

Asma had to admit to herself that the chaos of the ER did seem preferable to dealing with difficult parents. But she was reluctant to acknowledge that to Maryam, so she just nodded.

"But of course, you don't care," said Maryam.

"Of course I care." Asma kept her voice soft to sound convincing. "Why would you say I don't?"

"Because you don't even check in about my life. Like you forgot to ask me about Zahra's mendhi last night." Maryam held up her hands to show faded henna in an intricate design. "The mendhi lady was so terrible, it looks like I have leprosy."

"You went? I thought you were sick."

"Of course I went, there would've been so much drama if I didn't. Zahra's super pissed that you didn't go."

"I told her I had to work. I don't know why she even invited me. She's your friend, not mine," said Asma.

"You didn't miss much. These mendhis are all the

same. I went with Aunty and the girls, who of course spent the entire time in the middle of the dance floor."

"Aunty Bushra told me that they've been practicing their dance for weeks."

"They shouldn't have had that friend of theirs join them. Her jumps were embarrassing. Everything was jiggling."

"That's so mean! What is wrong with you?"

"I'm the one you should feel bad for," Maryam said. "We had to pick her up on the way and I was crammed in the back seat with her, totally squished by the window. Not to mention she was sneezing and blowing her nose the whole time." Maryam sniffled. "That's probably how I got sick."

Asma patted Maryam's arm, exhausted from their conversation. "Probably."

ASMA HEARD THE GIGGLES BEFORE SHE OPENED her eyes. When she did, she was startled by her twin nephews, Zayd and Zaki, standing over her, their matching thick black hair falling onto their foreheads and over their eyes.

"She's up!"

"We were waiting for you!"

"Patiently!"

Asma struggled to sit up on the partially deflated air mattress wedged on the floor between the twins' bunk beds and their dresser. Asma had offered to sleep on the floor of Hassan's home office, but there were so many boxes jammed into the room that it was barely possible to step into it, let alone enough room to sleep.

Zaki pulled a picture out from behind his back and thrust it at Asma, just inches away from her face. "Who is this?"

Asma jumped at the sight: the photo booth strip with shots of a much younger Asma and Farooq.

"Where did you find this?" Asma said to Zaki, more sharply than she intended.

"Mama said not to touch her stuff," Zayd told Zaki.

"I sorry," Zaki said, bottom lip quivering. He wasn't used to his Asma Khala yelling at him. "I got it here." Zaki held up a copy of the book *The Rumi Collection*.

Asma snatched the book from Zaki, but before she could console him—or chastise him any further—they heard the front door open and Hassan yelling, "I'm home! Boys?"

"Daddy!"

The boys ran out of the room. Asma tried to stand up but tripped, her foot catching in a fold of the air mattress. She lay sprawled on the floor as their footsteps receded, the picture and book still in her iron grip.

Asma looked at the picture a second, marveling at how happy she and Farooq looked. She sat up and opened the cover of the book. There, inscribed on the title page:

I'm no poet, but I love you. (Hope you know it.)—FW

Asma traced the outline of the inscription with her finger. The book had been a gift from Farooq shortly after he proposed. She flipped through the highlighted and dog-eared pages, stopping at a passage underlined in red: the poem "This Marriage." It described the blessings of marriage with spiritual reverence, evoking imagery and language of the Quran.

She had read the poem out loud to Farooq on one of their hiking trips. After agreeing that it encapsulated their marriage goals and that someone needed to read it at their wedding, Farooq had said that the last couple of lines—describing the limitations of words to convey the spirit of the union—perfectly captured how he felt about her. It was clear from the circumstances of their meeting and the way they had clicked together so easily that they had always been destined for each other.

Her thoughts were interrupted by Maryam calling from downstairs.

"Asma? Asma, where are you?"

Asma slammed the book shut and pushed it under her mattress.

"WHAT DO YOU THINK?"

Saba held the iPhone up so close to Asma's face that she had to guide her hand away to see the picture.

It was an unflattering close-up of Lubna. Lubna's eyes were closed, her mouth was open, and her hair was wrapped up in a towel turban. The picture was affixed with the hashtag #GoodMorning.

"OMG, don't post that!" Lubna lunged for Saba's phone. "It's bad for my brand!"

Saba was quicker, darting out of Lubna's reach and around Asma, using her as a human shield. "It's great for mine!" She laughed.

Lubna ran toward Saba, almost knocking over her mother, who was standing at the stove over a pot of bubbling daal.

"Stop this nonsense!" Bushra swatted Lubna on the arm before turning her attention back to her cooking.

Now untangled, Asma finished chopping an onion that she slipped into the daal. Hassan's mother, Bushra Qureishi, was known throughout the Bay Area's Pakistani community for her excellent cooking—her dishes were the first gobbled up at potlucks, and unannounced visitors around mealtimes weren't a rare occurrence at the Qureishi home. Asma couldn't get enough of Aunty Bushra's food—home-cooked Desi meals she learned never to take for granted after her mother's passing. Aunty Bushra, in turn, loved Asma's interest in learning from her—unlike her own daughters or daughter-in-law. And so, despite pleas from friends and acquaintances near and far, Bushra never shared her recipes with anyone—Asma was the notable exception.

Unfortunately, she wasn't the best of teachers.

"Just throw a little haldi in," Bushra said, standing on her toes to pull the turmeric off the top shelf of a cupboard.

"How much is a little?" asked Asma, thumbs poised to take notes in her cell phone.

"Just a pinch." Bushra dumped more than a pinch into the pot. As Asma typed into her phone, Bushra pulled a few more bottles out of the cupboard and threw more spices into the pot.

"What was that, Aunty?"

"What was what?" Bushra asked, genuinely confused.

She removed her apron from around her waist. "Beta, please watch the pot, I have to say my zuhur namaz."

"You have the patience of a saint," Saba said to Asma, as soon as her mother had left the kitchen.

Lubna and Saba sat at the kitchen table, neither looking up from her phone. They were just fifteen months apart and practically joined at the hip, in spite of their differences. Saba, an aspiring stand-up comedian, thrived off the perceived disconnect between her physical appearance—small, slender, and hijab wearing— and her onstage persona, loud and goofy. Saba stood a petite five feet in contrast to her older sister, who towered over her by more than half a foot. Lubna, with her bubbly personality and low-key glamour, seemed predestined to be a social media star. She had a special gift for connecting with people, her earnest and genuine posts inspiring adoring comments from her followers with nary a snarky comment in sight.

"Asma, you should Instagram your cooking lessons with Ammi," Lubna suggested. "Desi cooking is so hot right now."

"It's been hot for hundreds of years," said Maryam, entering the kitchen with Hassan. "People on Instagram didn't just invent it."

"Gen Z invented everything, Maryam," Hassan said, the two of them sharing a smile.

Saba rolled her eyes, then became distracted by her phone. "Ooh, Lubna! Your morning portrait already has 162 likes. An instant classic!"

Lubna lunged for Saba's phone again as Maryam narrowed her eyes on Zayd and Zaki, sitting inches away from the TV in the adjoining family room. "Boys! I told you to turn off the TV ten minutes ago."

"But Dadi said we can watch!"

"Boys!" Hassan clapped his hands. "Give your poor mother a break. Let's go outside, Dada is picking oranges from the tree, we can help."

At this, the twins jumped from the couch, turned off the TV, and raced out the glass sliding doors into the backyard ahead of their father.

"Enjoy the peace and quiet." Hassan kissed Maryam on the head before calling over his back ominously, "They'll be back."

"They never listen to me," Maryam grumbled. "Only Hassan."

"At least they listen to *someone*," said Lubna under her breath.

"What's that supposed to mean?" Maryam asked.

Asma flinched. Maryam was notoriously defensive about her parenting.

She turned to the girls to change the subject. "What have you two been up to?"

"I've been trying to hit up five open mic nights a week. Plus, studying for the GRE," said Saba. "So basically I haven't been sleeping."

"I'm editing some fun new videos and posts," said Lubna. "If you get to two hundred fifty thousand followers your sponsorship opportunities really expand."

"As do your chances of finding a man," said Saba.

"I have to work it somehow. Not all of us were lucky enough to find a nice guy in our MSA," Lubna teased Saba.

Saba grinned. It was an open family secret that Saba had been talking to Tariq Badawy, whom she had met her freshman year at a meeting of San Jose State's Muslim Student Association. Although the two were not officially engaged, things had been progressing fairly seriously.

"Don't worry, Lubna, you're pretty cute. You'll have your pick," Saba said, reaching out to tousle Lubna's hair. "Too bad Farooq Waheed is dating some Arab supermodel."

Asma felt herself shocked to attention at the mention of Farooq's name. She'd been mulling how to engineer an encounter with him since his failure to show up at Yusef's book launch. With her family moved out of the house, and her life now stretched thin between residency and spending time with Maryam, the odds of her unexpectedly crossing paths with him again weren't high. She would have to make her own luck.

"Farooq Waheed again," said Maryam. "What's his deal?"

"Yeah, Asma, what do you know?" Saba asked. "Hassan said you went to Cal with him."

"I didn't know him well," Asma lied. She and Farooq had been careful never to behave like a couple in public—their classmates assumed they were just platonic hiking buddies. Asma wondered if that was when she developed such a skill for lying, one that was serving her well now.

"He's not on Instagram, Facebook, or Twitter," said Saba while staring at her phone. "But his office is in Menlo Park. So we'll have to find our way over there to commence Operation Get Lubna Married."

"Are you serious?" Asma asked, before she could stop herself. In no way did Maryam's sisters-in-law factor into her plans to reconnect with Farooq. She wasn't going to stand by and watch them pursue him as marriage material. "You really think Farooq Waheed is a good option for you?"

"He's rich, he's handsome, he owns his own company,"

Lubna said with a skeptical, arched eyebrow. "If he's not a good option, our standards might be a little high."

"No, I mean, he's not right for you, Lubna," she said. "I heard he's a jerk. Really arrogant. Totally not your type." Asma grimaced, hoping the girls read her face as distaste for Farooq, not self-loathing for her lie.

"It figures," said Lubna. "Startup guys are the worst."

Asma was saved by the simultaneous return of the twins, Hassan, and Bushra. As Maryam took the boys into the bathroom to wash up for lunch, Bushra sent the girls into the garage to get some folding chairs. With everyone out of earshot, it was Bushra's turn to complain.

"Beta," Bushra said to Hassan, "the boys are out of control. Maryam doesn't discipline them properly."

Hassan laughed. "Ammi, they're three! All three-year-olds are out of control. Maryam's doing her best."

"There's just so much talking. You can't reason with children!"

Asma pretended not to hear the conversation, focusing intently on stirring the daal. At that moment, the boys came out of the bathroom, hands still wet and fighting over a small towel. Zayd yanked the towel out of Zaki's hand so forcefully that it went flying, almost knocking over a glass bowl perched on the edge of the table.

"Badtameez!"

Bushra's screech made the boys stop dead in their tracks.

"What did I tell you two about fighting?"

"But, Dadi, Zayd was—"

Hassan stepped in.

"Boys, let's go help Saba and Lubna Phuppo get some chairs from the garage," he said, ushering the twins out of the kitchen.

Asma pushed the bowl to the middle of the table before returning to her place beside Bushra at the stove, just in time to see her throw something else into the pot of daal.

"What was that you just threw in, Aunty?"

"Just a bit of chili."

"How much is a—"

"See what I was saying about the boys? I am just so tired. Can you please talk to Maryam?"

"Talk to me about what?" Maryam stood at the kitchen door.

"Nothing. Can you help me set the table?" Asma handed Maryam a stack of plates and pushed her into the dining room. Bushra threw a few more things into the pot, and Asma officially gave up taking notes.

EIGHT

The restaurant was so dark as Asma stepped inside that her eyes didn't have time to adjust before she bumped into a table. She apologized to the diners as the water in the goblet closest to her sloshed about, then turned and nearly knocked over a waiter balancing four plates of salad. Asma breathed a sigh of relief when she reached the private room in the back of the restaurant.

One of the unexpected annoyances of living with Maryam and Hassan was being badgered into joining their social engagements. Asma's father and Iman never seemed to mind when she turned down invitations to family functions—in fact, it happened so often that they usually didn't even bother asking her to join them in the first place. But Maryam had memorized Asma's work schedule and seemed to be planning a spate of events around Asma's availability. After years of tagging along with her big sisters, Maryam seemed to relish this new role as the one setting the social agenda.

As much as she might have preferred to spend her one night off in her pajamas, streaming something mindless featuring twenty-somethings on an island, Asma couldn't refuse Maryam's latest invitation. It was Hassan's thirtieth birthday and Maryam had gathered a group of his college friends for dinner at a trendy new seafood restaurant in downtown San Jose. And much to Asma's dismay, Maryam had made a specific point of not inviting her in-laws to the dinner.

"Aunty will complain that the food is bland, and the girls will put all our business up on Instagram," she'd said.

But Asma wished for the company of Qureishis when she arrived and saw that the only spot left was at the head of the table—right next to Maryam's friend Zahra, whose mendhi and wedding Asma had recently missed. Zahra's eyes narrowed when she saw Asma.

"Oh, hey, Asma!" Zahra said, a fake, strained smile on her face. "So nice to see you. Glad you're not too busy to join us tonight."

"I told you she was pissed," Maryam said to Asma as she took her seat.

Zahra looked at Maryam. "You told her?"

"Was I not supposed to?" Maryam said. "I thought that's why you kept complaining about it to me."

"Can I get a drink?" Asma flagged down a waitress, semi-wishing she drank alcohol so she could have something to get her through dinner—she didn't understand the strange dynamics of Maryam's friendships. It was going to be a long night.

From there, the conversation devolved as it does in a group of married couples, especially when most have small children.

"I can't potty-train soon enough. I am so tired of washing someone else's butt."

"Kids are so disgusting! I found the toddler drinking out of the lota yesterday."

Appetizers hadn't even been served yet and Asma had already lost her appetite. What was it about being a parent that suddenly made it okay to discuss bowel movements at the dinner table?

"Sorry, Asma, I know this conversation is no fun for you," said one of Maryam's friends with a sympathetic look. What was her name? Asma had met the woman a number of times over the years at Maryam's house— well past the time that she should have learned her name. It would be too awkward for her to ask for it now.

"Don't worry about her, she's used to being the only single one," said Maryam.

"You never really get used to it," Asma joked.

"Oh! That's so sad," said What's-her-name. "Don't worry, InshAllah you'll find someone."

"InshAllah," Asma said, solemnly raising her hands up in prayer, aware that the women at the table viewed her search for a husband with almost the same gravity as one would a sick person looking for a bone marrow donor.

"You should really get out more," Zahra said. "Maybe don't turn down invitations where you can actually meet people."

"She's a doctor." It was Hassan, from the other side of the table, who came to Asma's defense. "She didn't miss your wedding because she was sitting at home watching TV."

"I know why you haven't found someone," said another one of Maryam's friends. "Men are intimidated by strong, independent women."

The women around the table murmured in assent.

"Looks like all you strong, independent ladies managed to find the last of the good ones," said Asma, smiling so brightly that no one caught her dig.

"MashAllah, we really are blessed." Zahra spoke with a level of gratefulness found only in a woman recently married.

Thankfully, by the time the entrées arrived the conversation had moved off the subjects of children and Asma's single status. Unfortunately, it was on to another topic that gave Asma indigestion.

Farooq.

"I totally remember him from Cal. We used to play *Street Fighter* together."

"We met when we were on the board of the MSA. Really cool guy."

"We went snowboarding in Tahoe over winter break one year. He was really impressive on those double black diamonds."

Asma wanted to roll her eyes as the men at the table jostled for position close to Farooq, each with a more elaborate false memory. None of these men had been friends with Farooq during the short time he'd been a student at Berkeley. Not to mention, Farooq wasn't into video games, had never served on the board of the MSA, and had messed up his knee so badly playing soccer in high school that his doctor had forbidden him from snowboarding. She was amazed how his success had suddenly given everyone a license to rewrite history.

And now everyone wanted a piece of him. Especially for marriage.

"He would be so great with my cousin. She's just a little bit shorter than him, and they both have nice smiles."

"My mom is so bummed, he would've been perfect for my sister. His family is from our family's village, but she just started talking to this other guy."

"I would have loved to set him up with my niece. But she lives in Doha and long distance is so hard."

Asma couldn't believe the inane reasons proffered for why Farooq would be a good match. And that everyone at the table seemed to have forgotten that she was single. Asma knew that their failure to see her as a prospect for Farooq wasn't rooted in malice. It was pure neglect. Men became more desirable as they aged— women, not so much. Career and income stability were seen as good qualities in men, but for women they were a liability—evidence not of competence or success but of a "strong, independent" woman whom no one wanted for the men in their lives.

"My sister-in-law Lubna has made Farooq her project," Maryam said. "My mother-in-law just met his mother at a party and they got on really well. And our families would be a good match."

Asma nearly choked on her drink at Maryam's words. Asma could barely contain her indignation, although Maryam had no knowledge of their history. Suddenly Farooq was considered an ideal match, and the only thing that had changed was that now he had money.

Before she could say anything, however, Asma felt a sharp pain in her back, as though she had been stabbed. It was only when the waitress squealed, "Ohmygod!" that Asma realized what had happened. The waitress had knocked over a mug of coffee, a stream of it landing on Asma's back and scalding her. It was an opportune—if painful—excuse for escape. Asma waved off Maryam, who was furiously mopping the coffee off Asma's shirt, and excused herself to go home.

SINCE THE BEGINNING OF HER RESIDENCY, ASMA had learned that there were two kinds of patients in the emergency room: one-offs and repeat customers. The one-offs tended to be on the extreme ends of the spectrum—either having the most severe trauma or the most minor ailments. Car accidents or vertigo. Random allergic reactions. Heart attacks. Children with small objects stuck up their noses.

The doctors addressed these various crises, bandaged people up, and sent them on their way—the goal was to never again see the person in the ER. Asma sometimes wondered about how things turned out for some of the patients she saw, especially those with particularly memorable emergencies. Like the valedictorian suffering from a panic attack on graduation day or the civics teacher who had a pencil stabbed through his hand during the Pledge of Allegiance. She'd never forget the couple on their honeymoon whose sexual experimentation resulted in inflammation in some very sensitive places.

Then there were the repeat customers. People whose problems were neither as urgent nor as minor as the one-offs, familiar faces that showed up again and again with issues of varying seriousness. And it seemed Mr. Shepard had become a repeat customer.

It was a lingering fever this time. Asma recognized him immediately when he was admitted, noting with a certain amount of pride that the suture job she'd done on his split chin had healed up with a rather insignificant scar, all things considered.

"Dr. Ibrahim," he said, when she pulled back the curtain of the exam room. He turned to another elderly man, who was sitting in the chair by his bed. "Henry, this is the doctor I was telling you about."

Mr. Shepard's friend, an old man with big Coke-bottle glasses held together with tape, peered at Asma. "Oh, the Indian doctor."

"She's Pakistani." Mr. Shepard corrected Henry with a wag of his finger. "American. She was born here."

Henry waved his hand like he couldn't be bothered with the details. "I saw the Chinese doctor. Funny guy, always with the jokes."

"You must be talking about my colleague Dr. Wong," said Asma with a smile.

"Never been to China. Always wanted to go," said Henry. "I've been to India, though. Gloria and I went to see the Taj Mahal in 1984. Beautiful, just beautiful."

"I told you. She's not Indian," Mr. Shepard said, glancing at Asma apologetically. Asma shook her head to indicate she wasn't bothered. It wasn't the worst comment she'd heard from someone in the ER—and at least he hadn't questioned her competence. Not like the handful of patients she'd had over the course of her residency who had demanded that they been seen by a "real" doctor.

"I hear you have a fever?" Asma took a seat on the stool opposite his bed and looked at Mr. Shepard with concern.

"I'm fine, was just feeling a little short of breath. They said I was running a temperature, so they brought me here," said Mr. Shepard. "I probably got whatever it is from Henry."

"You've been sick too, Henry?" Asma asked, turning to the other man. "Is that why you came in to see Dr. Wong?"

"We've all been sick," he replied. "There's a bug going around Green Meadows. People keep passing it back and forth."

"And is that how you broke your glasses?" Asma asked, motioning to the tape holding them together. "From a fall?"

"That was nothing," Henry replied. "I got up too fast." He waved his hand, as if it were the last thing Asma should be concerned about. But Asma had worked in the ER long enough to know never to ignore an alarm bell going off in her head, and there was one ringing now.

"Weren't there nurses at Green Meadows to help you get up when you were sick?" Asma asked. A fall was a serious concern at Henry's age, and a nursing home should've known better than to let a geriatric patient with a fever get out of bed unaccompanied. But Henry only huffed.

"Once upon a time," he replied. "But not anymore. It's no real bother, though. I can get up on my own." He exchanged a loaded look with Mr. Shepard.

"Staffing shortages?" Asma asked, trying to prod for more information.

"New owners," Mr. Shepard replied. "They claim we're fully staffed. And maybe they're right. But the guy I used to share a room with got some pretty nasty bedsores from not being turned enough."

Asma examined Mr. Shepard, ordered some labs and a chest X-ray, and went to find Jackson. Luckily, she didn't have far to look. Her friend was at the nurse's station, raiding a box of donuts.

"Jackson," she said, and he nearly leapt half a foot into the air, as if he'd been caught raiding the pharmacy of its painkillers.

"Don't sneak up on me like that," he replied, a hand on his chest. "I thought you were one of the nurses. They get so territorial about their baked goods."

"You know that patient that you reported on in our meeting a few weeks back, the one who presented with a fever and stomach pains? The one whose family lives on the East Coast?" She followed him into the doctors' lounge, where he dropped onto one of the sofas.

"How on earth do you remember that?" Jackson asked, but Asma only gave a little shrug.

"What nursing home did he live in?" Asma asked.

"I don't remember," Jackson replied. "Some of us don't have savant-like recall of minor details, Asma."

"Can you look it up?"

"I have like fifteen minutes tops until Mrs. McKinney's labs come in," he complained.

"Jackson," Asma replied, "look it up or I'll narc you out to the nurses for stealing their sugar."

Jackson gave a long sigh and then took a seat at one

of the nearby computers. He typed with one hand, eating his donut with the other.

"Green Meadows Care Center," he said after a moment, spinning around triumphantly on his stool. "Happy now?"

"Oh God, I have two other patients who live there presenting with similar symptoms. You treated one of them for an injury from a fall," Asma said. She glanced up when the lounge door opened and Dr. Saucedo appeared. She nodded at Asma, who motioned for her to come over.

"It could be a common virus," Jackson said. "Nursing homes can be like petri dishes when something gets in."

"I don't think so," Asma said. "We haven't seen any of these symptoms in the general public. Whatever it is, it's confined to residents of Green Meadows."

"What's going on?" Dr. Saucedo asked.

"We have a cluster of nursing home residents coming in with similar symptoms over the past month or so," Asma replied. "Stomach pains, fever, shortness of breath."

"And nobody at the facility has taken any notice?" Dr. Saucedo asked.

"The residents claim they've cut down on the nursing staff since the place was sold," Asma replied. "It's possible that they're too short-staffed to realize that there's a problem." Dr. Saucedo nodded, and thought for a second.

"Bacterial pneumonia?" Dr. Saucedo asked.

"That's what I'm thinking," Asma replied. "Maybe Legionnaires'?"

"That's a sound theory, if it's localized to one facility," Dr. Saucedo replied. "How would you confirm?"

"A simple urine sample should do the trick," Asma said with a snap of her fingers. She felt a thrill as all the pieces came together, a medical puzzle solved.

"Legionnaires' disease?" Jackson asked, slumping down in his seat. "Damn, Asma. How would you even think to diagnose that?"

"Taking the bird's-eye view," said Dr. Saucedo, nodding with approval as a nurse came in, summoning Jackson with Mrs. McKinney's labs. "It's good work, Asma," she said, when Jackson had left and the two of them were alone. "Exactly the kind of instincts we're looking for here. I know you're planning on relocating to Sacramento after residency, but I just want to reiterate one more time how much I'd like you to stay."

"Thank you, Dr. Saucedo," Asma said, swelling with pride. She thought about the past few weeks. She felt completely in her element—in spite of her current living arrangement with Maryam. It was a relief, in some ways, to have Iman and her father two hours away by car. To not have to be the responsible one in the house—figuring out what they were going to eat for dinner, administering her father's medication, and making sure that they weren't spending money they didn't have on things they didn't need. And, most importantly, to not constantly be reminded of how her father had veered her life off course, especially after crossing paths with Farooq once more. "To be honest, I'm not set on the move to Sacramento," Asma said, surprising herself with the decision she felt herself making in that moment. "If a position does open up here in the next few months, I would love to be considered for it."

NINE

Asma sat on the couch, remote in hand, watching a reality show where families look for a new home because their current house is bursting at the seams. It created a strange sense of symmetry for her, because just that morning, Asma had left early to tour the new luxury apartment complex down the street from the hospital. If Dr. Saucedo was right and a job was about to open up in her ER, she could probably afford a two-bedroom place. Big enough for her father to stay with her when he visited from Sacramento. And even if she had to find a job at one of the other Bay Area hospitals after graduation, it would still be worth it. She couldn't mentally afford to live with Maryam.

"You're not ready?" Maryam was standing in the doorway dressed in a hot-pink salwar kameez and holding a gold clutch. "We're supposed to be at Aunty Bushra's house in twenty minutes."

"I'm staying in tonight," Asma replied.

"What's wrong?"

"Work was exhausting," Asma said, though really, it had been a good day overall. She arrived that morning to discover that she'd correctly diagnosed Mr. Shepard with Legionnaires' disease, and it was likely that many of the residents at Green Meadows had been exposed. She'd contacted the nursing home's administrator herself with the news, and he'd assured her that they would find the source of the infection and address it.

But even the best of days left Asma tired, and she'd earned a night of vegging out on the couch instead of dealing with another of Maryam's social events.

"That's not a good enough reason," said Maryam. "We're all tired. I've been handling the house and the boys all day."

"Please, Maryam, just cover for me."

"It's low-key, Asma, not some huge party."

"Then why are you dressed like you're going to a wedding?"

"I always dress like this." Maryam twirled to show off her outfit.

"Well, I'll be dressed like *this*"—Asma motioned to the flannel pajama bottoms that she was wearing along with a ratty med school T-shirt—"and be right here when you return."

"Fine! Leave me all alone to handle the boys and help Aunty," Maryam grumbled. "Hassan's not even going to be there. He says I didn't remind him about it and he scheduled back-to-back patients." Maryam had her hands on her hips. "Why should I have to remind him? Who reminds me?"

The question was rhetorical and Asma had the sense to keep her mouth shut.

"It's called the mental load," Maryam answered herself. "Women are expected to be the keepers of the family's to-do list, to make sure all the stuff that needs to get done gets done."

Maryam was monologuing to the room, to an audience that was not there. Asma didn't have the energy to engage. She slowly shifted her eyes back to the TV.

"I mean, just in this past week, I took the boys to their annual checkups, put together their outfits for spirit day, and filled out their field trip permission forms. Does Hassan even know all that stuff is happening?"

Asma shrugged, her eyes still on the TV.

"No, the answer is no," Maryam said. "But he knows that when he's hungry, there's food in the fridge and on the table. Does he think it appears by magic?"

It kind of does, Asma thought, *and Aunty Bushra is the magician.* She answered Maryam with another shrug.

"I just ask that he makes time for things that are important. Like tonight. He really should meet Farooq. It's rude not to be there at a dinner his parents are throwing for him."

Asma jerked her head back to Maryam so quickly she almost strained her neck.

"Wait, Aunty is having a dinner for Farooq?" Asma asked.

"Seriously, Asma?" Maryam glared at her. "Now I have to carry the mental load for you too?"

"Sorry, no one told me."

"What are you talking about?" Maryam said, her voice rising. "*I* told you."

Asma was certain she would have remembered if Maryam had, but that was beside the point.

"Never mind," Asma said. "Why Farooq?"

"For Lubna."

Oh no.

"I told you guys, I heard he was a jerk!" Asma said, trying to contain her sudden panic. This couldn't be happening. Asma could force herself to get over the fact that Farooq probably had to end up with somebody, but the prospect of it being someone in Asma's family was intolerable. The fact that her family was embracing him now with Lubna, after he'd made his millions, would all but prove to him how shallow they were all those years ago. And Asma desperately wanted him to know that it hadn't been about the money. At least not for her.

"Lubna met him at some gathering and said he was really nice. He must have changed since college."

"But isn't it weird, just inviting some rando over for dinner?"

"Aunty invited Sophia and Yusef too. I mean, Sophia is our tenant."

"I don't remember a clause in the lease that says we have to invite them over for dinner," Asma said.

"What's your problem?" Maryam suddenly looked curious. "I thought you didn't even know him."

Asma realized she was having what must appear to Maryam as an outsized reaction. "I didn't." Now was not the time to fill Maryam in.

"Then why do you even care?" said Maryam.

"I just think the whole thing is so strange. Like, come have dinner with us and our single daughter."

"Oh please, Asma." Maryam turned on her heel. "You know how this game is played."

I do, Asma thought as she watched Maryam walk down the hall. She turned off the TV.

Which is why I need to be there tonight.

ASMA STEPPED OUT OF THE SHOWER ONTO THE bath mat, her wet feet making soggy footprints in the gray shag. She tightened the towel around her, then grabbed an extra one from the back of the door to wrap her hair. The bathroom mirrors were fogged up in a way that suggested the water she had used was much hotter than it had felt when she was standing under it. She stood in front of the medicine cabinet for a few seconds before swiping her hand across it.

Her path to this point professionally had resulted in so many casualties, starting with her face. Her eyes, once bright and framed by long lashes, looked tired, accentuating the dark circles below them. Small wrinkles paved a path across her forehead and down between her eyebrows, unruly after months of missed threadings. Her hair had started to thin and break, baby hairs peeking out from the front and back of her towel turban.

All those years of residency-induced stress and sleep deprivation had taken their toll.

But she was a doctor—and a damn good one, at that. And wasn't that the goal when she ended things with Farooq so many years ago? Tonight, she would have the chance to let him know. To prove to him that she hadn't broken up with him because of money, but because she wanted to be the person treating Mr. Shepard when he came into the ER. Maybe, finally, she could make him understand. And maybe, hopefully, it could lead to a second chance.

She finished her pep talk and marched to the closet to dig deep into one of her many U-Haul boxes. She scrounged up an old and tattered bag, then took stock of the pathetic mess of makeup inside. Was her skin color still the same shade as this foundation? Did mascara have an expiration date? Where were the boys' school supplies? She needed a pencil sharpener for her eyeliner.

As she stood up, her hand brushed against one of her salwar kameez—a crimson tunic with embroidery. It was the color Asma was wearing the first time Farooq told her that he loved her—a spontaneous declaration during a stroll around campus on a crisp spring day that had taken them both by surprise. They spent the rest of the afternoon on a romantic high, the two of them sitting side by side on a bench and holding hands as they watched the sun set on the Berkeley hills. Asma had teased Farooq later that he had turned the color of her shirt.

Asma stood looking at the outfit, the vividness of the memory washing over her as if it had happened just yesterday. She wondered if seeing this color would remind Farooq of that afternoon too.

There was only one way to find out.

She pulled the salwar kameez off its hanger, pressed it flat against her body, then stuck her head out of the door.

"Maryam, where's your iron?"

BUSHRA HAD OUTDONE HERSELF. PLATTERS OF kabobs and bowls of salan crowded the kitchen counters, with several pots and pans still on the stove. Bushra, bustling around, paused for a second when Maryam and Asma entered the kitchen, the warm air enveloping them in the familiar embrace of spices that made Asma feel as though she were home.

"Girls, you look beautiful!"

"We clean up well, huh?" Maryam helped herself to a pakora from a tray on the island, then settled onto a barstool. "I helped Asma with her makeup. She's the only almost-thirty-year-old I know who hasn't watched a single YouTube tutorial."

"I think I read that article—by thirty you must have two times your salary in your retirement account and know how to properly apply eyeliner." Asma rummaged in the drawer underneath the microwave. She found an apron and slipped it over her head. "What can I do, Aunty?"

"Nothing, beti, the girls should be helping me. Lubna! Saba!"

Asma followed Bushra around the kitchen until she gave her a cucumber to chop for the salad. Maryam, who had now moved on to sampling the samosas, made no move to assist Bushra or Asma, instead muttering under her breath, "I swear, I've never seen Lubna or Saba help Aunty during one of her dinner parties."

The girls didn't make their appearance until the guests were at the front door, bounding down the stairs at the sound of the doorbell. Asma noted that they were especially dressed up for the occasion, wearing the custom-made clothes they had worn last Eid with so much embroidery that they made Asma's outfit look plain by comparison.

Asma was moving aside dishes to make room for the steaming platter of biryani that Bushra was carrying out of the oven when Yusef and Sophia entered the kitchen.

"Oh my goodness!"

"This is quite the spread!"

Asma didn't see Farooq enter behind them and startled at the sound of his voice, a deep murmur giving salaams. She saw him out of the corner of her eye, looking sharp and well put together in a button-down shirt with slacks, his hands clasped together in greeting, holding out a gorgeous bouquet of flowers to Aunty Bushra. She couldn't get over how much he had come into himself, how he stood so confident and assured. His first view of her tonight would be the same as his last one: her back, now adorned with the clumsy bow of her apron. She slowly untied the apron, preparing for the big reveal of her outfit and made-up face. But before she could slip it off her neck, Bushra handed her a platter piled high with naan. "Asma beti, can you please put this next to the biryani?"

Asma took the platter with one hand and attempted to yank off the apron with the other, just as the twins came racing into the kitchen. They stopped when they saw Farooq.

"It's you!" said Zayd.

"It's me!" Farooq answered, amused. His eyes crinkled at the side as he smiled, just as Asma remembered.

Zaki stuck out his tongue and crossed his eyes.

"Zaki—stop it!" Maryam said. "Why are you doing that?"

Asma looked at the boys in confusion before it dawned on her what was going on. Zaki was imitating Farooq's face from the photo booth strip he had found in her book.

"Zaki!" Asma said, trying to hide her anxiety. "Can you please take this apron and give it to Dadi?"

Asma pulled the apron off over her head and held out her hand to Zaki. He ignored her, still staring at Farooq.

"You're in the picture," said Zayd.

"What picture?" asked Farooq.

"From the book," said Zaki.

"What book?" asked Aunty Bushra.

"From the box."

"What box?" Maryam asked.

The boys turned to look at Asma.

"What are you talking about?" Asma smiled at them in a sinister, threatening way. No one noticed—except Farooq, who looked at her sharply. It was clear he knew exactly what the boys meant. The look sent a jolt through her to the point that she barely realized it when the platter of naan slipped from her hand. It fell to the floor and shattered, shards of white Corning-Ware decked with small yellow and orange flowers flying everywhere.

ASMA SAT NEXT TO BUSHRA ON THE COUCH, THE rest of the family and guests sprawled around the living room, their plates heaped with food. The destruction of the naan had mercifully distracted her family, who didn't seem to wonder why she had dropped the platter in the first place. By the time they had cleaned up the mess, they had long forgotten the picture of Farooq. Although Asma knew, much to her distress, that Farooq hadn't.

Now Bushra waved off Asma's apology, her ire directed toward the twins and Maryam.

"This is what I was saying." Asma was still so flustered that she didn't realize Bushra was talking to her.

"What were you saying, Aunty?"

"Maryam! She doesn't watch these boys and—"

Asma nodded as Bushra complained but tuned her out as she tried to listen in on the conversation Farooq was having with the girls and Sophia across the room.

"It was in the garage," Sophia said.

"Of course it was," Lubna said. "Isn't that where all startups begin?"

"It seems like a million years ago," Farooq said. "Working hard with just an idea and no guarantee of success."

Farooq had shared his idea with Asma shortly after they met, hesitant at first.

"So people in the Central Valley have no money and no accessible healthcare," Farooq had said. "They basically see someone only when it's an emergency. And by then, it's too late.

"It sounds crazy," he continued. "But what if there was a way I could build a network of medical professionals across the country—doctors and nurses—who want to help?" He had pulled out his phone and held it up. "And then develop some way for the people who need medical care to access that network through their phone, no matter where they are or how little money they have?"

"It's not crazy," Asma had assured him. "It's brilliant." She felt a rush of love thinking about his big heart and how their career ambitions so closely mirrored each other in helping people through medicine.

Asma knew it was her early support that had propelled him forward and factored into his decision to drop out of college and work on his idea full time. A decision that ultimately came back to haunt him, when her family used that as a reason for them not to be together.

Asma wondered if his comment to Lubna was directed at her, but he continued to look at Lubna.

"I remember those days," Yusef said, coming back into the room from the kitchen, his plate piled high with seconds. "We had them too."

"The life of a struggling artist," Sophia said. "You pretend like studio apartments are romantic."

It turned out Asma wasn't the only one halfway invested in her conversation with Bushra. Bushra cut herself off midsentence.

"Uncle and I lived in a small apartment when we first came to this country," she said. "Our rent was two hundred dollars a month. It was a fortune! Uncle wasn't making much."

"But they didn't care because they were so in looooooooove," Saba crooned. "You know Ammi and

Abu had a love marriage. I have a whole bit about it in my routine. *He was so handsome,*" Saba said with a slight accent, imitating her mother.

Bushra smiled, then wagged her finger at Saba.

This piqued everyone's attention, especially Farooq's.

"Aunty, if you don't mind me asking—what did your family say?" he asked. "Marrying a man who didn't have much money?"

Lubna put up her hand. "Nooo, don't get her started, she won't stop!" But Asma felt herself flush with embarrassment.

"My parents didn't mind," Bushra started. "He was a good man, they knew it would work out. We were getting married for ourselves, not for other people."

"That must have been unheard of when you married, Aunty," said Sophia. "I don't think that's the case with many Desi families even today."

"I know how these ladies talk," said Bushra. "But if you raise your children right and trust them, then you don't have to worry."

"I'll remember that the next time you yell at me for performing somewhere you don't like," said Saba.

"Beta, you shouldn't be in bars," said Bushra with a shake of her head.

"My last one is this weekend," said Saba. "I promise!"

"Cancel it, please, Saba! I need you at my event." Lubna's face brightened as she turned to Farooq. "Farooq! You should totally be on my panel. It's for PIMPS!"

Farooq choked on his kabob. He coughed and

pounded on his chest with his fist, glancing at Aunty Bushra, then at Lubna, in barely restrained horror.

"PIMPS—Pakistanis in Many Professions," Lubna explained, seemingly oblivious to Farooq's reaction. "It's a networking group for Pakistani American professionals."

"A bunch of Desi kids from rich South Bay families who talk and dress like they were raised on the streets of Oakland," said Maryam.

Asma stifled a laugh and noticed that the guests did the same. Maryam's bluntness could sometimes be refreshing.

"Don't be a hater, Maryam," said Saba.

Lubna ignored Maryam's comment, her focus still on Farooq. "I'm hosting a career panel at their mixer. You would be such a big draw. Please say yes!"

"Sounds interesting," said Farooq. "I'd be happy to."

"Awesome! Asma's going to be on the panel too. We couldn't have a career panel without a doctor."

Asma smiled and tried to meet his gaze, but Farooq no longer looked as pleased with his invitation. He wouldn't meet her eyes.

"Like half the attendees will be Berkeley grads, I'm sure they'll have tons of questions for you guys," said Lubna. "I can't remember—were you two friends in college?"

"No."

Farooq said no so quickly and forcefully that Asma understood. It had colored every interaction they'd had since they'd first seen each other in the Ibrahim back-yard. Farooq was still angry with her. That she was a doctor now, and that years had passed, made no differ-ence. Asma felt like an idiot for thinking otherwise. She looked down at her plate and didn't look up until the conversation turned elsewhere.

ASMA STOOD BY HERSELF IN THE KITCHEN. SHE hadn't been able to sit with the group any longer and had left to make chai, which she was pouring into cups when Farooq came out of the bathroom. He looked surprised to see her. Their eyes met, finally. Asma willed herself not to break his gaze.

"We weren't friends?" she asked.

"That's what we were?"

Farooq's answer, and his tone—cold and harsh—caught Asma off guard. He had never spoken to her like that before. She overfilled one of the teacups.

"You need help?" he asked, his voice softening.

An olive branch. She nodded.

Farooq took his place beside her. He held the cups steady as she poured the tea, her arm brushing against his sleeve as she moved from cup to cup. Her skin seemed to prickle with awareness of how close he was to her again, after so long. She had yearned for this moment, dreamed of it for years—and now that she was here, she wished she could freeze time and stay next to him forever.

Asma realized this might be her only chance to be alone with Farooq. She needed to talk to him now. She took a deep breath, the faint, familiar scent of Farooq's aftershave only slightly soothing her nerves.

"Farooq, I'm sorry," she said.

Farooq kept his hands and eyes on the cups. He didn't reply.

Asma put down the teapot and turned to him. "I regret so much the way things ended between us, but I want you to know that I thought I was doing the right thing at the time. I thought I was doing what my mother . . ."

Asma trailed off, a knot forming in her throat as Farooq stayed quiet.

"I'm not the same person I was eight years ago."

And there it was. As the words left her mouth, Asma realized that was what she needed Farooq to know. That if she were given a chance to do things all over again, she really would do them differently.

She needed him to believe her because she needed to believe it herself.

"It's fine," he said finally. Dispassionately. "Water under the bridge."

She realized she had been holding her breath, and exhaled.

"That's it?" Asma asked, her voice still taut with emotion.

Lubna popped her head into the kitchen. "Farooq!

We're waiting for you. Saba is shooting down my movie ideas, I need backup."

"She keeps picking old movies!" Saba called out from the living room.

"I'll be there in a second," Farooq said, as Lubna disappeared back into the living room. His smile faded as he turned back around to face Asma.

"Everything happened so long ago," Farooq said with a shrug, his tone matter-of-fact, his face unreadable. He picked up the tea tray. "I don't even think about it anymore. I've moved on."

Asma remained still as Farooq left the kitchen, the wind knocked out of her. Unable to move. As afraid as she'd been that he was still angry at her for their breakup, this—the revelation of his indifference—was so much worse.

In her mind, he, too, had spent the last eight years mourning the end of their relationship. Wishing things might have been different. But he hadn't. And, worse yet, he now knew that she had.

Asma had known Farooq intimately for two years and, as much time as had passed, she still knew from his face exactly what he meant and what he had left unsaid:

I've moved on. And you should too.

TEN

If there was one thing their short conversation in the kitchen had given Asma, it was time. Hours and hours in that special form of insomnia that seemed to always follow humiliation. Asma spent her days going through the motions at work and her nights turning the interaction over and over again in her mind. Farooq had moved on. She had not.

She was grateful that Jackson had pried her history with Farooq out of her because now he was there to make her feel better, gently disparaging Farooq as a fool and bringing her donuts and coffee from the stand in the hospital lobby. "Who cares if he has hundreds of millions," Jackson muttered. "Money can't buy you a good woman." Fatima searched for the silver lining, convinced that this would give Asma the closure she needed to move on once and for all. But every time Asma thought about Farooq's face—removed and indifferent—as she made her pathetic attempt at an apology, she felt a wave of embarrassment so strong that she wanted to curl up into a fetal position and wait for the end of time.

She finally pulled herself out of her self-flagellating funk by focusing her attention on another problem—her father and Iman. They'd been suspiciously quiet since their move. Asma decided to spend a long week-end checking in on them in Sacramento. Though the drive was only two hours, it somehow seemed longer to Asma. By the time she exited the freeway in Sacra-mento, Asma felt like she was in a different world. It had been years since she'd seen the little house her mother had insisted they purchase early on in her par-ents' marriage—her mother, a visionary, even decades ago. Asma barely recognized the streets she took to the house—the vast stretches of open and vacant lots in the sleepy state capital in the middle-of-nowhere-California of her memory paved over by generic strip malls and gated housing communities that all looked exactly the same.

She checked her phone as she pulled into the driveway. *Ran to the store. Side door is open*, Iman had texted.

The house was smaller than Asma remembered when she stepped inside. She'd only been there once or twice as an adult, as the family had been renting it out for most of her childhood. She walked through the living room and into the kitchen, where swatches of wallpa-per and paint samples lay strewn across the table. Of course Iman was already planning a remodel. Asma rifled through the stack of unopened mail on the island.

She slid open her father's credit card bill and winced at the charges Iman and her father had managed to rack up in the few weeks they had been in Sacramento. She carefully closed the envelope, not that anyone would notice it had been opened in the first place—her father and sister didn't pay attention to bills until envelopes threatened collection. Old habits, already resurfacing.

She stepped through the glass sliding door into the backyard, a small patch of grass fringed on three sides by flower and vegetable beds. Over the years their various tenants had done a decent job of taking care of the little yard that Asma's mother had set up when they first moved into the house, but Asma could see that Iman and Mr. Ibrahim had ignored it since they arrived. Moldy oranges littered the ground near the orange tree, and overripe figs rotted from their branches. Asma surveyed the damage before settling down in front of the rosebushes against the opposite fence, carefully navigating the thorns to remove the weeds.

Asma's mother had loved spending time outdoors, in nature. She spent hours in their Palo Alto garden, tending to the array of fruits and vegetables that she'd planted to remind her of home—everything from pomegranates and mulberries to okra and eggplant. She was so proud of her bounty, gifting bags of fruit to anyone who stopped by for a visit and leaving baskets of vegetables on the front stoops of their neighbors' homes. Asma was the only one who ever joined her in the garden—her father and sisters preferring the entertainment of the flat-screen TV in their air-conditioned home—and who enjoyed the family road trips her mother insisted they take to national parks. Asma always felt the presence of her mother when she was in nature—the scent of the earth, the greenery, the rustle of the wind through the trees.

And then she had met Farooq—the only person in her life who shared her mother's love of the outdoors. Their meeting in Yosemite was kismet—he fit so easily into the piece of her that had been missing since her mother's passing. The time they spent together hiking and exploring the outdoors was a balm to her soul.

Asma was so focused on her gardening—and batting away memories of her mother and Farooq—that she lost track of time, looking up almost an hour later at the sound of voices coming from inside the house. Iman and her father must have gotten home from shopping.

She brushed the dirt off her hands on the side of her jeans and stepped back through the glass patio door into the kitchen, stopping midstep at the sight in front of her. There, sitting at the kitchen table with her family, sipping a cup of tea, was one of the handsomest men Asma had ever seen. She was so taken aback that she stumbled when she stepped inside, looking from the man to Iman to her father, and forgot to greet anyone.

"Omar, you remember Asma," Mr. Ibrahim said, with no shortage of amusement at Asma's clumsy entrance.

Omar—Asma couldn't remember ever knowing someone this good-looking named Omar. She looked desperately at Iman.

Iman furrowed her brows at Asma, incredulous. *Omar Khan*, she finally mouthed.

Omar Khan? Asma looked at the man in amazement as he stood to greet her. Recognition flared almost immediately. How had she not made the connection? Because the Omar Khan of her memory had undergone some sort of radical transformation. He towered over her, well over six feet tall, with a wide smile, perfect teeth, broad chest, and a full head of carefully tousled jet-black hair. Had he always been this good-looking?

"Asma, so great to see you!"

He greeted Asma like a long-lost friend, a fact that stunned her even further as they had barely spoken two words to each other in all the years their fathers had known each other. She had written him off as intended for Iman, not bothering to get to know him any further. No wonder none of Iman's prospects after him had ever caught her fancy.

Omar handed Asma a cup of tea. "You take sugar?"

Asma nodded, noting that this may have been the first time in her life she'd ever been served tea in her family home. Omar took the cup back from her to add the sugar, then pulled out a chair and gestured for her to sit down.

She did. Then blurted out, "What are you doing here?"

"I heard your father and sister had moved out here," Omar said smoothly, patting Mr. Ibrahim on the hand. "I came to see if there was anything I could do to help."

"He's introduced us to so many people in the local community," Mr. Ibrahim said, returning Omar's look of affection. "He's in finance, you know."

As Mr. Ibrahim began listing their social engagements since arriving in Sacramento—the reason, Asma realized, they'd been so quiet since the move—Omar looked at Asma. Catching her eye, he winked and smiled. Asma, still unsettled by the sight of him in her family's kitchen, didn't smile back.

"WHAT DOES HE WANT?" ASMA ASKED IMAN THE minute the front door closed behind Omar.

"Anything is fine, really," Mr. Ibrahim said, padding toward the kitchen in his house slippers. "I'm not that hungry."

"Me neither," said Iman.

"Not for dinner, you guys! I mean Omar Khan!"

"What do you mean?"

"His father swindled you out of a lot of money, he cut us off, and you're just welcoming him back?"

"That's not what happened," Mr. Ibrahim said.

Asma was exasperated. "That's exactly what happened."

Unbeknownst to the Ibrahim daughters, Omar's father had convinced Mr. Ibrahim to take a loan out against his business, ostensibly to invest in a high-return investment fund. Mr. Ibrahim was excited that the investment would result in a windfall and hasten his retirement—which it did, just not in the way Mr. Ibrahim had anticipated. The money disappeared, along with Omar's father. The family later found out that Omar's father owed a significant gambling debt and had betrayed his longtime friend and client in a desperate attempt to save himself. Despite Asma's exhortations and Mr. Shafiq's pleas, Mr. Ibrahim refused to press charges. He said it was no use because the money was gone. But Asma knew the truth—Mr. Ibrahim didn't want news about the fraud to get out. What would people say if they knew how he had been duped?

"Omar didn't have anything to do with his father's business," Mr. Ibrahim said. "And now that his father is sick, he wants to make amends to the family."

This was the first Asma had heard of Omar's father since his disappearance.

"They found Uncle?" Asma asked. "And he's sick?"

"A stroke, a few months ago. In Pakistan," Mr. Ibrahim replied. "They brought him back here. You know Sacramento is where we first met. He's basically a vegetable, Allah tauba."

"So sad." Iman shook her head.

"Omar's back and forth most weekends from San Francisco to take care of him," Mr. Ibrahim continued. "He's working for a venture capital firm. Very successful, I hear."

"His father is literally a criminal!" Asma said. She was shocked that Omar's family disgrace didn't seem to register with her father, who judged other families for lesser infractions, such as a working-class background or a son dropping out of college.

"Wow, Asma, so judgy," Iman said. Then, with a pointed look, she added, "We can't help who we're related to."

"Yes, beta, you can't hold a son responsible for a father's sin," her father added.

"So that's it?" Asma asked. "He's our best friend again?"

Mr. Ibrahim smiled at Iman. "InshAllah."

"Abu!" Iman waved her hand at her father. "That ship has sailed."

But now Asma understood. Her father had chosen to forgive Omar—or at least chosen not to ask him the hard questions—because apparently his father's illness absolved him of his sin. And because he was rich and good-looking, Omar was once again a marriage prospect for Iman. The idea turned Asma's stomach.

Iman walked past her father to the fridge.

"Actually, I am kind of hungry," she said. "I think we still have food from Bombay Express—or we could order out again?"

As Asma watched her father and Iman discuss dinner plans, Iman scrolling through her phone trying to figure out what they should eat even when there was a fridge full of leftovers, she couldn't shake the feeling that things didn't add up. She could sort of understand her father's motivation for forgiving Omar, even if she didn't agree. But Omar hadn't cared enough about Iman to continue their relationship after the financial scandal had severed their fathers' friendship. Why would he want to be back in touch with them now?

THE NEXT MORNING, MR. IBRAHIM INFORMED Asma and Iman that Mrs. Gulnaz Dadabhoy—one of their most influential and distinguished relatives in Sacramento—had extended an invitation for lunch that weekend. Asma, of course, had never heard of her before, nor had she heard of Zubayr Dadabhoy, Gulnaz's son, who was apparently the richest Desi man in all of Sacramento. Mr. Ibrahim had set to work on reconnecting with that particular branch of the family tree since they'd moved to the state capital. So he and Iman jumped at the chance for a visit, particularly while Asma was in town.

The Dadabhoys lived in one of Sacramento's wealthier suburbs, their home accessible only by a road winding past gated-off properties with bold *no trespassing* signs. Mr. Ibrahim and Iman gasped at the appearance of the mansion at the end of a gravel path, beyond the elaborate fountains in the front yard and driveway where multiple luxury cars were parked. But Asma found the porcelain-white columns rising to a huge balcony and the huge front porch distasteful. They reminded her of the antebellum South.

The front door was opened by a maid. They took off their shoes and walked on cool marble floors past two spiral staircases and a formal dining room with plastic-covered furniture into a less formal sitting room where the furniture was also covered with plastic. The maid excused herself, telling them that Mrs. Dadabhoy was on her way down. As they waited for their host to arrive, the Ibrahims took in their surroundings.

"Beautiful! Beautiful!" said Mr. Ibrahim, looking around the room.

Iman also seemed impressed by the backdrop, unbelievably even more ostentatious and over-the-top than the Ibrahims' Palo Alto house. Intricate Persian rugs adorned the floor, and the walls were covered by gold-plated frames and embroidered hangings of verses from the Quran. Everything was framed by gold filigree. Asma couldn't help but note that they had been in the house for over ten minutes and Mrs. Dadabhoy still had not made an appearance. She couldn't imagine leaving expected company waiting for so long on plastic-covered furniture.

When she did appear, it was clear that Mrs. Gulnaz Dadabhoy may have been a handsome woman in her youth, but time and a sour disposition had done a number on her face. The frown lines across her forehead and on her cheeks were accentuated by the generous dusting of face powder five shades lighter than the skin color on her neck. Mr. Ibrahim leapt to his feet, heaping his warmest salaams and praise upon her as she settled on the couch across from the Ibrahims. She interrupted Mr. Ibrahim's lavish praise with a curt wave of her hand and a nod toward Iman sitting on the couch.

"This is the girl?"

Asma couldn't help but hold back a smile. Clearly the excuse of visiting long-lost relatives was just a ruse to get Iman in front of this matchmaking aunty. She wondered if Iman was in on it too, but when she glanced at her sister, Iman appeared just as surprised as Asma. That is, until her father cleared his throat.

"No," Mr. Ibrahim said, then looked pointedly at Asma.

Mrs. Dadabhoy turned her attention in Asma's direction. Oh no.

"How old are you?"

Asma felt annoyance prickle along her skin, her former amusement evaporated. So it turned out Iman wasn't the target of this little consultation. Perhaps Omar's renewed presence in their lives made her less of a marital concern for their father, and he was turning his attentions to his other—equally single—daughter.

"Twenty-seven." Asma was terse, hoping that she conveyed she wasn't interested in whatever her father had arranged here. She wasn't going to go from Farooq to a match made by her father and Mrs. Dadabhoy.

Mrs. Dadabhoy clucked her tongue.

"What are you waiting for?" she asked Mr. Ibrahim. Asma sat, silent, anger toward her father rising.

"She's been in medical school."

"She should have married and *then* gone to medical school." Mrs. Dadabhoy turned her attention back to Asma. "How tall are you? Stand up."

Asma's eyes widened at the gall of Mrs. Dadabhoy. She settled into her seat and crossed her arms as Mr. Ibrahim raised his eyebrows and nodded at Asma to stand up. It was one thing to be polite while visiting distant relatives. It was quite another to submit to this woman's inspection under false pretenses, and after being made to wait like they'd dropped in unannounced.

Asma was saved from having to make a scene by the appearance of a heavily made-up young woman in leggings and an oversized cashmere cardigan. At the sight of her, Mr. Ibrahim jumped up from his seat.

"Salaam, beti," he addressed the young woman, before turning his attention to Mrs. Dadabhoy. "That's your granddaughter, right? We've heard so much about her."

"Yes," Mrs. Dadabhoy said, without a glance at the girl. "That's Shagufta."

Asma watched in disbelief as Shagufta walked by without even acknowledging the guests in the house. She passed through the room and toward the front door, eyes glued to her phone and seemingly oblivious to Mr. Ibrahim or her grandmother. Asma could only imagine what Rehana—or worse, their mother—might have done if any of the Ibrahim girls had behaved so impolitely as teenagers.

"She's nineteen and we're already looking for her," Mrs. Dadabhoy continued. "If you wait too long, no one will want them."

"I have another daughter too," Mr. Ibrahim offered. "My youngest. She was engaged at nineteen."

Mrs. Dadabhoy looked vaguely interested.

"Where is she?"

"Near San Francisco. She has two children. Boys."

"What does her husband do?"

"He's a doctor," Mr. Ibrahim announced proudly.

"What kind?"

"A dentist."

Mrs. Dadabhoy snorted. "That's not a real doctor."

It was then—and only then—that the group received its first acknowledgment from Shagufta. A loud snicker, before the young woman left the house and slammed the door behind her.

ELEVEN

✦

The following weekend was Asma's first PIMPS event, and as soon as she arrived, she realized she was grossly underdressed. Women sporting headwraps and fresh blowouts mingled with each other and men wearing oversized tortoiseshell glasses and pocket squares. Waiters circled the room with trays of shot glasses filled with mango lassi. The DJ was playing music so loud everyone seemed to be yelling. It was a swirl of selfies, mocktails, and hashtags. Asma wavered between amusement and awe.

"Gorgeous Asma!" Lubna swept in from somewhere with a big hug. It was Lubna who looked amazing. Her hair was swept up into a high ponytail, the better to showcase her flawless complexion and perfectly applied makeup. She looked like a makeover after picture. Lubna was one of those people who made you feel, at least for a second, that you were just as cool as her. "Come with me, I want to introduce you to some people!"

Lubna steered Asma through the room, the crowd parting as they came through. Lubna stopped every few feet to shout out a salaam or give someone a hug. It seemed like she knew everyone in the room and everyone knew her. To all, she gave the same greeting: "This is my rock star sister-in-law, Asma. She's on the panel tonight!" Asma felt proud each time she said it, aware of how rare it was that her professional accomplishments were appreciated so publicly by members of her family.

Lubna guided Asma to a cordoned-off section near the stage. "This is for VIPs—you guys have your own facilities."

Several leather couches were set up on the other side of the velvet ropes. A big *NO PICTURES!* sign was displayed prominently near the entrance. A few people were mingling inside, drinks in hand.

"They are all major influencers," Lubna explained. "We're giving them their space so people don't try to take uncompensated pictures." Lubna scanned the room. "I need to find Farooq, he just got here a few minutes ago too."

As Lubna wafted away, Asma headed to the bathroom. She was dreading seeing Farooq and had even contemplated canceling on the event altogether to get out of seeing him. They had avoided each other for the rest of Aunty Bushra's dinner before Asma tapped out entirely, going back to Maryam's early by claiming residency-related exhaustion.

Asma returned in time to find that two chairs had been set up close together on a small stage at the front of the room. Farooq was already sitting in one of them and Lubna was standing near the mic. Were they the entirety of the panel? She squared her shoulders and approached the stage. If she was going to stay in the Bay after graduation, he would be back in her social orbit whether she liked it or not. She'd have to learn to act as though it didn't bother her, and she might as well start now.

Farooq stood up and gave his salaams without looking. Asma noticed that he pushed his chair back, widening the distance from where she was to sit.

So that was how it was going to be?

Asma made sure to push her chair back too. By the time she took her seat, they were sitting on opposite sides of Lubna's mic.

Lubna covered the mic and leaned toward them.

"Hey, guys, we'll be filming so we need you to scoot closer to one another."

Neither of them moved.

"Guys!" Lubna repeated, a bit louder. "Please, we have to start. Closer together."

It was a game of chicken and Asma was definitely not going to lose. Farooq finally broke at Lubna's increasingly insistent hand waving.

"Asma! You have to move in too."

Asma moved her chair in as the commotion caught the attention of a few people closest to the stage.

"Look like you're a couple about to sign your nik-kah," someone joked. "Close enough to be halal but one signature away from being haram."

Their chairs came to an abrupt standstill.

But they were apparently close enough for Lubna's liking. She flashed them a magnetic smile and thumbs-up before turning to face the crowd. "Hey, y'all—I'm Lubna Qureishi."

The crowd clapped and cheered as Lubna spoke, someone yelling "We love you!" from the middle of the room.

"Love you too! So glad to see you all come out. I know we're all here to have fun, but PIMPS is really all about making sure we have social and professional contacts and networks." Lubna spoke with big hand gestures, her face open and animated. A small camera crew offstage filmed her, a big furry boom mic hovering above them as the camera rolled. "We're super excited about today's panel, featuring two Cal alums who have gone on to do such amazing things. We had a third panelist too, but unfortunately she just wasn't feeling it tonight. She's learning self-care and we support her on her journey."

The crowd snapped their fingers. Why did this ever become a thing, Asma wondered, wishing they would just clap. It was going to be hard to keep a straight face for the duration of the panel.

"We really want this to be a conversation between our panelists and the audience," said Lubna. "So I'll kick off the discussion and then we'll open it up to questions from the crowd. Sound good?"

The audience cheered again. This was an easy group, Asma thought.

"Let's start off by getting to know our panelists. Asma, did you always want to be a doctor?"

"I did," Asma said, thinking of the photograph of her and her mother. "In fact, it felt like it was the only thing I can remember I wanted to be. I've always felt a calling to help people. Health and medicine struck me as the most fundamental way to do that." She didn't mention her mother, but she wondered if Farooq remembered. Ever since her conversation with Rehana, that part of her history had become murky for Asma. The steadfast conviction she'd held for so many years— that her mother had wanted her to be a doctor above all else, above even being someone's wife—had suddenly been shaken by her aunt's revisionist qualifications. But still, there was the photograph. Asma dressed as a doctor, her mother smiling. It would have to be enough, even now, with the cost of her unwavering ambition sitting next to her. For his part, Farooq glanced around the room as she spoke, looking everywhere but at her.

"Farooq, how about you—were you always into computers?" Lubna asked. "What went into your decision to drop out of Cal?"

"Yeah, I've always been that nerdy computer guy," Farooq said. "But after my first year, I knew that I didn't need a degree."

Asma had been there through that entire deliberation process and knew that dropping out wasn't a choice that came easy to him. He had agonized over it, turning the decision over and over with Asma. And she had consistently told him the same thing: "I believe in you, whatever you decide." Asma winced as she remembered his face as he said, *"This is how you believe in me?"*

"My siblings and I were the first ones in our family to go to college," Farooq continued, "so it was a big deal when I left the Bay. It was really hard, although my family understood and was supportive. But it took me years to figure things out."

"Deep, deep," Lubna said with a nod. There were more snaps from the audience. Asma stared straight ahead, afraid that if she moved, Farooq would see the impact of his words.

"Thanks for those intros. We're going to take a few questions from the audience and then unleash our panelists into the crowd so y'all can hang and mingle. Just yell out your questions, don't be shy."

"Asma, I remember you were all over the news a few years ago during the nurses' strike at your hospital." The woman speaking at the front of the crowd had a glittering nose ring. "I, too, really want to make a difference. How can I get on TV?"

"Do you want to make a difference or be on TV?" asked Asma. "Sometimes the people who are doing the most amazing work aren't necessarily the ones we know about. It was cool to be on TV, but that hasn't been the highlight of my career."

The woman nodded like she'd never before heard anything so profound.

"Farooq, what was your first purchase after you sold your company?" The guy asking the question had one of those big beards Asma could never tell whether was motivated by trend or religious orthodoxy.

"A watch." Farooq held up his arm to show off an ordinary-looking, bling-free black watch.

Typical, practical Farooq, Asma thought. The guy with the beard looked disappointed.

Lubna looked out at the crowd. "Any other questions? Come on, guys, don't be shy."

"Okay, not to be that person, but I know we're all thinking it: How do you two deal with all the pressure from your families to marry?" The woman's voice came from the back of the room. "I really want to be a lawyer, but my mom is always on my case about finding a man."

"Right?" yelled out several people at the same time. There were nervous titters across the room.

"Think about what you want—what are your priorities?" Asma said just as Farooq answered, "They aren't mutually exclusive."

"That's easy for guys to say," said Asma, turning to Farooq.

"It can be for women too."

"Men don't have the same kinds of pressure that women do."

"You're right. We have more," Farooq said, looking out into the audience as if looking for confirmation that his statement was basic fact.

"*Excuse* me?" Asma couldn't believe what she heard.

"Everyone is on our case to marry and have kids too. But we have the added pressure of career success."

"Maybe back in the old days, but not anymore."

"You know that's not true," Farooq said. "Women say they're looking for a good, kind guy—someone to be their partner through all of life's challenges. But really, that's not enough. They also want a man who makes money, who can financially take care of them."

There were boos from several women in the audience mingled with a few yeahs from men.

"That's sexist. And a complete generalization," Asma said. She felt the humiliation of her encounter with Farooq slip away, replaced by anger. He had once been her greatest champion and a witness to her ambition. Who had he become?

"Wow, conflict among our panelists!" said Lubna, with a nervous laugh. "I love it!"

"I'm not trying to be a jerk," Farooq said. "I'm just sharing from my own personal experience. I grew up in a working-class family, so I know what it's like to suddenly come into money. It's not the person with money who changes. It's the people around you."

"Money isn't what makes a relationship."

"I know that. But it seems to make all the difference for some people." Farooq turned and looked straight at Asma. "Some people who didn't want anything to do with me before suddenly wanting me back in their lives."

They sat for a minute staring at each other, the look on Farooq's face the same as on the day they broke up. He was angry—so very angry. It was what Asma had suspected all along—Farooq was furious with her, because he truly believed she'd ended their engagement over his lack of wealth.

But at least anger was a step up from the total indifference he'd claimed the other night.

Farooq looked away. Asma felt out of breath. She turned to see the crowd staring at them, unsure how to react to their discussion.

"Wow," Lubna finally said. "It's like a Twitter fight—but in real life."

ASMA WAS HALFWAY DOWN THE STAIRS THE next morning when she overheard Maryam talking in the kitchen.

"I'm happy that Lubna likes him," said Maryam. "But I hope she doesn't do anything dumb like post a picture of them on Instagram until they're officially engaged. Your mom would freak."

Asma slipped quietly down a few more steps so she could hear better, curious about what Lubna had said to Maryam after the PIMPS event.

"I think Ammi would just be happy that all her influencer activities actually resulted in finding someone," said Hassan.

"PIMPS is so dumb, but Saba really should make an effort to go so she can meet someone too."

"What are you talking about?" Hassan asked this question so frequently of Maryam that Asma could picture his face without even seeing it: scrunched-up nose, furrowed brows, and lips twisted in amusement. It was precisely the things Asma found so annoying about Maryam that Hassan thought were charming. "She's with Tariq."

"I mean with a professional," said Maryam. "Someone who doesn't work at Walmart."

"Part time!" said Hassan. "It's not his life dream, it's a college job."

"Oh right, while he becomes an *actor*." Maryam pronounced the word with an affected accent. "Hard to believe there's a job out there that makes working at Walmart seem like a stable career."

"Saba's right, you *are* a hater."

"I don't hate anyone. I just think she could do better."

"He's a good guy."

"That's what people always say about men without money. It's like saying a girl has a good personality. That means she's ugly."

"Jeez, Maryam," said Hassan. "Don't be a snob."

"I'm just saying that when it comes to marriage, you

have to stay in your lane. Everyone knows out-of-league marriages don't work."

"You're mixing metaphors," said Hassan. "And you sound like your father."

Hassan was right on that account. Maryam's criticism of Tariq sounded exactly like her father's and Rehana's past objections to Farooq. That he didn't have money or an education or come from the right family. Asma bit down hard on the inside of her cheek, her anger rising once more.

And now history was repeating itself with Saba and Tariq.

"Saba's a good girl and I think she knows she can find someone better for her and for our family," Maryam said. "If only we could find another Farooq."

"Well," said Hassan, "maybe Farooq can marry them both!"

"Guys love talking about having more than one wife. As if you could handle it," said Maryam.

"He does have enough money," Hassan continued.

"Having a wife isn't just about having enough money."

"True, it's also about patience." Hassan cleared his throat with exaggeration.

"And respect and responsibility," said Maryam.

"Which, you're right, *is* a lot to handle."

"Ha," Maryam deadpanned. "Maybe Farooq has some friends he could introduce Saba to. She's so young. She doesn't have to settle for Tariq when she could do better."

"Instead of worrying about Saba, why don't you worry about Asma?" Hassan's voice dropped. Asma had to slip down a few more steps and lean in closer to hear him. "I feel bad for her; my mom is trying to set her up with some old guy *again*."

Asma was surprised to hear Hassan talking about her. He usually kept his opinions on Asma's life to himself during family discussions—and Asma assumed it was because she'd turned down his family's rishta and left him open for Maryam to swoop in and catch his attention. So it was jarring that, six years later, here they were discussing *her* marriage prospects at the breakfast table.

"I told your mom not to bother," said Maryam. "She's not looking."

"Because of her job?"

"Because she's Asma. You know how she is."

Asma wondered what Maryam meant—how *was* she?

"She doesn't want to get married," Maryam said. "She never has."

So her younger sister clearly knew nothing about Farooq. Not even a sense that there had been a prospect, once. While Asma always wondered how much Iman knew about their broken engagement, Asma realized now that, if she knew anything, she wasn't sharing the information with Maryam.

"There are single Desi men in Sacramento," continued Maryam. "She can find someone if she really wants to."

"Doesn't seem like it's really her scene," said Hassan.

"What is her scene besides work?"

It was strange to hear herself spoken about. She didn't like it. Asma crept up the stairs and crawled back into bed.

Did Maryam really think she didn't ever want to marry? Asma had always been clear that her plan was to marry after she became a doctor. It seemed like one of the few decisions her family actually respected—or, at least, Asma assumed they did, because apart from the occasional conversation with Rehana, they had largely left her alone during med school. And she'd justified it to herself that, if she'd broken up with Farooq because becoming a doctor was more important to her than love, it made no sense to consider any other romantic possibilities until she'd achieved her goal.

But still, Asma *was* a doctor. She had been a doctor for three years, and she'd never seriously considered trying to find a husband in that time. She was exhausted, she worked too much, the potential suitors were never what she wanted. She had plenty of excuses. But beneath that justification there was the truth. There was only one person she had ever considered marrying. And she'd broken his heart eight years ago. Did she even deserve another chance?

She thought about her organic chem test in college, Farooq's arms around her as he told her he was proud of her. And she wondered if any success would ever feel as sweet as that, if she had nobody to share it with.

———

ASMA DRUMMED HER FINGERS ON HER DESK AND waited for the page to load. She was terribly behind on her charting. She'd come in early for her shift because the remote connection to the hospital's server was loading too slowly at home. But the computer software wasn't any quicker at the hospital, and now it kept freezing.

When the spinning wheel appeared onscreen for the fifth time, Asma opened up a browser window. She had once been a news junkie, but no more. Staying up-to-date on breaking news—immigration raids and hate crimes and police shootings on the regular—made her feel helpless. She was only able to function in her job, with her family, and as a sane citizen, by focusing on work and her local community and staying only marginally informed through limited doses of news consumption. Headlines read, she was about to close the browser when an ad in the corner of the screen caught her eye—it was for a dating app. These ads had become unnervingly accurate. How did this news website know she was single?

Asma thought back to the conversation she'd overheard between Hassan and Maryam and the comments Farooq had made during the PIMPS panel. Farooq had changed. And, based on what he said, not necessarily for the better. Maybe it was time for her to change too—let go of the past and imagine a future for herself beyond Farooq.

Asma googled Love & Salaam on her phone, one of the Muslim dating apps Lubna had recently plugged on her Instagram page. She was curious to see what type of men she'd find online. Maybe this was where she could start her effort to meet someone. She could prove to her family—and herself—that she wasn't committed to a life of solitude and celibacy.

Asma hunched a bit in her chair and glanced around to make sure nobody was behind her as the app downloaded—she would die if any of her colleagues saw what was on her phone screen.

So many questions, she thought, as the app prompted her to enter pithy answers to profile prompts, inform-ing her that *better profiles mean more matches!* and *make sure to show your whole face in your photos!* It was like a computer-generated aunty. Paranoid that the account could somehow be linked to her personally, she entered a fake name, birthday, and location and up-loaded an old, somewhat blurry photograph of Iman from Asma's birthday a few years back.

She leaned back and examined her profile—it was generic, uninformative, and untraceable, complete with a *new user!* banner welcoming her to the app. She started swiping through the seemingly endless stream of pro-files the app presented to her.

Was this man her father's age seriously looking for a woman in her twenties?

People who say they don't want drama are usually the ones with the most drama.

Wow, look at this guy's stomach! But why wasn't he wearing a shirt?

The profiles were overwhelming. Iman was right. Anyone could—and apparently did—go online. Perhaps she should ask Aunty Uzma for a spot in her matchmaking book.

"Ooh, he's fine. Nice abs."

Asma swiveled around to find Jackson, peering over her shoulder at her phone, a big shit-eating grin on his face.

"Oh my God," Asma said, mortified.

"Now, this is what I'm talking about! Get back on that horse, Asma!" Jackson laughed, then lowered his voice to a whisper. "But don't look at porn in here, the nurses are really nosy!"

"I'm going to kill you."

Asma shoved Jackson away from her, then held her finger down on the app to delete it. She cleared her browser history and logged out of the computer. She'd finish her charting in the privacy of her home tonight— which was where she should've ventured into the dating pool in the first place.

"ASMA, THIS WOULD LOOK GREAT ON YOU—TRY it on."

Fatima pulled a top from the rack she'd been searching through and tossed it at Asma. The two of them had spent the afternoon shopping, Fatima trying to find a dress to wear for a high school friend's wedding the next weekend.

Asma held up the top, a long-sleeved emerald green silk blouse, and admired it until she saw the number on the price tag. It nearly made her choke.

"I don't need it," she said, putting the blouse back on the rack.

"What about for your residency graduation?"

"I'm going to just borrow something from Maryam," Asma said. "Where will I ever wear this again?"

"Maybe on a date with a hot guy you meet online." Fatima smiled slyly.

"I should never have told you about that."

Fatima laughed. "Well, it's a better idea than whoever the aunties try to set you up with."

"That remains to be seen," Asma said dryly.

Asma took a stack of dresses from Fatima, then went in search of the fitting rooms. They were all locked and of course the salesclerk, who had been flitting relentlessly all around them earlier, was nowhere in sight. Asma walked up and down the aisles, looking for her in vain—and ran directly into the infamous Aunty Uzma, whom she had managed to avoid since her father's party.

Asma cursed her luck.

"Asma! I saw you earlier looking at shoes but I wasn't sure it was you. You've gained some weight."

Asma contemplated tossing the dresses at Uzma and bolting but knew that she would never be able to outrun Uzma's penchant for gossip.

"Salaam, Aunty, I'm doing well, thanks. How are you?"

Asma's passive-aggressive reply sailed over Aunty Uzma's orange, henna-dyed hair.

"Fine, fine," Uzma said. "Good I ran into you. We haven't heard from you about the wedding."

"Which wedding?"

"My nephew."

Her nephew? The one she kept trying to set Asma up with? Asma's confusion must have been evident on her face.

"The one you never contacted," Uzma said helpfully. "Alhamdulillah, it was for the best." Uzma nodded, relieved. "He met a nice young lady, MashAllah. She's very fair. She's a doctor. So is her father. And her two brothers."

"Aunty, you know I'm also a—"

"He's starting a fellowship next month. In Omaha. At a very good hospital. It's the third best in Nebraska. MashAllah."

"Omaha, huh?" Too bad it didn't work out, thought Asma, trying not to giggle. She had missed her chance of leaving the Bay for a flyover state.

"Your father still hasn't responded to the invitation."

"Did you send it to our Palo Alto address?" Asma asked. "Abu left for Sacramento last month and I'm staying with Maryam."

"Acha. Right. Right." Uzma waggled her head. "You must come at least. Bring your sister."

Oh hell no, Asma thought. "I'll try, Aunty," she said with a fake smile. "I've just been so busy, with work and everything."

Uzma's eyes narrowed, Asma's mention of work making Uzma momentarily forget all about the wedding.

"You girls and work. Put that on hold. You'll have time for work later, now you must find someone and settle down."

Asma spotted the salesclerk walking to the women's section. She subtly lifted the clothes in her arms and nodded toward the fitting room, wondering if her strained smile conveyed that she was being held hostage by an aunty.

"I said the same thing to your sister Iman," Uzma continued. "I thought she was serious about looking. I don't know why she asked me to take her picture out of my book."

"She did?" Asma had barely spoken to her sister since her visit to Sacramento, other than to text her reminders about overdue bills and their father's medication. She wondered why Iman would have asked such a thing—she'd seemed to have such high hopes for Uzma's matchmaking skills. Unless . . . could it have something to do with Omar Khan's sudden reappearance in their lives? "When was that?" Asma asked.

"Last week. I told her, Iman beti, you can't be picky, you'll be thirty next year!"

Uzma's comment actually made Asma feel sorry for her sister. To be sure, Iman was generally a snob when it came to looking for a life partner—she had previously turned down suitors based on what Asma thought were shallow reasons, such as height below six feet and an income in the low six figures. And yet Asma resented Uzma's implication that Iman couldn't be selective about who and what she was looking for in a husband just because she was almost thirty.

"Ma'am, can I help you with those?" A salesclerk appeared from around the corner, motioning to the stack of dresses Asma carried.

"Yes, please!" Asma lunged at the woman as though she were a first responder. "Excuse me, Aunty, I have to get a room for my friend. It was nice seeing you."

"Give my salaams to your father," Uzma called out as Asma rushed off without a backward glance. "And let me know about the wedding!"

"I will!" Asma lied, slamming the fitting room door behind her.

TWELVE

Asma's last overnight shift was brutal. There was a multicar pileup on the San Mateo Bridge and it seemed as though the ambulances carrying injured drivers and passengers were never going to stop arriving at the hospital. The ER was in chaos, with doctors, residents, and nurses being summoned from all over the hospital to pitch in. Asma ran back and forth between the injured all night, with hardly enough time to attend to one patient before being summoned to assist with another. The last of the patients wasn't stabilized until hours after Asma's shift was supposed to end in the morning.

Despite her exhaustion, Asma couldn't fall asleep when she got home, still high from the adrenaline of her shift, her body clock thrown off by the overnight activity and the late-morning sunlight streaming through the ineffective curtains in the twins' bedroom. After an hour of staring at the ceiling, growing more frustrated as each minute passed, she got off her air mattress and headed downstairs. Perhaps going for a run would tire her out. She was desperate—Asma was not usually one for running.

But here she was, sitting on the front steps of Maryam's house lacing up her shoes, when Lubna and Saba walked out of their front door across the street, their faces lighting up when they saw her.

"We're going to pick up Tariq from work and get some lunch," Saba said.

"Give him my salaams," Asma answered.

She grabbed the handrail and was pulling herself up from the stoop when Maryam opened the door. "I thought I heard voices out here," she said. "Where are the girls going?"

"Just out," Asma answered. She knew Maryam didn't approve of Tariq, and she didn't want to hear any complaining.

"Where are you guys going?" Maryam called out to the girls.

Lubna and Saba glanced at each other.

"Just out."

"I want to come!" said Maryam. It was one of Maryam's least attractive qualities, Asma thought with annoyance, how she was perpetually the youngest sister even now that she was married with children. She'd never grown out of demanding to be included when she felt she was being left out, or pretending to be ill so she might be tended to. Asma had hoped she would age out of that behavior one day, but it seemed even well into Maryam's twenties, she was still a seven-year-old at heart.

"We're going to get lunch, so we'll be gone for a while!" Lubna called back, and Asma knew it was a mistake not to simply refuse Maryam her demand outright. But Lubna was too polite for that and would be made to indulge Maryam as a result.

"No worries," Maryam said. "I don't have the boys right now. Your parents are picking them up from soccer and then taking them to run a few errands."

Saba frowned and whispered to Lubna.

"We're actually going to be walking," Lubna said, slipping her car keys into her purse.

"Sounds good to me!" said Maryam.

"A super-long walk—maybe three miles!"

Maryam didn't get the hint. Asma thought of the vague headaches and low-grade fevers Maryam was perpetually complaining about, despite the fact that Asma never found anything wrong with her. Clearly, Maryam had forgotten that she was supposed to be in "delicate" health, when faced with a three-mile hike.

"I'll just grab my shoes," Maryam replied.

The girls looked at Asma in desperation as Maryam disappeared into the house. Asma held up her hands at them and nodded, indicating that she would handle the situation.

"Why are they acting like I can't walk?" Maryam

muttered as she rummaged through the hall closet for her shoes. "I'm not some lazy housewife who doesn't leave my couch!"

"They just want some sister time," Asma said.

"They're always hanging out with each other. I'm their sister too."

Asma considered her options. If Maryam joined the girls, she would mess up their plans to see Tariq. Maryam was not one to hold her tongue when faced with a situation she deemed inappropriate. Maybe Asma should go with them to run interference for Saba and Tariq. It would be a good deed and, more importantly, it would get her out of her run.

"You know what, I'll come with you guys," Asma said, though she was already feeling fatigue pulling at the backs of her eyes, her long, taxing night in the ER beginning to catch up to her. A three-mile walk didn't exactly sound appealing. But still, she couldn't leave poor Tariq at Maryam's mercy.

When they emerged from the house, there was a black BMW parked in the Qureishis' driveway. Beside the car, a figure stood talking to Lubna. Asma recognized him immediately, even with his back to her. Farooq. He'd been invited to join their little excursion.

His presence startled Asma and brought on a rush of hot panic. After all, if this was meant to be a double date with Tariq and Saba, then Farooq and Lubna were clearly seeing each other—a reality that Asma had refused to take seriously even after hearing it discussed by Hassan and Maryam. But her denial had now caught her off guard.

"You're sure you want to come?" Lubna called to Maryam, as Farooq turned and caught sight of Asma. He seemed not to react, though Asma was flooded with another wave of regret. This was actually happening . . . the love of her life had moved on and was now dating a member of her family. She felt like she might be sick. She bent down, pretending to check her laces, then stayed down to slow her breathing.

"Definitely!" Maryam said. "Asma's coming too."

"Great," Saba said, though her tone didn't reflect enthusiasm. "It's a party."

As the little group started down the street, Asma's phone rang. She'd never been so happy to see the hospital in her caller ID. She waved at the group to go ahead and stopped to take the call.

"Sorry, I know you're off, Dr. Ibrahim," apologized the intern on the other end of the line. "But Mr. Shepard was just readmitted."

Asma felt a flare of concern. The last she'd heard, Green Meadows had identified their air-conditioning system as the source of the Legionnaires' outbreak and were taking steps to address the situation. Either Mr. Shepard was being admitted for something unrelated, or perhaps the situation hadn't been thoroughly corrected. Legionnaires' was a serious public health concern. Asma resolved to check in with the health department if Mr. Shepard still had signs of bacterial pneumonia.

"Please keep me posted as to his condition," Asma instructed the intern, before she hung up and hurried to rejoin the group.

Maryam was speed-walking ahead—perhaps to show that she was a great walker—with Saba following, walking, talking, *and* texting on her phone. Farooq and Lubna brought up the rear. Asma caught up to them at a stoplight and fell into place behind them so quietly that they didn't notice that she had joined them.

"They drove down to Santa Cruz last night for his reading," Farooq said. "They said they'd meet us at the restaurant." Asma realized that he must have been talking about Sophia and Yusef. Her stomach dropped further—this was meant to be a lunch date where they introduced their siblings, she realized. Things were moving quickly, then.

"I love Santa Cruz," said Lubna. "Such a fun town."

"I've never been," Farooq said, and the lie made Asma catch her breath.

Santa Cruz was where the two of them had gone after Asma received her organic chem grade. They had walked along a deserted trail with a gorgeous vista of the ocean when they had taken a break, spreading a picnic blanket in a clearing on the side of the path. It was the happiest Asma could ever remember feeling. She had turned to share that with Farooq but hadn't needed to. She knew from the look on his face—that big lopsided grin and the way he had gazed so intently at her—that he felt the same.

"Oh, Asma!" Lubna turned around, sabotaging Asma's plan to eavesdrop. "Is everything all right? You look a little pale."

"It's nothing, that was just the hospital."

"Do you have to go in? I thought you just worked all night." Lubna looked concerned. Farooq stared at the ground ahead of him. His face was expressionless, but Asma knew from the slight clench of his jaw that he was aggravated.

"No, it was just a consult about one of my regular patients," Asma said. "I'll follow up on it tomorrow. I don't think I have it in me to go back in now." In truth, Asma was feeling her exhaustion. She wondered, particularly compared to Lubna's bright twenty-something-who-gets-good-sleep glow, if she looked as haggard as she felt.

"Oh my gosh, you must be so tired," Lubna said.

"You get used to it after a while," Asma replied. "Kind of."

The light had turned green but Farooq didn't move. It was a second before Asma realized that he was waiting for her to walk ahead. Embarrassment flared. It was clear that he wanted her to go so he could be alone with Lubna. She quickened her step to pass them and catch up with Maryam.

Maryam was throwing a temper tantrum. During their walk down the hill to the town center—a glorified strip mall—she had overheard Saba on the phone and realized the real reason the girls had left home in the first place and why they didn't want Maryam to join them.

"I don't shop at Walmart," she announced. "They're terrible to their workers and their plastic Chinese goods are destroying the ocean."

"I didn't realize you were such an environmentalist," said Asma. "Especially after your rant the other day about paper straws."

"They turn into pulp in your drink, who thinks of these things?" Maryam said. "Asma, come with me to Carter's instead. The boys need new shoes and I prefer to buy ones that weren't made in sweatshops by other children."

Asma didn't protest. She needed to get away from Farooq, even for a few minutes. Her memory of their Santa Cruz trip had left her feeling raw in his presence, especially now that he seemed like a completely different person with her. Cold and distant, the opposite of the warm, sweet boy she'd known, with his encouraging words and arms full of flowers.

"I don't understand why Hassan's family is encouraging this," Maryam said as they entered the shoe store.

"Tariq is a good guy."

"I'm sick of people saying that! There are lots of good guys, that doesn't mean you should marry all of them."

"What exactly is your problem with him?"

"It's not personal. I'm just saying she can do better."

"Better, how? He's smart, close to his family, and, most importantly, he's good to her."

"Marriage is a lot of work, even when you're with someone who has so much in common with you," said Maryam. "Why make things harder by marrying someone from such a different family and background?"

Did all married people really feel this way about marriage? Were they speaking some universal truth that she couldn't understand because she was single? Or was her family especially preoccupied with wealth and status?

And then there it was. "You don't understand these things because you're not married, Asma."

"Oh right. Because you're married to the right man from the right background. So your life should be our aspiration." Asma let out a little laugh, though she knew she was being cruel.

"What's that supposed to mean?"

"Nothing."

"No, please tell me, Asma. What about my life is so terrible that you wouldn't want any part of it?"

"Maybe you should ask yourself. You're the one always whining and complaining."

"That's a really bitchy thing to say." It was, and Asma regretted it almost immediately. But the combination of her fatigue and Farooq's indifference had left her short-tempered and prickly. Especially since the only reason Asma was crashing this double date was because Maryam had horned her way in on Lubna and Saba's plans and was too self-involved to realize it.

"I'm tired," Asma replied. "I shouldn't have come."

Asma put down the mini-Crocs she had been holding and left Maryam alone in the store. She felt dizzy from fatigue. She went in search of the go-to suburban strip mall refuge—Starbucks. She opened the door, greeted by a blast of cool air and the overwhelming aroma of roasted coffee beans. But then she saw that she wasn't the only one who'd had that idea. Farooq and Lubna were there, waiting at the counter for their drinks. So deep in conversation that they hadn't seen her come in.

Asma ducked her head and quickly passed them on the way to the alcove where the bathroom was located. She stood next to the wall, hoping they would leave without noticing her and she could get her caffeine fix.

"I mean, he's practically supporting his entire family," said Lubna.

"He seems like a nice guy."

"Nice guy is an understatement. Tariq's the best."

"So you don't think Saba could do better?" Farooq asked.

"Because he works retail?" Lubna asked. "Who cares? Saba likes him."

"What about your parents?"

"They like him too."

"I mean, they don't care about his job or that he's not Desi?"

"Please, Ammi and Abu are so chill. They just want us to marry good people."

"Unpretentious Pakistani parents—how refreshing."

Asma winced. It was clear that this was less a compliment of the Qureishis than it was a dig at the Ibrahims. A customer approached the bathroom. Asma moved aside, pressing herself against the wall to remain out of sight.

"I don't think I could handle it if our parents were super judgy. Like Maryam," Lubna continued. "She drives me nuts sometimes. She can be such a snob. She's so much like her older sister, Iman. Have you met her?"

"No."

"It's that whole family, really. Except for Asma."

"How so?" Farooq asked.

"She's more like their mother was, apparently. Down-to-earth, and humble even though she's the most accomplished one. I wonder how things would've been if Hassan had married her instead. You know they were set up, right?"

"I didn't," Farooq said, carefully. "When was that?"

"Maybe a year or two before he married Maryam— so, six years ago?"

"How come it didn't work out?" Farooq asked, and Asma could tell his curiosity had gotten the better of him. Despite how much he'd changed, Asma realized she still knew him so well. And it didn't hurt that his curiosity was about her.

"Asma's always been really focused on her career and isn't interested in marriage. Which, I get, but still. Sometimes it seems like she's lonely."

"Maybe she hasn't met the right person?"

"Maybe. Saba and I wonder sometimes, but we've never asked her. Saba's theory is that she had a great love who left her permanently heartbroken."

"Like Miss Havisham?"

"Who?"

"You know, from *Great Expectations*," said Farooq.

"I haven't seen it."

"Not important," said Farooq. "Do you have a theory about her?"

"I don't know. I think it's cool that she's a doctor, but I wonder if the aunties are right in some ways. Follow your career aspirations but only at your own peril if you want to get married."

Asma took in a sharp breath just as the barista called out Farooq's and Lubna's names. The last thing Asma wanted to be was a cautionary tale for the career-minded young women in her life. She wanted Lubna to know that it was possible to have both—that Saba was right, and Asma had chosen not to marry because of heartbreak and not indifference—but their voices faded as they took their drinks and headed out the door.

IT WAS ONLY WHEN ASMA GOT TO THE FRONT OF the line that she realized she'd forgotten to bring her wallet with her. It was the fatigue of the long night shift—she felt herself blush and apologized to the barista, heading quickly for the door. By the time Asma got outside, the entire group had reassembled in the parking lot by a small black convertible with its top down. Asma could see Yusef and Sophia behind the windshield. Sophia waved at her as she approached.

When Maryam caught sight of her, she pointedly looked at her phone.

"I actually don't think I can do lunch. If I'm not home when your mom arrives with the boys, I'll never hear the end of it," she said to Lubna. "And I can't take another person yelling at me today."

Asma knew the comment was directed at her.

"I'm sorry, Maryam," Asma said.

"Whatever," Maryam said with a wave of her hand. This was her way of accepting Asma's apology.

"I should probably go too," Asma added, grateful for the escape. "I think I'm a lot more tired than I realized."

"Do you want us to drop you two at home?" Sophia asked. "We're a little early for our reservation anyway, and it won't take long."

"That's okay," Maryam said, as if to prove once more that she was physically able. "I could use the walk. But, Asma, you go. You look terrible."

There was no time for Asma to refuse. Sophia was out of the car, pulling up her seat.

"Sure, I apprecia—" Asma said, as she awkwardly began to climb into the back. But her fatigue got the better of her as she misjudged the width of the car's little doorframe, and her foot slipped. Before she could topple over, however, Farooq's steadying hand caught hers. She gripped it, startled both by her clumsiness and by the sudden contact. That familiar hand, the one she'd held so many times and then had not touched in eight years after it had been yanked away from her in anger. Warm and firm, it slipped perfectly into place with hers. Farooq helped her into the car and then released her. Asma hoped that it appeared she was blushing from the near fall and not from her sudden proximity to him. And then, without any prelude, he handed her the cup of coffee he had been holding, two packets of raw sugar and a wooden mixing stick balanced on the lid. A grande skim latte.

It was the only drink Asma ever got at Starbucks. Asma looked at him blankly for a moment, before she realized that he had ordered it for her. Perhaps he had been listening when she and Lubna were discussing her exhausting overnight shift. But by the time she thought to thank him, he had already closed the door and was walking away to join Lubna on the sidewalk.

THE CAR RACED DOWN AN EMPTY FREEWAY.

The top was down but Asma couldn't even enjoy the feel of the wind in her face and hair. She tried focusing on the moving landscape, the small rolling hills on either side of the freeway lush and green after several days of rain. She kept replaying the conversation between Lubna and Farooq as she sipped the drink he had given her, her hand still tingling from where it had met his.

He got her coffee. He even remembered her order. Had the memory of their trip to Santa Cruz triggered feelings in him too?

"Well, that didn't take long," Yusef said.

"You mean Farooq and Lubna?" Sophia asked. "Did he say something to you?"

"No, but he seems really into her. I think he's found a match."

"I thought so too. Although it's surprising considering how strongly he used to feel about Desi women," Sophia said.

Sophia caught Asma's eye in the rearview mirror and mistook her grimace for curiosity.

"Farooq was head over heels in love with this girl in college. Did you hear about that back in the day?"

Asma shook her head, trying to play it cool.

"We never met her. I guess she was keeping the relationship a secret from her family, so it was all very hush-hush at the time," Sophia said with a look of pity. "And I guess for good reason. They were such snobs that as soon as she told them about Farooq, they made her dump him. I guess they thought he wasn't good enough for her. Can you imagine?"

"I bet they are regretting it now!" Yusef laughed.

"I really hope so," Sophia said. "Awful people. It took him years to get over it. God, he was so depressed.

He swore that he'd never marry a Desi woman, because he didn't want to deal with another family like that."

Asma looked out at the green hills, grateful when they passed a semitruck so loud that it excused her from having to respond.

THIRTEEN

A sma tiptoed down the stairs. She rummaged around the front hall closet, but unable to find shoes in the dark—and not wanting to wake anyone by turning on any lights—she slipped out the front door barefoot. The night air was cool, the breeze hitting her bare arms and her legs through her pajama pants. She ran on her tiptoes over the dew-covered front lawn to the car parked curbside.

Asma's phone had rung shortly after midnight, blending into her dream. When it rang the second time, it roused her from her sleep. She bolted upright on her air mattress and felt underneath her pillow for her phone, answering it quickly so as to not wake the twins.

It was Fatima, in tears. Asma couldn't understand what she was saying, only that she needed to talk and was on her way to Maryam's house.

She was still crying as Asma slipped into the passenger seat.

"Salman's cheating."

Asma felt her stomach drop. She remembered Fatima's suspicions and how she had tried to downplay them. She had been so wrapped up with work and Farooq that she hadn't wanted to worry about anything else, convinced that Salman would never be foolish enough to betray a wife like Fatima.

"How do you know?" Asma asked.

"He admitted it. He was on the phone with her when he thought I was in the shower, and I heard everything."

"Oh, Fatima," Asma began, but her friend was talking quickly before she could say more.

"She was a summer associate at his firm," Fatima said. "It's been going on for a year, Asma! I missed the signs for an entire year!"

Fatima's voice cracked.

"I feel so stupid."

"*You* feel stupid?" Asma said. "*He's* the stupid one!"

"Here I was, going about my days in total denial. Trying for a baby! And he was cheating on me the entire time."

Asma held Fatima's hand as she doubled over in sobs, a sliver of a memory sharpening in her mind: Fatima, a huge smile on her face, holding up an acceptance letter to Columbia's School of Architecture. The opportunity she'd given up when Salman's priorities got in the way.

Fatima had sacrificed her entire life when she married Salman. Any personal or career aspirations she had had been put on hold to become a loving and a supportive wife as he worked countless hours to become a partner at his firm. And this bastard had cheated on her?

"What are you going to do?" Asma asked.

"My parents told me to pray and not make any rash decisions because it won't look good if I just leave."

Fatima looked at Asma, tears streaked across her cheeks.

"*He* cheated on *me*! And my parents said *I* won't look good for leaving?" She shook her head. "I'm heading to Oakland to stay at my cousin's."

"Now?" Asma asked. "It's late! Stay here."

"I can't—your sister and Hassan's family. They'll want to know what's going on. And I don't want to answer any questions."

"Okay, then wait. I'm coming with you."

"You have work."

"I'll Uber back tomorrow morning."

"It's okay. I need to be alone," Fatima replied, wiping her face. "I have to figure out what I'm going to do."

Even once Fatima had left, Asma didn't sleep, staying up to wait for Fatima to text that she'd made it to her cousin's. When the text came in, Asma switched off her phone and settled into bed. But sleep didn't come. She tossed and turned, ruminating about the situation. It wasn't lost on her that Fatima had done everything she was supposed to. She'd married the man her parents had wanted for her and been a loyal and devoted wife to Salman for years. He had taken her for granted all that time, and then betrayed her. And yet, after all that, her parents' first concern was saving face. For whom? Asma wondered. Was keeping up appearances more important than their daughter's happiness?

And then, as Asma was finally drifting off to sleep, the answer came: of course. After all, it had been for her family too.

AUNTY BUSHRA'S DUPATTA WAS SLIPPING DOWN the back of her head as she opened the door. "Thank you, Asma beti," she said, pulling Asma in for a hug. "I'll be back in less than an hour."

Asma had been enjoying a rare morning off after waking up to an unusually empty house. Hassan was working and Maryam had taken the boys to their soccer game. But a minute after she had brewed a fresh cup of coffee, she got a call from Maryam that Zayd was running a fever, she'd dropped him at Bushra's house, but Bushra needed to run to the store to pick up groceries for a dinner party she was hosting later that night. Nothing like a sick child to entirely throw off everyone's well-laid plans.

"Zayd is upstairs asleep and there's food in the fridge." Bushra squeezed past Asma and out the door. "Please eat!"

Bushra didn't need to tell her twice. Asma rummaged through the fridge. Only Bushra, with a kitchen full of food, would be cooking up a fresh feast to serve guests.

Asma had just finished pulling out all her favorites—chicken jalfrezi, saag paneer, and roti—when the landline rang. The caller ID announced that it was Lubna.

"Salaam, Lubna," Asma said, answering the phone. "It's Asma."

"Asma! Hey, salaam! Is my mom there?"

"She went to the store—I'm here with Zayd. Everything okay?"

"Yes, fine, fine! I just ran to get a mani because I have to film later today. It's for this amazing new lip gloss, Smooches. It goes on so smoothly and doesn't get all sticky."

"That's a good testimonial," Asma said. "I don't even wear lip gloss and I'm tempted to get some."

"Don't buy it, Asma!" Lubna said, alarmed. "They are sending me so many boxes, I can totally hook you up."

Asma laughed. "Thanks, Lubna, I appreciate that."

"Of course! Hey, you'll be there for a bit longer, right?" Lubna continued. "Farooq is stopping by in a minute. My laptop was acting crazy so he took it yesterday to fix it—he said he'd drop it off on his way to work."

Farooq? Coming here? Now? Asma scanned what she was wearing. A total mess. Sweats, a hoodie, and her old, scratched-up glasses.

"Asma? You still there?"

"Still here!"

"Can you please let him in? Don't let him leave! I texted and called but his phone went straight to voicemail. I'll be home in like fifteen minutes."

Asma hung up the phone, panicked. She pulled up the hood on her sweatshirt and tied the string tightly under her chin. Maybe Aunty had a dupatta lying around that she could throw on her head?

The doorbell rang.

Asma ran into the living room, then the guest room, scanning for a scarf, but none were to be found.

The doorbell rang again. No time to check upstairs. It was inevitable. She dragged herself toward the front hallway, catching a glimpse of herself in the mirror by the front door. Her hoodie was on so tight she looked like the kid from South Park.

She untied the hoodie and pulled it down, along with the rubber band holding together a sloppy bun. She quickly combed through her hair with her fingers. There was not much else she could do.

She took a deep breath and opened the door.

Farooq was standing on the doorstep, laptop in one hand and a small stack of newspapers and flyers in the other—items that had been littering the Qureishis' driveway and front stoop all week that no one had bothered to bend down and pick up. He was freshly shaved and wearing a sharp, well-tailored navy suit and aviator sunglasses—the most put together she'd seen him. Ever.

"Asma?" He looked completely startled to see her.

He stepped back in confusion, took off his sunglasses, and looked around, seemingly in search of the house number.

"You're in the right place," she said. Something about how disoriented he was by her presence made her feel a bit better about her disheveled appearance. "I'm baby-sitting a sick kid. Lubna's on her way home, she should be back soon."

Farooq nodded, still looking thrown. They stood uncomfortably for a second, before Farooq gestured toward the driveway. "I can just wait in my car."

She needed to stop making this awkward. "No, no. Come in, come in."

Asma opened the door wider and he followed her into the house. Now what?

"I was just about to get some food, let me make you a plate." She gestured toward the table as they entered the kitchen.

She knew exactly what he liked—chicken tikka masala and roti. His no-fail staple order whenever they went to Big Biryani, the terrible Desi restaurant near campus they frequented whenever he felt homesick. Despite her encouragement—and much to her dismay—he never ate a single vegetable. She pointed to the Tupperware of spinach on the counter in front of her to confirm. "No saag, right?"

"Right, no saag," he said with a small smile.

They didn't speak as the food warmed. Asma stared at the microwave while Farooq glanced through the flyers he had brought in with him from the front door, like he was in the market for a gardener and a new roof.

Asma brought the food to the table when it was ready, taking the seat across the table from him.

"Thanks," Farooq said. "Aunty Bushra's food is amazing. I've been thinking about it since the dinner we had."

"It's my favorite," Asma said.

They ate for a few minutes in silence before Asma couldn't take the quiet anymore.

"I wanted to—"

"What do you—"

Of course, they both had felt the awkwardness at the same time. Farooq motioned to Asma to go ahead.

"Thank you for the coffee the other day."

Farooq nodded. "You seemed pretty exhausted after your all-nighter. Saving lives?"

"One or two," Asma demurred.

"You're off today?"

"On tonight," she replied. "You?"

"I have a few meetings. Then we're having a team dinner at that new, fancy Lebanese restaurant, Le Palais Zaatar." Farooq gestured to his suit self-consciously. "That's why I'm dressed like this."

"Ah, I was wondering," Asma smiled. "Le Palais Zaatar is good, you'll like it. Fatima and I went there a few weeks ago."

Farooq looked at Asma with curiosity. Of course, he had no idea who Fatima was—they had met after the breakup, *because* of the breakup. How strange that two of the most important people in her life had never met.

"Fatima's one of my best friends. She went to Cal too. We met junior year."

Farooq seemed to instantly understand. He nodded slightly.

"She was at Yusef's book launch." *Why weren't you?* she wanted to ask.

Farooq answered the unspoken question.

"I was sorry to miss it," he said. "I was at my parents' place in Stockton dealing with their contractors and it was too late by the time we wrapped up."

So his absence had nothing to do with her, after all. She felt relief. His mention of Stockton made her nostalgic. He had fiercely defended the small city while in the Bay. By his account, he'd had a charmed, idyllic childhood, in a city he claimed was diverse, down-to-earth, and a great place to raise a family. An unsubtle campaign, Asma teased him, for one of the cities on their short list of places to settle down after they got married.

"How's Hamza?" she asked before overthinking the overfamiliarity of the question. Hamza was Farooq's childhood best friend, one of the few people in his life she'd felt comfortable meeting during their time together. Mainly because Farooq referred to him as his security detail. Quiet and big, he was obsessed with bodybuilding.

"He's great," Farooq said. "Married, one kid—

another one on the way. His dad just retired, so he's taken over the store."

"No way!" Asma replied, more enthusiastically than she intended. "Do they carry beef jerky now?" Hamza's father owned a small halal market in Stockton that Hamza was forever trying to modernize. He had been convinced that halal beef jerky was the key to the store's patronage by a new generation of clientele, presumably young Muslims like him also obsessed with weight training and portable protein.

Farooq laughed. "It was the first order he put in as the new owner."

"Good for him." Asma felt the nostalgia grow, enveloping her. There was so much more she wanted to ask, but she didn't want to push. It seemed as though they had come to a tentative truce after Farooq's anger at the PIMPS event and the awkwardness during their walk. Perhaps the coffee had been a peace offering.

They sat in a comfortable silence, finishing their food. The quiet was interrupted by Zayd, coming into the kitchen, his blanket trailing behind him.

"Hi, sweetie, you feeling better?" Asma touched his forehead—his fever had broken.

Zayd held up his iPad. "I need the password."

Asma punched the password into his iPad as Farooq pulled out the chair next to him and helped Zayd into it.

"I remember you," he said to Farooq.

"I remember you too," Farooq responded with his big lopsided grin. "Zayd, right?"

Zayd nodded, his eyes back on his iPad.

Farooq gestured toward Zayd. "Your target demographic," he said to Asma with a hesitant smile.

Asma, surprised by the reference, could only nod. She felt whiplash. It was just days ago that Farooq had lied about never visiting Santa Cruz. And now, here he was referencing an intimate shared memory.

During one of their late-night, marathon phone sessions in college, the conversation had shifted to the family they envisioned for themselves.

"I have a confession," Asma said. She continued only after Farooq had promised not to judge her. "I'm not into babies."

"Not into babies? What does that even mean?"

"I like kids. A lot. But I don't really get all the fuss about babies. I never know what to do with them."

"You just cuddle them," Farooq had replied. "They're like comfort animals. They make you feel better."

"Yeah, until they start that inconsolable crying. Then they make you feel totally useless." Asma had shaken her head. "I love kids in those preschool years. They are so funny. Such wild conversationalists."

"Well, you're in luck," Farooq had said. "I'm super into babies. So I'll hold our babies and then, when they get older, you can have deep conversations with them."

Asma's heart had swelled at the thought of Farooq holding their children.

"Sounds like we make a good team," Asma had replied. "I'm going to hold you to the baby thing."

"InshAllah," Farooq had said. *InshAllah* was a word that promised disappointment when said by most of the people in her life—a way for people to say no without confrontation. But coming out of Farooq's mouth, it felt like a promise. How easy it is to make promises when you're young and in love. How easy to imagine a world where babies could be dreamed into existence. Not like the reality of Maryam's first few years with the twins or Fatima's struggle with infertility.

Asma looked at the man in front of her. The man who said InshAllah and meant it.

Zayd glanced up from his iPad. "Who is your wife?" The spell had been broken. By a middle-aged aunty in the body of a three-year-old.

Farooq's eyebrows shot up. "I'm not married."

"Neither is Asma Khala." Zayd motioned to Asma as though introducing her to Farooq for the first time. Asma felt herself blush.

"Is that right?" Farooq said. Then he said to Asma with a twinkle in his eye, "Here's that preschooler conversation you're so fond of."

Asma laughed in spite of herself.

Zayd continued. "My dadi said she's not sure why Asma Khala's not married because she's such a nice girl."

"Zayd!" Asma said, trying to sound stern. She wanted to slip under the table.

Farooq laughed, his face lighting up with amusement. "What else does your dadi say?"

"Farooq!" Asma held up her hands in admonishment, but Farooq's laughter made her laugh too. She was completely and totally mortified.

Zayd looked at the adults laughing at the table around him, confused. Not to be left behind, he joined in too.

"Hi, guys! What's so funny?" They didn't hear Lubna enter the kitchen over their laughter.

Lubna's presence immediately sobered Asma. Lubna had asked her to open the door for Farooq, and Asma had—why did she feel like she had been doing something wrong? Asma grabbed their empty plates and took them to the sink, busying herself with loading the dishwasher to soothe her guilt.

"Zayd," Farooq said, affectionally tapping Zayd on the shoulder. "Zayd is so funny."

Zayd beamed at Farooq's praise and then held up his iPad. "Farooq Uncle, look—I just got a high score."

As Farooq and Lubna crowded around Zayd to admire his score, Asma slipped out of the kitchen. She wanted to escape before the jealousy of seeing Lubna and Farooq together supplanted the nostalgia and warmth of memories that had made her feel, just for a bit, the comfort of old times and what she once thought her future might be.

THE BOWLING BALL WASN'T EVEN HALFWAY down the lane before Asma turned around to give

Hassan a thumbs-up. And, sure enough, a second later, she heard the familiar clatter of the pins. Friday night at San Jose Lanes was loud and chaotic, but Asma could hear Hassan cheer above the din of the teenagers on group dates and schoolkids up past their bedtimes.

"Another strike!" Hassan raised his hand in the air to give Asma a high five.

Bowling wasn't the original plan for the evening. Hassan and Maryam were supposed to be on a double date to watch the newest superhero blockbuster with Lubna and Farooq, but Farooq had texted a few minutes before they were to leave that he was stuck in a meeting and wouldn't be able to make it after all. Saba was busy studying for a GRE practice exam, but after much cajoling, Lubna was able to coax Asma out of her pajamas and the house. The change of plans took time. By the time they got to the theater, all the showings of the movie were sold out. It was Maryam who suggested they go bowling, excited to be out without the kids.

"This is crazy. Who knew that Asma was such a great bowler?" Lubna wondered aloud.

"She was on an intramural bowling team in college," said Maryam.

Lubna looked at Asma, exasperated. "How come you didn't say anything when we were picking teams?"

"That's what you get for picking Maryam," Asma replied.

"What was your team name, Asma?" Maryam said. "I can't remember, I just remember it was dumb."

"The Pin Pals."

Lubna groaned. "Oh man!"

Asma took a deep bow, then laughed and headed to the snack bar. She was actually having fun, and not only because she was leading the scoreboard by such a margin that she could miss her next three turns and still win by at least a hundred points.

She was waiting for a vanilla shake when she saw Farooq enter the bowling alley. Wasn't he supposed to be at work? He had certainly dressed the part of a Silicon Valley CEO—jeans and a hoodie. It was more in line with how he used to dress, unlike the last time she'd seen him, in a fancy suit.

Farooq scanned the crowd, spotted Asma, and smiled. She felt her heart pounding as he headed toward the snack bar, an amused look on his face.

"I assume bowling was your idea?"

Farooq had laughed hysterically the first time he saw Asma wearing her bowling team jacket—he had never heard a cornier name, he'd told her. But he stopped laughing when he saw her in action. She'd beaten him badly the first time they went bowling together, and subsequently he had nothing but the utmost respect for the Pals.

"Maryam's, actually. I haven't been bowling in ages."

"Don't tell me you're rusty," Farooq said, with mock optimism and a raised eyebrow.

"Of course not," Asma replied. Farooq smiled.

Asma smiled back, unsure of exactly what was

happening. Farooq made no move toward joining the others, and she could feel them slipping back into old rhythms. The shorthand of people who knew each other intimately. Just like earlier in the week at Aunty Bushra's. But it felt wrong in these surroundings, especially considering the fact that Farooq was here for a date with Lubna. Asma found she was relieved when her order was called. It made it seem less like the two of them were drawing close to an edge, like the steep slopes of the cliffs where they used to hike together. There they were, giddy at the view, but apt to tumble down with one wrong move. She was reaching across the counter for her shake and a wad of napkins when she heard a familiar voice behind her.

"Farooq? Farooq Waheed!" Asma was taken aback to see Dr. Saucedo, greeting Farooq like a long-lost friend. "I thought that was you—how *are* you?"

"Melinda! I'm great! It's been years!"

Dr. Saucedo caught sight of Asma and looked as surprised to see her as Asma felt.

"Asma!" Dr. Saucedo looked from Asma to Farooq then back at Asma, her face breaking into a grin. "What a small world! I didn't realize you two were—" She gestured from Farooq to Asma suggestively.

Asma felt herself flush.

"We're not, we're—"

"We know each other from college," Farooq finished smoothly.

Asma nodded.

"What are you doing here?"

"Birthday party," Dr. Saucedo replied. "So many birthday parties!"

"And how do you know each other?" Asma pointed from Dr. Saucedo to Farooq.

"Farooq and my husband were at the same company years ago."

"You two work together?" Farooq asked in return.

"Asma's our star resident. And"—Dr. Saucedo smiled big and leaned in—"the lead candidate for a position that just opened up." She looked at Farooq. "If you can help convince her to stay in the Bay Area instead of moving to the middle of nowhere."

Asma swallowed hard. There was a job opening at her hospital, just as Dr. Saucedo had been promising. She thought about staying in the Bay, the prospect of continuing to work at the ER that had become her second home. And, of course, of her father's disapproval if she did.

"The middle of nowhere?" Farooq asked.

"Staying with my sister was supposed to be temporary," Asma explained, disoriented by the choice now presented to her. "I was going to move to Sacramento after graduation. But . . ." She paused, meeting Dr. Saucedo's smile. "I don't think I could pass up the opportunity to stay, if I got the job."

"That's exactly what I wanted to hear," Dr. Saucedo replied, smiling wide. "Come over to our place for dinner tomorrow. We can discuss your application."

"That would be great!" said Asma.

"Farooq—come too!" Dr. Saucedo continued. "Hector would love to see you."

Farooq seemed flustered at the invitation. He gestured to his phone.

"Thanks for the invitation . . . but, um—"

"Wonderful!" Dr. Saucedo was distracted by two small girls behind her—mini versions of herself—who were tugging on her jacket. "Hector will text you the address. I better run, these two are up way past their bedtime."

Dr. Saucedo gathered the girls and headed toward the exit, calling over her shoulder, "We'll see you both tomorrow night!"

Farooq stared after Dr. Saucedo until she left the bowling alley, then started punching the dinner into his calendar. Asma felt overwhelmed by the news about the job opening and her worlds colliding. But she knew that one thing needed to be addressed immediately.

"Farooq?"

He looked up from his phone.

"If you wouldn't mind keeping this to yourself for now, I'd appreciate it. I haven't told my family about the job."

Asma saw a flicker of the familiar coldness in Farooq's eyes, and the smile faded from his face. More secrets. More conflict between what she wanted and what her family would allow. If he thought that nothing had changed since they were in college—that Asma was still more than willing to indulge in dishonesty and avoidance rather than disappoint her father—he would be justified in thinking so.

"I won't say anything," he said, his tone clipped and terse.

He put his phone in his pocket and walked off toward her family at the back of the bowling alley. Asma felt her excitement over her job opportunity slip away as the warmth that had begun to build between them dissipated. She stood staring after him until she felt something cool and sticky on her arm. Her milkshake had sprung a leak and was dripping down her sleeve.

FOURTEEN

Asma glanced at the apartment brochure lying on the bed in front of her, its glossy cover marred with the Sharpie that Asma had used to jot down notes. She hadn't been able to get Farooq's look from the prior night out of her mind. Especially because he was right to be angry. Nothing had changed since college, no matter how many years had passed or how accomplished Asma had become. So, in an attempt to prove to herself that she was willing to live her own life, she'd walked into the leasing office of the apartment building near the hospital that morning and applied for a two-bedroom, two-bath unit.

Asma knew her father would be angry that she had gone behind his back, but she also knew she would have to withstand his anger. She had to tell her father that she was not moving to Sacramento. He might be mad at her initially, but he would soften eventually—at the very least, he wouldn't come to the Bay and force her to move. Would he?

She decided to break the news over the phone—if he yelled too loudly, she could just move the phone away from her ear. She mumbled a prayer before punching in her father's number.

"Salaam, beta! I was just on the phone with Gulnaz Bhabi," said Mr. Ibrahim. "We must make sure to visit again next time you're in town. It's so wonderful to have such distinguished relatives so close by."

Distinguished, of course, was always code for *rich*. Asma decided to let the comment go, though she knew she would rather shave her head than sit under Gulnaz Dadabhoy's haughty inspection ever again.

"Abu, I have to talk to you about something." She needed to get it out before she lost her nerve. "There's a job opening at the hospital, and my attending believes I'd be a top candidate for it."

"What hospital?"

"My hospital. Palo Alto General."

"MashAllah." She could hear the smile on his face. "That's good news."

"It is?"

"Of course. It's a great achievement to be the best one."

"Abu, I'm so happy to hear you say that. I can't tell you how much I want this job." Asma felt herself relax. "I can introduce you to Dr. Saucedo when you come up here for my graduation. She's been wanting to meet my family. And I applied for an apartment, it's right by the—"

"An apartment?"

"Near the hospital."

"What are you talking about? You're moving here."

"What?" Asma asked, stumbling a bit. "I just told you there's a job opportunity here and you said that's good news."

"Yes. Now you see how easy it is for you to get a job. You won't have any trouble finding one in Sacramento. Something more prestigious than emergency medicine. Private practice, maybe."

"Abu! *This* is the job I want, not to work in private practice in Sacramento."

"Asma, you didn't even try to apply for a job here."

"But why would I?"

"Because this is where you're going to live," Mr. Ibrahim said. "Not some apartment by yourself."

"Abu—"

"I'll call Gulnaz Bhabi back now, you know her husband was one of the most distinguished surgeons in Pakistan. I'm sure he has many contacts in Sacramento too."

And before Asma could respond, her father hung up the phone.

ASMA SAT IN HER CAR, PARKED AROUND THE corner from Dr. Saucedo's house in an old, moneyed neighborhood of Palo Alto filled with stately homes. She was trying not to dwell on her phone call with her father. He had never hung up on her before. She'd called him back immediately, but he'd ignored her phone calls and then told Iman to tell her that he was out—even though she could hear him in the background.

Her father seemed incapable of even considering an alternative to his plan for her, no matter what Asma might have preferred. She remembered Farooq's disappointed look at the bowling alley. At the time, Asma assumed he was reacting to her secrecy, but maybe it was more than that. Maybe Farooq realized how much Asma's father still influenced her choices, and how unhappy his decisions had made Asma over the years. It was a thought that had not occurred to Asma before— she could gain her father's approval once more by leaving her job in emergency medicine, but it would cost her what little happiness and satisfaction she had left. And the half-block walk to Dr. Saucedo's house wasn't exactly long enough to clear her head.

"Asma! You look great!" Dr. Saucedo swung open the front door. "Come in, come in!"

Asma had spent more time than usual selecting an outfit and getting dressed for dinner, going so far as to wear a ruby earring-and-necklace set that had once belonged to her mother. Maryam, so impressed by how Asma looked for what Asma told her was a work function, had even offered to do her makeup, loudly narrating as she applied concealer and eyeliner, making sure Asma was paying attention to her tutorial.

Dr. Saucedo led Asma down a long, narrow hallway,

the floor covered by a Persian carpet runner and the walls filled with framed family portraits.

She opened the heavy mahogany pocket doors at the end of the hall to reveal a huge living room with red velvet couches and rows and rows of wood-paneled shelves filled with books. Farooq stood at one corner of the room, flipping through a book. He closed the book when Asma entered and murmured salaams.

Dr. Saucedo led Asma into the room, then turned toward the adjoining kitchen. Asma panicked at the thought of being left alone with Farooq.

"What can I do to help?"

"I have everything taken care of." Dr. Saucedo motioned for Asma to sit down. "Hector is putting the girls to bed, he'll be down in a minute. What can I get you to drink?"

"I'll just have some water. Here, let me get it."

"No problem, just make yourself comfortable."

Asma and Farooq stood awkwardly, neither of them talking. The easy rapport that had emerged over the impromptu brunch at the Qureishis' house and the bowling alley was gone, and Asma was unsure where things were supposed to go from here. She looked around the room, an overflowing vase of pink and white lilies on the table catching her eye.

"These flowers are beautiful!"

"Aren't they gorgeous?" Dr. Saucedo called out from the other room. "Farooq brought them."

Asma remembered the bouquet Farooq had given

her after their first official date, a modest bunch of purple peonies that meant more to her than if it had been a dozen long-stemmed roses. She looked at Farooq, who still hadn't moved from his spot at the bookshelf. He looked uncomfortable and was opening and closing the same book absent-mindedly. She wanted to ask him if he remembered, too, but just then, Dr. Saucedo reentered the room with a tray of drinks. Her husband, Hector, a tall man with a kind face and salt-and-pepper hair, followed shortly thereafter.

Despite Asma's initial trepidation, she found that Hector and Dr. Saucedo's company eased some of the tension between her and Farooq. As they sat down at the well-appointed dining table and began to eat, Hector peppered them both with questions that allowed them to talk around each other instead of engaging in direct conversation.

"We'd been in negotiations for months," Farooq said, when Hector asked about the buyout of his startup. "But I was still shocked when I got the call. I thought someone was playing a joke on me."

"Because it sounds like an unreal number. Half a *billion* dollars?" said Dr. Saucedo. "Not to sound crass, but what is it even like to be that rich?"

"It feels like it's happening to someone else. There's this public persona that I see people reacting to and it almost makes me laugh," Farooq said. "But my day-to-day is basically the same. I mean, obviously, the stress about paying bills is gone. It's nice to be able to take care of my parents, they've always been so supportive. And I'm trying to find good philanthropic causes to invest in. But I'm realizing I don't have particularly expensive tastes."

Asma remembered the disappointment of the crowd at Farooq's basic watch.

"And what about you, Asma?" Hector asked. "Why emergency medicine? Are you a secret adrenaline junkie, like my wife?"

A smile passed between Hector and Dr. Saucedo, the kind that made Asma simultaneously grateful to see such a supportive spouse, and envious beyond measure of Dr. Saucedo's marriage.

"Well, I'm not sure how exactly to answer," Asma replied. "If this were a job interview—"

"Which it very well might be," Hector interjected, giving Asma a mischievous smile while nudging his wife gently.

"I promise, it's not," Dr. Saucedo said, raising both hands in a posture of innocence. "But if it were . . ." she continued, and the rest of them laughed.

"I'd say that I thrive in an environment where I have to trust my instincts and rely on my training to make essential decisions in real time," Asma replied. "The pace, the stakes, the procedures, the excitement . . . it's intoxicating."

"So, an adrenaline junkie," Hector summarized, as the rest of them laughed again. "And if it wasn't an interview?"

"I'd say that I don't like being helpless," Asma replied, the words escaping before she could think her answer through. "Being in the ER makes me feel like I can make the difference between someone being safe and someone being at risk. Living or dying. And I like being the person who makes that call."

"Ah," Hector said, with a knowing smile. "An adrenaline junkie *and* a control freak."

"It's a shock that I'm not married, right?" Asma joked, as the rest of them laughed heartily at her self-deprecation, even Farooq. "No, it's funny, I remember in college, going on a hike with a friend. And there was an accident."

The smile dropped from Farooq's face. Asma wondered how often he thought of it. Hiking on Mount Diablo, the steep incline. How Farooq had lost his footing. Asma's scream caught in her throat as Farooq went over the side of the ravine. She could still feel the pulse of her heart in her throat, the rush of adrenaline as she'd scrabbled down after him. The same feeling of watching her mother slip away from her, only faster this time. In the space of a breath.

"They had to medevac us out," Asma continued. "I remember sitting there waiting for the helicopter, wishing I knew what to do. And I never wanted to feel so useless again."

She'd held his hand as the emergency crew made their way toward him, and he'd said something to her that was lost in the whirring of the helicopter blades.

"What?" she'd shouted over the noise, putting her ear close to his mouth.

"If I get out of this," he'd said, his voice threaded through with the pain of his fractured leg. "Promise you'll marry me."

She'd promised, right then and there. Promised him that she'd be his wife. Promised herself that she'd become the sort of doctor who'd never be helpless again. And she'd only kept one of those promises.

"Well," Dr. Saucedo said, raising her glass to Asma. "A bit of advice. That should be your interview answer."

They all raised their glasses, but when Asma glanced at Farooq, his eyes were down, his mouth in a hard line, and he wouldn't meet her gaze.

BEFORE ASMA KNEW IT, ALMOST THREE HOURS had passed. Hector started to clear the plates. Farooq got up to help, but Hector waved at him to sit back down.

"It's dessert—my course." Hector brought out a cake platter from the kitchen. "Baked Alaska!"

Asma and Farooq stared at it for a second before they both burst out laughing.

"Well, that wasn't the reaction I expected," Hector said.

"Sorry," Asma said between giggles. "The last time I had baked Alaska . . ."

Asma glanced at Farooq, who finished her sentence.

"It was a mess. More like fried Alaska," he said, re-counting the time he had attempted to make baked Alaska in college. He didn't mention that he had burned the dessert for Asma's nineteenth birthday in the small, cramped kitchen of the apartment he shared with three other Muslim students.

"I keep forgetting you two went to college together!" Dr. Saucedo said. "So, Farooq, you'll have to tell us: was Asma in college the same as the Dr. Ibrahim we know now—always at the top of her class?"

"Always," said Farooq. "She set the curve in organic chem by almost eight points. Everyone was so mad. She would've been the class outcast if she wasn't so—"

Farooq stopped.

"Brilliant, I think is the description you're looking for," Dr. Saucedo said with a wink at Asma.

Asma blushed.

"And, Asma." Hector turned to her. "I'm sure you knew—like the rest of us—that it was only a matter of time before Farooq was off to make millions with his startup."

Asma froze.

"She was definitely there at the beginning of it all," Farooq said with a strained smile.

Asma knew that this reminder of why their relationship had ended had upset him. But their hosts didn't seem to notice. They continued to chatter on about Farooq's buyout until he excused himself from the table and left the room.

Asma was helping clear the table when Farooq returned.

"Thank you both so much for dinner. Everything was great," he said.

Asma, too, took her leave and, a few minutes later, found herself standing on the front stoop with Farooq. She thought he would flee but instead he stood there, not moving.

"Where did you park?" he asked finally.

"Just around the corner."

Farooq nodded and started walking alongside Asma to her car.

It was surprisingly cool for a summer night. They walked in silence. Asma could hear Farooq breathing steadily next to her. For a second she closed her eyes and imagined that they were back strolling through campus on that crisp spring afternoon when Farooq first told her that he loved her.

"You still have the Camry?" Farooq asked when her car came into view. Asma had inherited Iman's car her freshman year after Iman convinced Mr. Ibrahim that Asma starting college was the perfect opportunity for Iman to upgrade to a Lexus.

"Two hundred twelve thousand miles and counting."

"Planning on getting a new one when you get that job?"

"No way. I'm driving this one until it doesn't drive anymore."

Farooq smiled, his eyes crinkling at the sides.

When they reached the car Farooq chuckled, seemingly in spite of himself, as he ran his hand over a small dent in the driver's-side door. One that had appeared the morning he'd borrowed her car to pick up a table he'd found on Craigslist during their freshman year. He'd apologized profusely and offered to pay for the damage, but Asma had shrugged it off.

"You never fixed it," he said.

"It's cosmetic," Asma said. "Adds character."

Asma expected another chuckle, finding humor in the memory. But when he looked up at her, she was startled to see that his eyes were glassy.

Asma stood for a moment, unsure what to do, then found herself reaching for him. She rested her hand on his arm and they stood just a few inches away from each other, silent.

"I haven't thought about breaking my leg in years," he said, his voice gravelly with emotion. "Being with you brings everything back." Asma wanted to move closer, to close the distance between them. But in the moment before she did, he cleared his throat, glancing at his buzzing cell phone. Asma saw Lubna's name flash across the screen before Farooq silenced his phone and slid it out of view.

Seeing Lubna's name jolted Asma. She pulled her hand back.

"It's late, I better get going."

She got in her car as Farooq stood at the door, holding it open. Asma willed him to say something—

anything—to acknowledge what had just happened. But, instead, he just said softly, "Good night, Asma," and closed the door.

Asma managed to drive to the end of the block before breaking down in sobs, overwhelmed by longing and regret. As she turned the corner and away from the man she'd been in love with for the past eight years, she caught a glimpse of him in her rearview mirror. He was where she'd left him—standing in the middle of the street, looking after her.

FIFTEEN

Asma pulled the carafe off the coffee maker and placed her stainless steel tumbler directly under the basket while it was still brewing. It was her third cup of coffee that morning and she didn't have the patience to sit around waiting for the entire pot to brew before getting her fix.

She had been working nonstop—so much for residents not working over eighty hours a week. The frenetic work schedule had her exhausted, as did constantly thinking about Farooq. When they first reconnected, Farooq said he'd moved on. But either he hadn't been entirely truthful or something had shifted between them; she just couldn't figure out how she might test these new waters to see if his feelings for her had, indeed, changed.

Her phone buzzed. She picked it up, expecting a return call from Fatima. She'd called her earlier in the day to check in after having to cancel dinner with her that night because of work. But it was Maryam.

"Can't talk, Maryam, I'm about to see a patient," Asma said by way of greeting.

"I need you to pick me up."

"Where are you?"

"In Daly City."

"Why are you in Daly City?"

"Long story."

"I'm at work."

"My car broke down."

"That's why we have Triple A."

"I don't have my card. And Hassan's not picking up. He's at work."

"As am I!"

"Oh my God, Asma! The boys' field trip to the zoo is this afternoon and I'm stranded."

"Call Saba, she doesn't have her GRE class today."

"You know I hate asking her for anything."

"Oh, Maryam, have you spoken to Abu?" It had been more than a week since she'd told her father about remaining in Palo Alto, and Mr. Ibrahim was still refusing to answer her calls. Despite Asma's request, Iman had refused to referee.

"So *now* you want my help?" she had asked. "You're perfectly fine going over my head to Abu to boss us around from out there. You're on your own for this one."

Asma wondered if she could get Maryam to intervene.

"No, why would I call Abu? He's in Sacramento.

You think it would be faster for him to come here and pick me up?"

Asma spotted Jackson gesturing at her from the nurse's station.

"Never mind. Maryam, I have to go."

Asma grabbed her tumbler and headed toward Jackson.

"What's going on?" Asma asked.

"We've just had another admit from Green Meadows," Jackson replied. "This one is an eighty-five-year-old woman with dizziness, a fever, and shortness of breath. Bacterial pneumonia, I'd bet my life on it."

"Just like the others," Asma said, glancing over the intake form in the woman's chart. "I thought the health department was investigating the Legionnaires' outbreak. The last I heard, they ordered Green Meadows to replace all the air-conditioning units in the building."

"I asked her about that," Jackson replied. "She said they started doing work on the air conditioners a month ago but only got through about a third of the building. The rest still have the old units. Apparently the administrative staff claims they're clear of Legionnaires', but people are starting to get sick again."

"I'll put another call in to the health department," Asma said, handing the chart back to Jackson. "Thanks for letting me know."

THE CAKE WAS IN THE SHAPE OF A QURAN. THIS was the cake du jour at ameen parties, gatherings that celebrated a child's reading of the entire Quran in Arabic, but Asma still thought it strange—and slightly sacrilegious—to bite into a chocolate page covered with God's word in icing.

A friend of Aunty Bushra's was throwing a huge party at her home to celebrate her granddaughter. Bushra insisted they all attend. She said it was important for Zaki and Zayd to see what they could look forward to once they, too, finished reading the Quran. How religious instruction had changed since she was growing up, Asma thought. Her Quran lessons had been with the hafiz at the local mosque, she and her sisters huddled around him reading under the threat of hellfire. The fire and brimstone of her youth had been replaced by frosting and Bavarian cream.

Asma, standing in the middle of a crowd of children struggling to get to the front of the dessert table, felt herself jostled by small bodies. She stood firm, holding up Zaki to help him get a better look at the cookie crescents and stars, cake pops in the shape of mini mosques, and tasbeehs made of chocolate-covered raisins.

"God, who doesn't have a Quran cake these days," said Maryam, staring at the table. She scooped up Zayd, who had been tugging at her sleeve, and pushed her way to the table, grabbing some dessert for herself and the boys. One look at the plates his mother was holding and Zaki scrambled out of Asma's arms.

Asma waited until the crowd dispersed before helping herself to some cake, taking extra slices for Lubna and Saba. The cake looked so delicious, she figured it would almost be a sin *not* to eat it.

Asma looked around the living room and saw Maryam heading over to a corner where Lubna and Saba sat on metal folding chairs, their eyes focused on their phones. Asma made her way over to them, dodging toys, half-empty plates and cups, and car seats with abandoned sleeping infants.

"This cake is amazing," Asma said, taking a bite as she settled into an empty seat next to Saba. "Here, I brought you some."

"No, thanks," Saba said, hand on her stomach. "I'm so stuffed."

"Me too," Lubna added, shaking her head as Asma held out the plate to her. "I want to leave already. This is so hella boring."

"Things have become infinitely more interesting since I started eating this cake," said Asma, marveling at the plate in her hand. "You sure you don't want some?"

"I don't know why Ammi drags us to these things," said Lubna, shaking her head. "We're too old for this."

"I know, there's literally no one else here our age."

"If you were at home, you'd be sitting on the couch on your phone," said Maryam.

"Which is what we're doing here," Saba said. "But

at home we could be in our PJs and wouldn't have to answer a bunch of questions from nosy aunties about when we're getting married."

"God, I can't wait for that line of questioning to be over," said Lubna.

"Me too!" replied Saba.

"How are things going with you and Farooq?" Maryam asked Lubna.

At the sound of Farooq's name, Asma stuffed the last of her cake into her mouth and started in on the second slice.

"He's been crazy busy with work," Lubna said. "I haven't seen him in two weeks."

Asma's ears perked up. That meant Lubna hadn't seen Farooq since their dinner at Dr. Saucedo's house.

"I've been wanting to talk to him about this sponsorship deal I was just offered. And usually he's so easy to talk to, but now that he's gone AWOL I'm starting to think that he doesn't feel the same way about me."

"It's probably just like you said, he's busy," said Saba.

"But it's not just that. I feel like I really open up with him, but he doesn't do the same."

"That's all men," said Maryam.

"You should just ask him directly," Saba said. "That's the healthiest thing to do in a relationship."

"Definitely don't do that," Maryam countered. "Honesty is generally good, but you don't want too much of it before you have a ring."

Asma felt her stomach turn at the conversation. There were the competing pulls of jealousy at the prospect of an engagement ring for Lubna, and also hope for herself. Hope, in that Farooq had perhaps begun to pull away from Lubna.

"I'll be right back," Asma said, getting up. "I'm going to the bathroom."

Once inside the tiny powder room, Asma threw some water on her face. When Farooq and Asma were together, she'd often heard him talk about the necessity for directness in undefined Muslim boy-girl friendships. She remembered Farooq telling his roommate not to waste time wondering where he stood with a mutual female friend—to clarify what was going on with her or move on. So if Farooq hadn't been clear with Lubna about the contours of their current relationship, maybe it meant that they didn't have one. Or maybe things had changed in the years since college. Maybe Farooq realized that relationships were less black-and-white than they'd seemed when he was twenty. Asma could go crazy, turning the implications of his silence over and over in her head.

Asma left and made a beeline for the percolator of chai in the kitchen. She rummaged around the table to find a clean, empty cup in between discarded sugar packet wrappers and used plastic teaspoons. Nothing noisy enough to stop her from overhearing the aunties congregated nearby.

"MashAllah, my daughter is pregnant with her third

child. That'll be eight grandchildren for me. Mash-Allah."

"Oh, MashAllah. I have ten grandchildren, they are such a blessing. My eldest grandson just made it into Dartmouth. MashAllah."

"Dartmouth? MashAllah. That's a good school. My grandson is premed—at Cornell! That's an Ivy League school, MashAllah."

"Dartmouth is in the Ivy League too. MashAllah."

Asma couldn't help but grin, despite her mood. In the mouths of the aunties, MashAllah could simultaneously ward off the evil eye and give a symbolic middle finger.

"That reminds me, did you hear about Huma's boy, Salman?"

"The one who went to Harvard?"

"Yes! His wife just left him!"

Asma's amusement was replaced by a cold wave of horror. They were talking about Fatima.

"She seemed to be the quiet type, but I heard she was very bossy, always complaining that he was working too much."

"Poor Salman is a lawyer, he has to work hard!"

"I heard she wanted to move to New York, even though his job is here!"

Asma felt her hand burning and looked down to see her mug overflowing with chai. She grabbed a dish towel from the counter and bent over to clean up the mess, choking back the rage gathering in her throat.

Fatima had abandoned her dream of going to grad school. And here, all these years later, these women were using that sacrifice against her, assuming *that* was why she had left him?

"These girls today!" One of the aunties gasped in mock outrage.

"That's not what happened!" Asma interrupted before she could stop herself. It was one thing for the aunties to gossip about her lack of marriage prospects or the personal price of her career ambitions. It was another for them to talk about Fatima, who had always played by their rules, done everything correctly, right up until the moment she couldn't anymore.

The aunties stopped talking.

"He cheated on her! He was sleeping with one of his co-workers."

No one responded, although she heard a few clucking tongues and whispered Astaghfirullahs.

Asma stood glaring at them before turning on her heel and storming out of the kitchen. But she could still hear the hushed comments even from the next room.

"I don't believe he did such a thing."

"He comes from such a good family."

"Sometimes these things happen, nothing to leave him for."

There was no way to win. Asma understood it now—none of the women she knew would be spared the gossip that accompanied even the slightest misstep, even if they'd sacrificed their own happiness to live by the rules, like Fatima had. Asma staggered out of the house and into the garden, just in time for the two slices of Quran cake to come back up in the bushes.

IT HAD BEEN OVER TWO MONTHS SINCE MR. Ibrahim and Iman had moved to Sacramento, and Sophia and Yusef's housewarming was Asma's first time back at her old home. How odd to be visiting as a guest, she thought, as she pulled into the driveway. But as she entered through the French doors with gold handles that her father had insisted on installing, Asma barely recognized the place. The Abdullahs had managed to make her father's ostentatious McMansion look chic. Free of the Ibrahims' clutter, the striking pillars, double grand staircase, and cool marble floors actually seemed modern and sleek, like a home in *Architectural Digest*.

Maryam, of course, wasn't impressed.

"I hate what they've done to the place," she said as they walked past the bare floors and sparse shelves on their way to the back patio, snapping pictures on her phone to send to Iman. "It's so cold and impersonal."

The transformation of their home extended to the outside. Except for her mother's garden—which Asma was relieved to see the Abdullahs had maintained—the backyard was the complete opposite of the last time it had seen a group of people, at her father's retirement party. This was a casual barbecue, with no caterer, ice sculpture, or miniature cakes in sight. The Qawwali singers on the stage had been replaced by a side table with an iPhone and small speakers. Children were not only invited, they ran underfoot, several splashing in the pool.

Asma, too, was different this time. She'd made an effort with her outfit and makeup, for starters. But something else had changed as well, in response to the gossip she'd overheard about Fatima. She didn't want to be like her, giving up something meaningful in order to please those who could never be pleased. She no longer cared that her father wanted her to move to Sacramento and get into private practice. She was proud of the life she'd built for herself and she intended to see it through.

Zayd and Zaki ran to join the other kids, while Hassan headed over to Yusef at the grill crowded with hot dogs, hamburgers, and kabobs. Asma took in the scene. A herd of men surrounded Yusef, drinking soda and talking loudly, focused more on their phones than the meat on the grill. Not far from the men sat their wives, chatting while tending to small children and periodically yelling across the backyard at the older ones. Across the lawn, as far as possible from the children and the married couples, were the young single women, Lubna and Saba among them.

To Asma's disappointment, Farooq was nowhere in sight. She was finally ready to face him, and had even been hoping that she could get him alone this afternoon so they could talk about what had happened at Dr. Saucedo's house.

"Reema Akhtar is here?" Maryam scoffed. "She said she was too busy to join the parents' committee at the boys' school. But she's such a social climber, of course she's not too busy to figure out a way to get herself invited to something like this." Maryam stalked off, leaving Asma to stand awkwardly by herself.

She was saved by Sophia, who seemed to appear out of nowhere, an empty tray in hand.

"Asma! I didn't see you come in," she said. "I am so behind. I haven't even finished the salad."

Asma admired Sophia's casual honesty. In their social circle, a hostess would never admit to not having everything together. In fact, Asma had been working one night when an acquaintance of Maryam's had come into the emergency room, complaining of stomach pain. The doctors had examined her closely, running multiple tests, sending her home hours later when they could find nothing. It was a nurse who told Asma the real reason for the woman's trip to the ER.

"She had a dinner party planned this evening for a hundred people," the nurse, an older white lady, said to Asma in the break room. "And an hour before the first guest was to arrive, she found out the caterer had mixed up the dates.

"Can you believe it?" the nurse had asked Asma with a shake of her head. "She pretended she was sick!

I told her, honey, you should've just ordered pizza or bought those rotisserie chicken dinners from the grocery store. Your guests would've understood!"

Asma had turned away to mask her smile, tickled by the image of Maryam's friends, dressed to the nines, chomping on drumsticks from Costco. The guests would've understood absolutely nothing—they would've spent the evening asking themselves and each other why the hostess hadn't double-, triple-, and quadruple-checked with the caterer. Who waits until an hour before a dinner party to have catered food delivered anyway?

"Need help?" Asma asked Sophia.

"Please, if you don't mind?"

In the kitchen, Asma chopped cucumbers and tomatoes while Sophia prepared the dressing. She held out a spoon to Asma, who leaned in for a taste.

"I'm so impressed by your spread," Asma said. "Aunty Bushra's been trying to teach me to cook, but the lessons aren't going so well. I think it's only partly my fault, though."

"Not like you've had anything else to do—you know, like being a doctor," Sophia said, picking up the salad. "I'll take this out. Do you mind grabbing the plate of kabobs in the fridge?"

Asma opened the door to the fridge as Sophia went outside. The plate was on the top shelf, wedged between a gallon of milk and an open bowl of yogurt. Asma had just maneuvered it out when she saw, through the crack in the door, Farooq enter the kitchen. She felt the same flutter in her stomach that used to accompany adolescent crushes—a feeling she'd long since thought she'd outgrown.

She shut the fridge, and Farooq jumped at the sudden movement. "Hi," Asma said, carefully. She didn't want to risk whatever had built up between them that night at Dr. Saucedo's house, and she didn't think she could take it if he looked at her as coldly as he had during the last conversation they'd had in a kitchen. When they'd poured out chai together, and he'd told her that he didn't think about her at all anymore. But to her relief, there was no coldness in his eyes this time when he looked at her. They were kind, even. Warm. Almost like the way he used to look at her.

"Hey," he replied softly. "If you have time today, we should probably talk."

"Okay," Asma said, something like anxiety—or even excitement—gripping her stomach.

But Maryam was nothing if not the master of ruining a moment, so Asma couldn't be surprised when her sister chose that instant to stick her head through the patio door.

"What are you guys doing?"

Farooq and Asma exchanged glances. Now was not the time.

"Bringing out more stuff," Farooq said. He grabbed a two-liter off the counter, then slipped out the door past Maryam.

Farooq took over Yusef's place at the grill and the crowd of men drifted away, quickly replaced by Lubna and Saba, who pounced the moment Farooq appeared. Apparently she wasn't the only one who'd been desperate to talk to Farooq today. Asma stood at the patio door, kabob plate in hand, and hesitated. And she realized, as she watched Lubna smile as she chatted with Farooq, that any reconciliation between Asma and Farooq would come at Lubna's expense. Asma, somehow, had become the other woman.

Lubna saw Asma standing at the patio door and excitedly waved her over. Asma headed toward them, heavy with guilt.

"Asma, you have to come too!"

"Where?" Asma asked, placing the platter on the table next to Farooq.

"To San Francisco! This weekend!"

"Farooq invited us," Lubna explained. "There's a huge tech conference. He's giving a presentation on Saturday morning. We can stay all weekend and hang out with a bunch of his friends!"

Despite Lubna's enthusiasm, and the fact that Asma loved San Francisco, Asma would happily have pulled a triple shift at the hospital if it meant that she could escape a weekend spent with Lubna and Farooq.

"Thanks for the invite," Amsa replied, feigning real regret, "but I don't think I can. Graduation is in three weeks and I have a lot going on with residency."

Lubna and Saba exchanged a distressed glance.

"Please, Asma, Ammi will totally let us go if you come!" Saba said. "Think of it as a favor to us."

"Yeah, you should come," added Farooq. Asma was surprised by the resolve in his voice. He seemed not to share her hesitance about spending the weekend together . . . with Lubna.

"You have to," Saba added, her smile already betraying the fact that she knew they were wearing Asma down.

"Come where?" Maryam materialized out of nowhere.

The delight on Lubna's and Saba's faces vanished. There was silence as Maryam looked from one person to the next. No one answered.

"Where? Asma, you have to come where?"

Asma shot Saba and Lubna an apologetic look before responding. "San Francisco."

"Ugh, I hate San Francisco," said Maryam. "It's so cold. And dirty. The sidewalks are always covered in poop."

Lubna and Saba looked relieved, their smiles returning.

"But if Asma is going, Hassan and I will come too," Maryam continued, as if there were no question in it at all. As if it were as simple as that.

Lubna and Saba sighed. But it was just a momentary disappointment, as the plan to spend the weekend in the city with Farooq and his friends was too exciting to permanently dampen their moods. As they chattered about the trip, Asma kept glancing over at Farooq, who was focused on the grill. What did he mean by inviting her to San Francisco? Was it simply so Saba and Lubna would be allowed to go? Or was he looking for the same thing as Asma: an excuse to spend time together, to figure out what on earth was going on with the two of them?

SIXTEEN

✦

They saw the fog rolling down the freeway before they saw the city, the skyline obscured by a haze. Between the clouds, Asma could see the outline of the familiar San Francisco landmarks—the peak of the Transamerica building, the outline of Coit Tower, the imposing Bay Bridge.

Although San Francisco was only about an hour from San Jose, Asma had spent very little time in the city. Her family hadn't taken trips to San Francisco when she was growing up, her parents preferring to turn the car southward toward the warmth of Los Angeles. In high school, she took the occasional trip up to the city with girlfriends to go shopping or to see a show, but the vast majority of her time in San Francisco had been spent during her four years at Berkeley.

"I could get used to this life," Lubna said, interrupting Asma's nostalgia.

"Me too!" Maryam chimed in.

Farooq insisted that their entire trip was on him—

hotels, meals, everything. Asma had tried to convince Maryam that they should pay their own way. But Maryam had no such qualms.

"Please, Asma, he's the one who invited us—he'll be insulted if we offer to pay."

It was already clear that Maryam planned to take full advantage of Farooq's generosity. She'd made reservations at Oasis, which she heard was the best spa in the city, and dropped heavy hints that she wanted to dine at Le Chateau, famous for its five-course tasting menu. She insisted on staying at the Fairmont Hotel, at the top of Nob Hill, where they had a breathtaking view of the city and the Bay spread in front of them— the tracks of the cable cars, the Victorian houses, and the outline of the bridge against the water.

Asma thought that Maryam would've been eager to get the weekend started. But she dawdled through the morning, planning her weekend itinerary. By the time she packed the boys off to the Qureishis', decided what outfits she wanted to bring, and what snacks they might need in the car, their whole group was running an hour late. By the time they finally all packed into the car with Saba and Lubna, and got through the traffic that started where the freeway met the route into the city, they were two hours behind. They had to abandon their plans to check into the hotel first and head straight to dinner instead. Asma, wearing faded khakis and an old med school sweatshirt, wished she'd had the foresight to have dressed for dinner instead of the car ride.

Dinner that night was at the family restaurant of one of Farooq's friends.

"Naveed moved here five years ago from Pakistan to go to business school at Stanford," Lubna said. "He's a banker, totally rich, went to Karachi Grammar School, you know the type."

"God, those KGS kids are such snobs," Maryam said.

Kettle, meet pot, thought Asma.

"He's got the craziest story, though. So his mom is totally trying to set him up with girls from home, but he falls in love with this Desi chick in his B-school class and they get engaged. At first his mom is freaking out, but then it turns out this girl is rich and from their hometown so it's like a perfect match."

"Rich and from your hometown—what more could any man want in a wife?" said Hassan with a wink at Maryam.

"Shhh, Hassan, let her finish!" said Saba.

"Yeah, Hassan! Let me finish! It's just getting good." Lubna took a deep breath, then launched back into her story. "So the wedding is all set up—it's this *huge* affair—everyone and their mom is invited. They have all these events planned over the course of three weeks—three dholkis, two mendhis, dawat after dawat. And everything is going great—until the bride doesn't show up to the shaadi!"

"Oh my God, did someone murder her?" Maryam

asked, twisting around to gape at Lubna with what seemed to be genuine concern.

"What? *No!* She stood him up! She was in love with some other dude."

"Oh." Maryam settled back into her seat, seemingly disappointed.

"So the guests are just sitting there, assuming she's late, because brides always show up late to their weddings. But then two hours turned into three, then four—then at hour five Naveed's dad comes out and tells everyone that the bride is sick."

"That is *so* sad," said Saba.

"I know, it's, like, my nightmare," added Lubna.

"*That's* your nightmare?" Hassan asked Lubna, amused.

"I'm glad you think this is so funny, Hassan," Lubna said, not amused. "How devastating for him. He had taken off all this time from work for the wedding and honeymoon and everything, and instead, he just came back to San Francisco. Apparently he was such a mess, he wasn't even able to go back to his apartment, he just moved in with his uncle."

"And we're having dinner with this guy?" asked Maryam. "Can't wait."

"It's actually his uncle's restaurant," Lubna said, brushing off Maryam's sarcasm. "Kamran. Apparently Farooq knows him pretty well too. He came here from Pakistan after his wife died. Which was fortunate for

Naveed, to have family in the Bay, after what he went through."

As they followed the GPS through the city and into the Tenderloin, their excitement over dinner simmered down considerably. Imagining a sleek modern restaurant worthy of a Food Network show, they fell silent when Hassan pulled in front of a battered storefront. The name of the restaurant on the red awning was obscured by bird droppings.

They stood close to the car as Hassan fed the meter, trying to ignore the stench of urine and weed coming from the group of men lighting up on the stoop of the neighboring building.

"Are we going to just hang out on the sidewalk?" Asma asked.

"Yeah, let's get a move on," said a grumpy Hassan, exhausted from the almost two-hour drive. "I'm hungry."

They hustled into the restaurant packed with cab-drivers and families and were immediately hit with the pungent aroma of Desi food that would likely stick on their clothes and follow them around for hours after dinner. Tables topped with cloudy pitchers of water and chipped plastic cups crowded the space in a haphazard manner, and a long line of people clutching sticky menus while waiting to order at the front counter snaked around the restaurant. Farooq was already there, staking out a big table in the back corner. He stood up when they entered and waved them over.

They navigated the crowd, pushing gingerly past the

stained plastic tablecloths and greasy napkin dispensers. Asma looked at Maryam with apprehension—the look on her face was one they were used to seeing before she said exactly what was on her mind.

"I don't know why people confuse dirty with authentic," she said, before Asma could stop her.

"Shhhh," Asma admonished Maryam.

Farooq didn't seem to notice their faces or hear Maryam. He was busy trying to wave someone down.

Asma followed his wave to behind the stove, where a chubby middle-aged man, covered in sweat, broke out into a grin. He yelled something over his shoulder toward the back kitchen before removing his apron and using it to wipe his face. On his way to meet them he stopped to give his salaams to a few of the patrons. They were reviewing the menu by the time he made it to their table. Farooq introduced him as Kamran, the owner of the restaurant, and he greeted each of them warmly, Lubna last.

"Lubna! So nice to meet you," Kamran said with a smile and a sly look at Farooq. Farooq smiled in response. Asma felt sharp disappointment mixed with jealousy. She couldn't keep up with the ping-ponging signals she was receiving from Farooq, and knew that she needed to have a private conversation about where things between them stood.

Asma turned her attention to the head of the table, where a sad-faced man was standing with a plate of samosas.

"This is Naveed, my nephew," Kamran said.

Asma recognized the expression on Naveed's face: utter pain and despair, the wounds of heartbreak. Realizing that the rest of the table—after their perfunctory salaams—were in too good a mood to pay attention to him, Asma pulled an empty chair from the neighboring table, brushed the crumbs off the seat, and motioned for Naveed to sit down.

"So," Asma said once Naveed was settled. "I hear you're an investment banker."

It was a pathetic attempt at conversation, but Asma couldn't think of anything else.

"I'm not sure I'm going back to my job," said Naveed. "I'm thinking about a career shift."

Asma waited for him to continue. When he didn't, she prodded gently.

"In what direction?"

"Writing," Naveed said, his voice defiant. It was clear from the way he said it that previous expressions of this new plan had not been met with excitement. But his look softened when he saw Asma's face light up.

"That's wonderful! What do you write?"

It was as if Asma had uttered the magic words. Naveed transformed, enthusiastically launching into a detailed description of his novel.

Over the course of dinner—which, Maryam conceded later, was delicious, "in spite of the grossness of the restaurant"—Naveed and Asma fell into an easy rapport, a relief for Asma to have someone to talk to.

By the end of the meal, Asma had even managed to make him laugh, a detail, she noticed, that was not lost on Farooq, who was observing them, intently, from the other side of the table.

ASMA WOKE EARLY THE NEXT MORNING TO A text from Lubna—*meet in lobby at 9*—and bright blue skies. The day was also unusually sunny, the streets outside the hotel still empty save for the occasional early-morning tourist bending backward to snap pictures of the flags flying above the hotel's porte cochere. Asma raised her face toward the sun, enjoying the warmth on her cheeks, the light breeze, and the soft clanging of the cable car that was making its way up the hill.

"Hey there, beautiful!" a homeless man called out from the corner.

Asma turned around.

"You, I'm talking to you!" he continued, pointing at Asma. "Isn't she beautiful?" he asked the valet attendant standing just a few feet away.

"She is, indeed!" the attendant agreed.

Asma mumbled thanks under her breath, embarrassed that she was actually flattered by the attention. She hurried back into the hotel just as Saba and Lubna were coming out of the elevator.

"You're looking nice this morning," Saba said. "Are you wearing makeup?"

"Just the lip gloss Lubna gave me."

"You should wear it more often."

"Clearly. It's getting a reaction out of everyone," Asma said. "Where are Hassan and Maryam?"

"Still asleep," Lubna said. "Here, Farooq left these for us."

Lubna held out name badges. "We better hurry, his presentation is at nine thirty."

They set off down the steep decline of California Street, careful to watch their step in between admiring the bird's-eye view of the Bay Bridge stretching over the sparkling water separating San Francisco and Oakland.

"I love everything about this city except for maybe these hills," Saba said. "Tariq and I were even talking about moving here after we get married."

"Wait—what? Are you engaged?" Asma asked.

"Basically. Tariq needs to come and officially ask Ammi and Abu, but we're good to go. Maryam even gave us her blessings."

"She did? When?"

"After the Walmart thing."

"What Walmart thing?"

"Maryam was at the Walmart in Daly City and her car broke down," Lubna said.

"I remember that day. She called me at work asking for a ride."

"Apparently she called everyone before calling me," Saba said. "And even I wasn't free. But Tariq was. And he picked her up."

"What was she doing at a Walmart in Daly City?"

"She needed to pick some stuff up for the boys' school but didn't want to be seen at any of the stores by our house."

"You know," Lubna said, "because she's such a crusader for workers' rights."

Asma chuckled. "Classic Maryam."

"I know, right? To her credit, she apologized to him. And me," said Saba. "I told her I wouldn't forgive her unless she gave me permission to use the story in one of my routines."

Asma laughed.

They made it to the Moscone Center a few minutes before Farooq was scheduled to take the stage. Attendees were swarming about wearing matching orange lanyards and carrying conference tote bags, enthusiastically greeting acquaintances they likely only saw once a year. Asma snagged a conference program she found abandoned on a table. She flipped through it and found Farooq's headshot—he was the keynote speaker for the morning session. She swelled with pride as she read his bio.

Asma, Lubna, and Saba found seats in the middle of the main hall.

"There are so many people here," Lubna said in awe.

The lights dimmed as the lectern in the middle of the stage was illuminated by a spotlight and projected onto two huge screens. A minute later, Farooq's face filled both of them.

"Everyone always wants to hear my origin story,"

Farooq began. "How did I get the idea for this platform that has already drastically transformed medical services for people living in rural areas?"

He was confident and calm as he shared the details of his family's journey from Pakistan to a small farming community in central California. Asma remembered the story. It was there that the death of his father's beloved sister—from a treatable illness that no one caught until it was too late—forever changed the course of his life.

"I grew up wondering if Aunty Zainab could've been saved if she only had access to a doctor and preventive care. There's no way to know. But I knew that I could make sure that what happened to her didn't happen to anyone else."

The massive audience seemed completely engaged—laughing, groaning, and clapping on cue as Farooq went into the details of his company's product. A way to connect people—no matter where they were or how much money they had—to the massive network of medical professionals that Farooq had built. Just as he had envisioned so many years before.

The only people who didn't seem to be listening were the two sitting next to Asma.

"Reception in here is so bad." Lubna was staring at her phone.

"None of my posts are uploading," Saba said.

Lubna swiveled around in her seat.

"I think there's Wi-Fi in the lobby."

"We'll be right back," Saba whispered, as the two of them scooted past her and out of the hall.

They hadn't made it back by the time Farooq wrapped up his talk. Asma looked around and wondered if she should try to find them in the lobby. But then she spotted Farooq near the front of the hall, ringed by security guards and a mob of what appeared to be tech groupies. She moved toward him—maybe she could pull him aside and finally get him alone.

She stood off to the side, waiting for the horde of people to disperse. It was almost as if Farooq sensed she was near. He found her face through a gap in the crowd and smiled. She smiled back, her heart racing. He excused himself and made his way to where she was standing.

"What did you think?"

"Very impressive," she said. "And moving." Asma's voice unexpectedly cracked with emotion.

"You remembered?"

"Of course." She had known Farooq for months before he had shared the story behind his idea for a startup, the pain that lived on the edges of his childhood. Grief that she shared that he didn't want to overshadow with details of his own. It was only with Farooq that she was able to sit with the sadness that had been her companion since her mother's death. In losing Farooq, she realized now, she had also closed herself off to that sadness.

A slight man wearing a polo shirt and khakis had come up beside Farooq and put his hand on his shoulder. "Good job, man."

"Thanks," Farooq said. "Asma, this is Patrick, our CFO. Patrick, this is Asma. She's known me forever. Before all of this." Farooq gestured around the room.

Asma smiled at the introduction as she shook Patrick's outstretched hand.

"Lubna and Saba didn't come?" Farooq asked, looking behind Asma.

"They did," she replied. "I lost them."

"We can meet them back at the hotel," he said. "Let's get breakfast." She nodded, too shocked by the invitation to respond audibly.

"We have that investors' meeting," Patrick said. Asma had forgotten he was still there. Apparently, so had Farooq.

"Can you handle it?" Farooq asked.

"You know they didn't come to hear from me," Patrick replied.

"Go," Asma said. "We'll catch up later."

"Are you sure?" Farooq asked.

Asma nodded as the mob closed in on Farooq again. She stood for a moment looking at him, surrounded by nerdy tech groupies, and felt herself swell with pride and hope.

HAVING BEEN UNABLE TO FIND SABA AND LUBNA in the packed lobby after the conference, Asma went back to her hotel room. She mindlessly flipped through the channels on the TV, smiling as she replayed her short conversation with Farooq over and over in her head. Particularly the prospect of Farooq blowing off a work meeting, and Lubna, to have breakfast with her. She was so proud of him—his confidence, his brilliance, and how he had used something so painful in his past to help others. Eventually Asma dozed off on the hotel bed, waking to the sound of her phone vibrating. It was one of four missed calls from Maryam, no message or text, of course. Hassan had the sense to text her that they would all be meeting at the hotel's patio restaurant for lunch at one. It was already twelve forty-five.

By the time Asma showered and changed her clothes, she was running late. She grabbed a scarf from her bag—the San Francisco fog could roll in at any minute—and dashed out of her room. She was checking her face in the mirror next to the elevators—it really *did* look like she was wearing makeup today. Apparently getting away from the hospital and catching up on sleep was doing her good.

The group was seated at a corner table on the patio, and had already started on appetizers, by the time Asma arrived. Lubna was sitting next to Farooq, animatedly showing him something on her phone. When he saw Asma, he stopped talking and motioned for her to sit in the empty seat on his other side. Naveed called out to her before she could.

"Asma! I saved you a seat."

It would be weird if she didn't take it. Naveed handed her a folder the minute she sat down.

"I wanted to share this with you. I wrote it last night."

Asma opened the folder but was distracted by the sound of Hassan's low whistle. There was a gleaming red sports car at the valet, visible from the table. The men strained their necks to stare.

"Amazing," said Naveed.

"Beautiful," marveled Hassan.

"I don't think you've ever used any of those words to describe me," replied Maryam.

A man made his way out of the hotel and walked around to the driver's side of the car. He tipped the valet before getting in, checked his hair in the rearview mirror, and sped off. But not before Asma recognized him—it was Omar Khan. The last time she'd seen him, he'd been sipping tea in the house in Sacramento with her father and Iman.

"I saw that guy at the conference this morning," said Farooq, glancing at Asma.

"He looks Desi," Hassan said.

"No, he looks Arab. Must be from the Gulf," said Maryam.

"He's Desi," said Saba. "I heard him checking out. His name is Omar Khan."

Asma's stomach dropped as Saba said the name. She hoped beyond hope that Maryam wouldn't recognize it. Asma didn't relish the idea of having to explain how they knew him—the Ponzi scheme, Iman's almost-engagement, their family's financial ruin—to the rest of their group.

But, as if on cue, Maryam's brow wrinkled.

"That name sounds familiar."

"Cuz, like, everyone is named Omar Khan," said Saba.

"No, I really know that name. Hassan?"

Hassan didn't respond, pretending to be engrossed by the menu. He raised his eyebrows imperceptibly, a detail lost on Maryam. She continued to repeat the name a few times before her face lit up with recognition.

"Omar Khan! I remember now! His father was Abu's financial advisor!"

Asma looked quickly at Maryam across the table and coughed, trying to get her attention. But Maryam ignored her and continued.

"What are the chances! I haven't seen him since— ow, Asma, did you just kick me? Watch where you're putting your foot!"

"Sorry," Asma said, and was beyond grateful when a perky waitress appeared, distracting Maryam from whatever she was about to say next.

"DO YOU THINK IMAN WOULD EVER FORGIVE Omar?" Maryam asked Asma as they walked along the sand-strewn path.

It was Farooq's idea for them to drive to the beach after lunch and walk along the cliffs at Ocean Beach.

The sun was still out, even though it was windy and fog was starting to roll up on the sand. Small groups of people dotted the beach, with beach chairs, coolers, and umbrellas clustered around bonfires. Waves crashed in the distance, the soothing sound of the ocean interrupted occasionally by the cries of seagulls.

Maryam and Asma brought up the rear as the group marched on ahead of them.

"I don't know," Asma replied. "She says she's over him. I don't think she blamed him necessarily for his father's crime. I think the bigger question is whether she wants to spare Abu the strain of being related to the Khan family after we lost so much because of them."

"But she loved him, didn't she?" Maryam asked. Asma considered the question. Was it possible that Iman had loved Omar—more than as just an ideal match? Asma couldn't imagine it at the time, but maybe that was only because she didn't give her sister enough credit. After all, thanks to Rehana, Asma had broken up with Farooq based on the simple implication that her mother wouldn't have approved of the match. But faced with a very live parent who might be hurt by the union? Asma couldn't imagine Iman would have made any other choice, whether she loved Omar or not.

"I don't know," Asma replied truthfully. "I guess, under circumstances like that, it doesn't even matter." But Maryam scoffed then.

"Of course it matters, Asma," she said, with her

usual bluntness. "If you find someone you actually love, it's stupid to just throw it away over a family squabble."

Asma wondered if Maryam would have said the same all those years ago about her relationship with Farooq. Probably not, hindsight being 20/20. She was never more grateful that Maryam was ignorant of her relationship with Farooq than in that moment.

As if thinking of him had conjured him, Asma noticed Farooq ahead slowing down from where he had been walking next to Lubna. It looked like he was lingering behind to join them. Now was the time to finally have their talk, that much was clear. But how to get rid of Maryam?

"Maryam, where's Hassan? This is such a nice stroll, you should join him." Asma hoped Maryam wouldn't notice that her departure would leave Asma alone with Farooq.

"He's walking with Naveed," Maryam said, oblivious. "No, thank you. That guy is such a downer."

"Well, he was dumped on his wedding day," said Farooq, catching up to them.

"Like six months ago. Thank God and move on already. There's nothing more irritating than when a person wallows in a relationship that didn't work out."

Asma and Farooq both winced simultaneously. But it was no use. Maryam wasn't going anywhere.

The group reached the end of the path and, one by one, descended the stairs to the beach below. There was a patch of sand and a small clearing where the waves crashed to the shore between rocks.

Maryam made Hassan give her his jacket before he followed Naveed and Kamran, who was practically dragging Farooq off toward some surfers at the far end of the beach. She plopped down directly on the sand and used the jacket to shield her face from the glare of the sun. Lubna and Saba kicked off their shoes and rolled up their pants.

"We're going to dip our toes in the water," said Lubna. "Come on, Asma!"

Asma declined, more interested in the tide pools at the opposite end of the clearing. She felt herself relax as she watched a small crab making its way out of a narrow hole in the sand. Asma rarely came to the beach. She had forgotten how calming the sound of the water could be, how therapeutic it was to comb her hands through the sand and watch the grains slip through her fingers. She was making a mental vow to visit more often when she heard Lubna squeal. Lubna was balanced precariously on a rock in the middle of the water.

"Farooq! Farooq!" Lubna yelled, as the group of men made their way back from where the surfers were bringing in their boards. "Take a picture of me!"

Asma brushed the sand off her hands and stood up, alarmed, as Lubna pulled her leg up behind her in an exaggerated yoga pose, clearly hoping for an Insta-ready photograph.

Asma took off jogging toward where the group was congregating, calling out to Lubna on her way.

"Lubna, be careful—

But Asma's premonition came to life before she could finish her warning. As they all watched, a wave crashed over the rock, throwing Lubna off-balance. She slipped and fell into the water, out of sight.

For a moment, their little group of shocked onlookers was frozen, perhaps hoping that she might pop right back up, laughing, with little more than seaweed tangled in her hair. But after that single held breath, they all seemed to realize at once that she hadn't resurfaced.

And then. Pandemonium.

"Lubna!"

"Oh my God!"

"She's drowning! She's drowning!"

Everyone raced toward the water. Farooq reached the edge of the ocean first and ran through the waves toward the rock where Lubna had been standing. He dove in and disappeared under the water, resurfacing a few seconds later with Lubna's lifeless body. Naveed and Hassan were close behind, waist-deep in the water as the three men hauled Lubna to shore. Asma pushed past them when they reached the sand, her instincts kicking in, assessing the situation with her years of trauma experience.

Lubna was bleeding from the side of her head. Asma pulled the scarf from around her shoulders and pressed it against Lubna's temple. She checked Lubna's pulse, then immediately began CPR, barking orders between chest compressions.

"Hassan, call 911! Farooq, Saba—*back up*! I need space. Maryam, stop screaming!"

Hassan pulled his phone out of his pocket, then yelled, "No reception!" Asma cursed silently. Lubna wasn't breathing. CPR would buy her time, but a head wound of this sort would bleed fast, causing Lubna's blood pressure to bottom out sooner rather than later. And that wasn't even taking into consideration the potential internal injuries—a brain injury, a bleed—that Asma couldn't evaluate here. Moments mattered in a situation like this. She needed help.

"Naveed—go—run! Flag someone down on PCH! Everyone else, try to get cell reception. We need an ambulance."

The rest of them scattered, searching for higher ground—with Maryam and Hassan prying Saba away from Lubna—except for Farooq. He paced back and forth next to them as Asma continued CPR, his hands covering his mouth. But through them, she could hear him speaking. At first she thought he was praying, but then as he drew closer the words became clearer. He was talking to her.

"Please, Asma. Don't let her die. Asma. Please. Save her."

SEVENTEEN

The hours after Lubna's accident were a blur. When the ambulance arrived, Asma jumped in to accompany Lubna to the emergency room. She stayed by her side for as long as she could until she was ushered out to join the family in the waiting room, a nurse placing a heavy blanket around her shoulders when she saw that her clothes were still wet from tending to Lubna in the water.

The minutes passed, the emotion in the room as taut as piano wire. It felt as if, at any moment, something might snap. Farooq paced, shaking his head and muttering under his breath. Saba texted furiously, looking up from her phone every time the doors to the ER swung open. Maryam sniffed loudly, then moaned, then sniffed loudly on repeat—an elaborate mixture of both show and genuine worry. Asma sat still and prayed, less for divine intervention than to occupy her mind; she couldn't stop thinking about the worst-case prognosis.

So many things could go wrong with a head injury. Lubna might never be the same, if she survived at all.

Finally, it was Lubna's doctor who emerged from the swinging ER doors. Everyone stood up.

The doctor, a small, slight man, took off his glasses and his scrub hat. "Her hip is fractured and she has an intracranial bleed. She hasn't yet regained consciousness."

Maryam collapsed into a chair while Saba put her hand to her mouth, speechless. Farooq bent over, his head in his hands.

"I should've stopped her," he mumbled.

Asma was the only one who remained calm enough to ask for more information. Where was the bleed located? Were they considering a craniectomy incision? What blood pressure medications had been administered? The doctor patiently answered her questions, clearly relieved to be talking shop with a fellow professional. But it all boiled down to one simple message.

"For now," the doctor said, "it's just a waiting game."

ASMA WAS IN THE HOSPITAL CAFETERIA SIPPING a cup of coffee when she received Hassan's text. Farooq had had Lubna moved to one of the VIP suites on the top floor of the hospital. The rooms were absurdly expensive and were not covered by insurance.

She walked down the hall, her unfinished cup of coffee still in her hands. She was at Lubna's suite, about to enter, when she heard whispers inside.

Asma pushed open the door to find Lubna in bed, hooked up to a ventilator, a heart rate monitor, and a central line. Her head was wrapped in bandages and the bottom half of her body was encased by blankets. Asma could make out the rise and fall of her chest, her breathing assisted by the whirring ventilator at her bedside, next to where Maryam and Hassan sat.

"Oh, it's you," Maryam said. "I thought it was Saba. I'm so ready to chew her out. These girls and social media, I'm sick of it. And look, it is actually dangerous."

"Maryam, now's not the time," Hassan said.

"She was acting stupid," Maryam replied. "She brought this upon herself."

Maryam handed her phone to Asma, her screen open to Instagram and a picture of Farooq and Lubna taken at lunch. It was captioned with a heart emoji. And had seven thousand likes.

Asma felt her heart nearly stop. Lubna took her page seriously—she never would've posted something like this unless there was something official between her and Farooq. And "official" was very different in their community than simply becoming exclusive or putting a label on it. Were they engaged?

"She posted it literally five minutes before she fell. She basically invited nazr."

"It was an accident," Hassan said. "It didn't happen because of the evil eye."

Farooq came into the room. Asma couldn't look at him. She stared at Lubna's enshrouded body and her eyes filled with tears. Lubna adored Asma and had never been anything but kind and loving. She was lying in a hospital bed and Asma was jealous about some picture on Instagram? What was wrong with her?

"The car's outside," Farooq said. "I'm taking Saba home to get Aunty Bushra. Maryam, I can take you too."

"I'll stay with Hassan."

"Maryam, the boys—" Hassan began.

"Asma can take care of them," Maryam said. "You really don't want me around Saba right now."

Asma didn't have the strength left to argue. Between Lubna's current condition and her undefined, and rapidly fading, relationship with Farooq, she felt a deep weariness overtake her. Part of her would gladly see Lubna and Farooq together if it meant that Lubna would recover. But the other part—the part of her that had reawakened since Farooq had reentered her life—would be devastated to see Farooq with anyone else, much less someone in her family. She immediately kicked herself for being selfish. Her mind flashed to Farooq onstage, tilting his head as he talked about his aunt. All the pain that she had put him through. He deserved better.

"Asma?" She flinched as Farooq said her name. "You ready?"

"I'll meet you downstairs in a minute," she managed to whisper.

The sun had set on the city. The fog and moonlight cast a gloomy shadow on the skyline. It was the complete opposite—in all ways—of the start of the day.

Farooq opened the front door of his car for Asma as Saba climbed into the back seat. They drove away from the hospital in silence. Farooq gazed straight ahead without a sideways look.

As they entered the freeway, out of the city traffic, Farooq hit the accelerator. He glanced back at Saba in the rearview mirror.

"You okay back there?"

"I guess. This day has been surreal. I can't get the image of Lubna floating in the water out of my mind."

"Me neither," Farooq said.

Asma looked out the window and bit her lip to prevent herself from crying. She could feel the adrenaline rush that had sustained her through the day wearing off. And, unlike the comedown after an intense shift in the ER, where she could shut off her brain and try to relax, Asma was now left to deal with the fallout of the day's events on her own family. And the waves of regret hitting her. It was an entirely different feeling, and one she was unprepared to handle.

The rest of the ride unfolded in interminable silence. When they arrived at the Qureishis' home, they were greeted by a flurry of activity as Bushra and Saba ran about, hurriedly packing bags for themselves and Lubna. Farooq and Asma stood at the foot of the stairs.

"Asma, if you hadn't been there today, I don't know—"

Farooq was interrupted by the doorbell. Asma couldn't help but be grateful that Farooq couldn't complete his sentiment. She was afraid that the slightest kindness from him might make her go to pieces right now, after the stress of the day, and the last thing she wanted was to put him in the position of having to comfort her.

Asma opened the door to find Tariq.

"Saba texted me."

At the sound of the door, Saba ran downstairs carrying a duffel bag and Bushra emerged from the kitchen carrying stacks of Tupperware.

"Hospital food is garbage," she explained.

Tariq took the Tupperware from Bushra's hands and headed out to his car, Saba and Bushra on his heels. For the first time in two days, Asma and Farooq were alone.

"Asma, we haven't had a chance to talk," Farooq began, but Asma cut him off.

"I can't," she said, feeling tears prick her eyes. "Not right now . . ."

She rubbed at her eyes before the tears had a chance to fall. If Lubna recovered, she would need Farooq's support. A brain injury could mean months of rehab, maybe more. Her speech might be affected, or her fine motor skills. She might have to relearn how to walk. If she recovered at all. Asma thought of the private hospital room, the state-of-the-art rehab centers that weren't covered by most insurance. The kind of care that Farooq could afford, that Lubna's family could not. And no matter how exhausted and desolate Asma was at the thought, she knew that right now, Lubna needed Farooq more than she did.

"I mean," she began, unsure of the exact words. "We've been dancing around each other for weeks now, but it's just rehashing the past. Our relationship was over a long time ago. You moved on, right?"

She could see Farooq hesitate at her words, something like agony playing over his face. He said nothing.

"And all of this back-and-forth isn't fair to Lubna. She doesn't know anything about what happened between us, and finding out that we've been reminiscing about the past would hurt her terribly. And she's had enough hurt, now."

"Right," Farooq said, the word harsh and clipped, as if Asma were being cruel. Farooq agreed? Did that mean what she thought it meant? She had to ask to be sure.

"So you're with Lubna?"

Farooq was quiet for a long, excruciating pause. "Yes," he finally replied. "I'm with Lubna." And then, without another word, he turned and left.

Asma felt all the air rush out of her body as Farooq walked out of her life, again. She fell to the floor as the door slammed behind him, her heart shattering into a million pieces.

EIGHTEEN

Asma remembered the first week after her college breakup with Farooq as calm. She had so convinced herself that she had done the right thing that she went about her days as usual. But the numbness wore off in the second week. Her regret mounted each day that passed and with each unanswered call and emailed apology to Farooq. The rest of the semester passed by in a lonely fog before the end of the school year brought some relief—the end to daily reminders of him around campus. She spent her summer days volunteering at the local hospital and her summer nights crying into her pillow at her father's house.

This time, the first week was the hardest. For the first time in her life, she called in sick to work and spent her days in bed. Lucky for her, she had the house to herself and didn't have to contend with unwanted questions from Maryam or the twins. Lubna had regained consciousness after a few days in the hospital, with thankfully no detectable brain damage although her hip was still in bad shape. Farooq had stepped in with the generous offer to house the entire family at the Fairmont until Lubna's doctors cleared her to come home. Maryam had jumped at the offer like she'd won an all-expenses-paid vacation to an exotic locale.

Asma rolled over and hit her phone. It had been ringing nonstop all morning. The latest call: her father. After weeks of silence, he was the last person she wanted to speak to. She ignored the call.

It was 11:48 a.m. She should go back to sleep. She had earned it. Even a week straight of sleep would barely make a dent in the deficit she'd accumulated over three years of residency.

More ringing. This time it was the doorbell. She ignored it, but when it continued—over and over—she realized it must be the twins. The family was back earlier than Maryam had predicted. Maybe Lubna's recovery had taken a turn for the better. Asma crawled out of bed, threw on a ratty bathrobe, and shuffled downstairs.

It wasn't the kids.

"Hey," Fatima said, her sad eyes filled with an understanding that Asma knew she couldn't find from anyone else. At the sight of her best friend, Asma burst into tears.

"Oh, Asma." Fatima wrapped her arms around her, rubbing her back. "I'm so, so sorry," she said.

Fatima led Asma into the kitchen and sat her down as though Asma were a visitor, not the other way around.

"I made you some soup." Fatima took out a Pyrex bowl from the tote she was carrying and placed it on the table in front of Asma with a spoon. "My mom used to make it for us when we were sick." Fatima took a seat next to Asma at the table.

"You want to talk?"

"Nothing to talk about. It's over. Again." Asma's eyes filled with tears. She brushed them away, then took a spoonful of the soup.

"And that's what you want?" Fatima asked.

Asma shrugged, as if she were indifferent. A week of bed rest had brought Asma some clarity.

"It's not really about what I want," she said. "I've thought about it from every angle, and either way, it's better that he's with Lubna."

"Even if he really wants to be with you?" Fatima asked.

"Then why was he with her in the first place?" Asma countered. "Was it just to get back at me for dumping him all those years ago?"

"Or maybe to get close to you again," Fatima said. "To figure out if he could get past his anger and hurt from all those years ago by being around you. It's not so outlandish, really."

"But what about Lubna?" Asma said. "If that's true, and he's just been using her to get close to me again, doesn't that make him just as devious as Salman?"

Fatima bristled at the sound of her estranged husband's name. She was still staying at her cousin's apartment in Oakland, where her days were spent fielding calls from her parents and relatives who were distraught that she had left Salman and were trying to convince her to come home. Salman, meanwhile, had taken a leave from work and disappeared. He was nowhere to be found.

"The difference is, he never made any promises to Lubna. He didn't stand in front of God and their families and swear to be faithful and loving for the rest of their lives."

"So it's just okay for me to be the other woman in their relationship, as long as they're not married?" Asma asked.

"I think you're trying to take a very complicated situation and make it black and white," Fatima replied. "I love you, Asma, but it's what you do. Things are either good or bad. People are right or wrong. You're a good person, but you never allow people to mess up or do the wrong thing, even if they're well intentioned. And you're not good at admitting your own mistakes either."

"What does that mean?" Asma asked, feeling a prickle of annoyance that her friend was being so ruthless—if accurate—when all Asma wanted was a compassionate shoulder to cry on.

"It means, it took you eight years to admit that breaking up with Farooq was a mistake," Fatima replied. "You broke his heart, and you believed you were justified in doing it because it was what your mother would have wanted. You were wrong for hurting him—and yourself—back then. And maybe he's wrong for using Lubna to get close to you again, or for thinking he'd teach you a lesson, or whatever it was he was doing. But at the end of the day, he shouldn't be with her just because you've decided it's the right thing to do. That's not fair to Lubna either."

Fatima went quiet, a pensive look on her face.

"Maybe this is an opportunity for you to disentangle yourself from Farooq once and for all," she finally said. "You used to be so focused on work and talk about your patients nonstop. But since Farooq reappeared, it's like you've lost yourself."

Asma was silent then, unsure of how to counter Fatima's argument.

"You know I'm right," Fatima said, sitting back, a self-satisfied smile crossing her face.

"Possibly," said Asma, unable to fully admit defeat. "Maybe."

"So, are you going to stop wallowing and actually try to take back control of your life?" Fatima asked.

"Possibly," Asma repeated, begrudgingly.

"When are you back at work?"

"Monday. Mainly because everyone is coming back from San Francisco this weekend."

"Do they know why you've been calling in sick?"

"Only Jackson," Asma replied. "I told everyone else

about the accident. I think they assume I'm in shock, or having some sort of breakdown."

"All of the above," Fatima said with a grin.

"Jackson has been keeping me up to date on what I've missed," Asma said. "There was another gender reveal snafu. Explosion. Shrapnel. The whole bit."

"More exciting than private practice in Sacramento, I gather."

"Yes," Asma said with a smile. "Just opioid overdoses and tractor injuries out there."

Fatima laughed.

"And I made a decision," Asma said, wanting to prove to Fatima that she wasn't planning on simply wallowing forever. That she'd already taken steps to move forward with her new life, the one that involved neither moving to Sacramento nor reuniting with Farooq. And, as heartbroken as she was, there was some excitement there. The promise of uncharted territory.

"I'm renting an apartment."

Fatima raised an eyebrow.

"Really? Not just looking, considering, pondering . . . ?"

"My application was accepted yesterday," Asma said, leaning into her own smugness. "Two bedrooms, close to the hospital."

"You got the job?"

"Not yet. Dr. Saucedo said they're making a final decision right after graduation. But, Fatima, I know I got it—I feel it. And I'll be all ready to go when I do. But I'm going to need some help decorating my apartment."

"Well, you've got the right woman for that," Fatima replied. They sat in amiable silence for a moment, just as they had in the bathroom all those years ago.

"Thanks for coming, Fatima." Asma held up her bowl of soup, her eyes filling with tears—this time out of love for her friend who had reached out to comfort her in the midst of her own heartache. "This is just what I needed."

ASMA STARED AT THE BLACK-AND-WHITE IN-structions for a few seconds before realizing they were upside down. She righted them, then made a new life resolution: no more furniture from IKEA. How had she been able to complete complicated surgical rotations but couldn't figure out how to put this dining room table together? After a few more minutes struggling to insert a screw into a hole clearly not big enough, Asma gave up. She balled up the instructions and aimed for the trash can across her new living room. She didn't need a dining room table. She wasn't planning on having anyone over for dinner anyway. She'd be eating most of her meals at the hospital cafeteria.

She'd unpack her books instead. An easy decision to make as the bookshelf, a hand-me-down from Maryam, was already assembled.

Asma had told Maryam about her new apartment

the night she came back from San Francisco. At first, Maryam had protested and begged Asma to stay, promising that they'd clean out Hassan's office so that she could have her own space. But Asma was one step ahead.

"Don't you want a place to escape when everyone is driving you crazy?" Asma countered. "I'll give you a key." Maryam was so delighted by the prospect that she gifted Asma her wedding china and took her on an IKEA shopping spree.

"What did Abu say?" Maryam asked.

"He doesn't want to talk about it," Asma responded.

Asma's father had called her nonstop for two days after Lubna's accident before she finally relented and answered the phone. She was bracing herself for the conversation to pick back up from where they left it last—him reprimanding her for trying to live on her own—but he changed the subject the minute she brought it up, inquiring after Lubna and the Qureishis. Genuine concern in his voice.

"He only started talking to me again because of Lubna's accident," Asma told Maryam.

Now Asma took her medical school textbooks from the box closest to her and kneeled down to put them on the shelf. She lined them up in the chronological order in which she had studied the topics in medical school, then leaned back in satisfaction. The apartment was starting to take shape. After months of living out of boxes at Maryam's place, it felt good to be able to stretch out and fill the expanse of her living space. Her bed would be delivered later that week, the morning of her residency graduation. An auspicious start to this new phase of her life.

Asma reached out to grab the open flap of another box. She dragged it toward her, then reached in without looking, her hand feeling not the familiar outline of her books but a shoebox.

She pulled the box closer and peered in, stopping at the sight of it: the shoebox filled with mementos of her time with Farooq. What had once seemed like a talisman now seemed like a curse. Farooq's reappearance in her life had brought nothing but heartache, an old wound reopened. And sentimentality would only impede her progress in moving on with her life. Asma propped open the door of her apartment with an old magazine and took the shoebox down the stairs to the garbage bins at the back of her building.

She stood in front of them for a minute, trying to figure out whether she should recycle everything in the box or send it to the landfill. She finally decided on the landfill; she couldn't risk any of this stuff reappearing in her future like Farooq.

She opened the garbage bin, then remembered the book of Rumi poetry. She couldn't throw it away— books were too precious to end up in the garbage, especially her favorite poet. She'd donate it to Goodwill after redacting all the comments in the margins. She pulled it out, then tossed the shoebox into the dumpster without hesitating. The lid opened and out spilled old cards, concert tickets, pictures, and cheap college-age jewelry, settling into a sticky pile of slime some kid had thrown away.

How fitting.

Asma slammed the garbage lid down, the last image she saw before it closed: the photo booth picture of her and Farooq, covered in goo.

ASMA STUDIED HER HAIR IN THE BATHROOM mirror. She turned the faucet on and wet her hand, just enough to smooth down a flyaway on the side of her head. Tucking it behind her ear, she silently wished that caps were worn at residency graduation ceremonies. She could have really used a hat today.

Asma spent the morning in her new apartment, waiting for her bed delivery and putting the finishing touches on her décor. The plan was to bring everyone here after the ceremony to show them the place, including her father and Iman, who were driving in from Sacramento for her graduation. When her father saw how close the apartment was to the hospital, he would understand that it was just like when she was on campus at Berkeley. She took it as a good sign that he was even coming— what would people say if he didn't show up for his own daughter's graduation?

Asma drove to the hotel by herself and sat in the parking lot, feeling sadness as she watched her fellow residents pass by her car accompanied by their families. Asma felt a small lump in her throat seeing a few of her classmates walk by with their mothers—another big occasion in her life without her mother by her side. Also not present: a partner. There was a small part of her that had been hoping, when things were beginning to thaw between her and Farooq, that he might have been here with her today. At the thought of him, her eyes filled with tears. She wiped them away and pushed the thought out of her mind, grabbing some tissues from her glove compartment. She chided herself for getting upset about something that was clearly never meant to be. No more Farooq. All of it was in the past; even her mementos of the relationship had been taken away with last week's garbage. This was the beginning of a new chapter. She would only look forward.

She got out of her car, plastered a huge smile on her face, and congratulated the residents she passed. The smile became genuine when she saw Dr. Saucedo. After giving her a congratulatory hug, Dr. Saucedo looked around behind her.

"Your family's not here?"

"They're on their way."

But they had still not arrived by the time Asma and the other residents were ushered onstage in the hotel ballroom. Asma scanned the audience as various members of the hospital faculty and administration took their places on the stage next to their small cohort.

"Your family on CPT?" Jackson asked, looking around the room with her.

Asma couldn't believe it. Her family was never on time for anything, but she thought they would make a special effort today. They were going to miss her graduation.

The hospital's president was the first of the speakers, and then Dr. Saucedo rose to address the graduates. She started with general congratulations to the group, then remarks that seemed directed to Asma.

"Some of you will be faced with tough decisions, forced to choose between what someone else thinks is right and what you believe to be the truth. Will you stand firm in your convictions? Or will you allow yourself to be persuaded?"

Dr. Saucedo's comments were like a beacon call, a clear sign to Asma that she was on the right path. For her entire life, she had been so worried about her family—making decisions based not on what she wanted or needed but on what she thought they did. And here she was, on one of the biggest days of her professional career, and they weren't even here. She felt completely and utterly alone.

"Enough from me," Dr. Saucedo wrapped up. "And now, what these doctors have all been waiting for—the end of residency!"

Dr. Saucedo shuffled the name cards on the lectern and read out the name of the first graduate. But before he could take his diploma, there was a commotion at the back of the room. The door swung open.

"I'm being quiet!" a little voice yelled.

"Shhhhhhh!" screamed another little voice. "You have to whisper!"

Dr. Saucedo stopped talking as the audience tittered. Asma instantly recognized the voices. And, sure enough, in stumbled Zaki and Zayd, followed closely by the rest of the Qureishis, her father, and Iman.

Asma was torn between relief at seeing her family and embarrassment at the disruption. The latter emotion took stronger hold when Zayd caught her eye and yelled, "Asma Khala! Asma Khala!"

Hassan clamped his hand over Zayd's mouth while the audience erupted into laughter. *Sorry!* mouthed Saba, as Maryam ushered the boys toward empty seats. Bushra waved from behind her iPad, with which she was filming the events on the stage. Mr. Ibrahim and Iman took their time walking to the front of the room in search of seats instead of slipping into the back like normal people.

The family settled, Dr. Saucedo again began to call out the names of the graduates. As they lined up to shake hands with Dr. Saucedo, the hospital president, and the other administrators onstage, the audience cheered and clapped, ignoring the request to save applause for the end. And, as embarrassed as Asma had been by her family's entrance, she choked up as she crossed the stage to shake Dr. Saucedo's hand, realizing she had the loudest cheering section of all.

THE MINUTES AFTER THE GRADUATION CEREMONY were a frenzied cacophony of hugs, flowers, and balloons. Asma scanned the crowd of graduates and their families and saw hers standing in a corner of the lobby talking to Dr. Saucedo. As she approached, she overheard her father:

"She's always been so responsible. I knew, even from a young age, that she would do whatever it is that she set her mind to."

Asma wondered if her father was telling the truth or if this was just for Dr. Saucedo's benefit. Either way, she was relieved he had come around. And she could hear the pride in his voice.

Someone grabbed her from behind, and she turned to find Jackson, looking a bit teary-eyed. Very uncharacteristic.

"This isn't the great Dr. Jackson Wong getting mushy on me, is it?" Asma asked, giving him a nudge to the shoulder.

"Of course not. I just don't know what you're going to do without me," Jackson said gruffly, hugging Asma.

"Me neither," Asma said, suddenly holding back tears once more.

By the time she'd said goodbye to her friend, her

family was no longer in the lobby. She picked up her phone to call her dad. There was a text from Hassan: everyone was waiting in the parking lot. To Asma's shock, Iman had made dinner reservations at Golden Panda.

Golden Panda was the only halal Chinese restaurant in the area. Bustling and chaotic, it was nestled between a nail salon and a dollar store in a Chinese strip mall. Its sprawling dining room walls were decorated with Chinese calligraphy and gold-lettered Quran verses on black velvet. The restaurant was filled almost entirely by non-Chinese patrons—mainly South Asian Muslim families who made the pilgrimage from all over Northern California for halal moo shu beef.

"I thought about putting together a real graduation party," Iman said as they arrived, "but I know you like this place even though it's so crowded and run-down."

Once seated, the twins immediately started spinning the lazy Susan in the middle of the table and poking each other with wooden chopsticks. As Hassan and Bushra tried their best to keep the kettle of green tea and saucer with hot sauce from flying off the table and injuring someone, Iman and Mr. Ibrahim directed the waiters—arms piled high with Asma's favorite dishes, which Iman had ordered before their arrival—to their table. Asma turned to Saba and Maryam for an update on Lubna, still at her physical therapy appointment. Asma felt guilty that she hadn't seen Lubna since the accident—a fact that no one seemed to notice given

Asma's hero status within the family. She knew she couldn't yet handle the chance of running into Farooq with Lubna.

"She's sooo much better," Saba said. "She can't remember the details of the accident, but otherwise she's okay—she's almost able to walk unassisted."

"She's back to her old self," said Maryam. "You should see how she's bossing everyone around."

"She's not bossing anyone around," Saba said, annoyed. "She just asked you to get her a cup of water because, you know, she can't walk."

"Well, I don't know why I have to hang around all her appointments anyway. She has Farooq and Naveed ready to wait on her hand and foot."

"Naveed is helping out too?" Asma asked.

"He's like Farooq's little sidekick," Maryam replied. "Always following him around."

"Don't be judgy," Saba said. "They've both been so awesome. Naveed's been helping Ammi by bringing us food, and Farooq keeps sending her these beautiful bouquets of flowers."

Saba held out her phone so Asma could see a picture of the Qureishis' living room, filled with elaborate arrangements.

"I guess he made the move Lubna was waiting for," Saba said with a wiggle of her eyebrows.

Asma spun the lazy Susan around to help herself to a slice of the puffy sesame seed bread the waitress had placed on the table. She focused on chewing. She didn't want to hear anything else about Farooq and Lubna. Even listening to her father and Iman drone on about their social life in Sacramento was preferable.

"You wouldn't think it, but people there appreciate a good party," Iman declared. "Although it's like they didn't know what luxury was until I showed up."

Iman's event planning business had taken off. Probably because she had less competition in Sacramento, and she flagrantly encouraged the people she knew to celebrate even the smallest of life's milestones in a valiant attempt to keep up with the proverbial Khans. Iman had already arranged a baby sprinkle, a sweet sixteen, and a divorce party.

"The circle of life," said Asma.

Mr. Ibrahim also found the company in Sacramento much to his liking.

"The people are healthy without spending too much time outside," he said. Mr. Ibrahim hadn't much cared for the Bay Area lifestyle—hikes, bikes, and running outdoors. Asma noticed that her father's hair was once again completely jet black and the wrinkles around his mouth had diminished. She wondered if he'd started using Botox but was afraid to ask.

"It's been so nice to reconnect with Gulnaz Bhabi," Mr. Ibrahim said. "You remember Gulnaz Dadabhoy?" Mr. Ibrahim asked Bushra. "She's one of our most distinguished relatives."

Mr. Ibrahim's discussion about the lives of their extended family was interrupted by a waitress walking toward their table with a cake. She placed it in front of Asma with a hearty congratulations and handed Iman a book of matches.

Asma peered at the cake, a giant 3D fortune cookie. A fortune was scrawled in black icing on a white chocolate fondant scroll: *You will find much success in your medical career.*

Asma was as touched as she was surprised—both that Iman had actually taken the trouble to organize a graduation dinner at one of her favorite restaurants, and that she knew Asma well enough to keep it as subdued as Iman could probably manage.

"Thank you, Iman," Asma said.

Iman smiled. "You did it!"

What a way to end the roller coaster of the last couple of weeks. After her first breakup with Farooq, Asma was completely alone. At the time, she had wondered if she'd ever feel happy again. She could never have imagined what would await her all these years later. Another heartbreak related to Farooq—but also love and support. She had deep friendships and was surrounded by family. For the first time in her entire life, she felt seen and appreciated by them. This was how it was supposed to be, how she'd always wanted it to be, when she first set her sights on med school.

Asma leaned over to grab her phone from her purse. She wanted to take a picture of the cake and memorialize the moment so she could look back on this day when she was feeling down.

As she rummaged through her bag, she heard dishes clattering.

"Nana?" said Zaki.

"Uncle?" Hassan sounded worried.

"Abu!" Maryam screeched.

Asma sat up to see her father, head planted, face-first, in a bowl of egg drop soup.

KIMBERLY WESTERLAND. THE NAME KEPT MOVING through Asma's head, over and over, to the rhythm of the ambulance's siren. Asma was in third grade when the girl down the street, Kimberly Westerland, told her that her parents were going through a divorce. Asma didn't know anyone who had divorced before. Kimberly tried to put a positive spin on it—she said she'd have two rooms and get double presents for her birthday and Christmas. Asma had thought at the time that parents splitting up was the worst thing she'd ever heard in her life. Of course that changed when she lost her mother years later.

And on the evening of her residency graduation, as Asma sat in the ambulance clutching the hand of her father, who had just suffered a massive heart attack, she thought back to third grade and how she would've never known then that there was something much worse than her parents not living together. Losing them both.

NINETEEN

⌒

The drive from San Jose to Sacramento was almost two hours of suburban wasteland, farms, fast food, and the occasional rest stop. Asma drove with all four of her windows down, the wind rushing by the car the soundtrack to her drive when the Bay Area's radio stations stopped receiving signal and faded to static. She focused on the freeway ahead of her, a straight shot as far as her eyes could see, her view periodically broken by semitrucks driving too slowly in the fast lane.

Two weeks. It took almost exactly two weeks after Mr. Ibrahim's heart attack for the doctors to clear him to go back to Sacramento. Just enough time for Asma to break her lease and withdraw her application for the position in the ER.

Asma exited the freeway in Fairfield to stretch her legs. She had left almost two hours later than she planned that morning, when Aunty Bushra insisted on packing a bag full of food for her drive. Asma had told her it wasn't necessary—it wasn't long enough to need to stop for food, and there were plenty of In-N-Outs that she'd pass on the road—but Bushra insisted. Between Mr. Ibrahim's heart attack and Asma's care of Lubna at the beach, she had been elevated to almost saintlike status in the Qureishis' home. Asma thanked Aunty Bushra silently as she pulled out a thermos of chai, watching a family at the table next to her sipping remnants of Big Gulps they had picked up from a freeway 7-Eleven.

When the thermos was empty, Asma threw her trash in a nearby bin and pulled onto the freeway again. As she drove, she reflected on the choice she had made. She was leaving the job she wanted and the life she had created, for the responsibility of taking care of her father. Asma could tell Dr. Saucedo was disappointed when she had made the call—a snap decision while in the ER next to her father—but Asma knew it was the right thing to do. And it would make everything easier. Easier to move on from her old life. To not have to see Farooq every time she met the Qureishis for dinner or saw Lubna socially.

But as Asma approached the Sacramento city limits, her resolve started to fade. She had made the decision in the chaos of her father's hospitalization. Between wrapping things up at work and deconstructing her just-assembled apartment, she'd had no time to sit and think through all the practical and emotional implications of her move. She had no job and no friends. As the weight of it all finally started to settle on her, she resisted the urge to pull off the freeway and head back west.

When she finally arrived at the house, her father was upstairs sleeping. Asma looked in on him and, careful not to wake him, checked his pulse. A normal, steady rhythm. He'd lost a lot of the water weight he'd gained after the surgery to insert a cardiac stent, and his color looked better than it had the day he was discharged. But Asma couldn't help but feel like this had happened because she hadn't come with him to Sacramento, hadn't kept up with monitoring his medical care. Well, that was all about to change, now that Asma was moving in. Her father's health wasn't going to deteriorate on her watch.

"How's cardiac rehab going?" Asma asked Iman, as she unpacked her boxes from her car and stacked them up in the corner of the garage.

"He complains," Iman replied, watching Asma but making no offer to help. "But I think it's good for him. Gives him something to do every day besides sleeping and watching TV."

"And the home-care nurse?"

Iman shrugged. "Seems fine."

"What about his diet? Is he eating enough? And staying away from fried food?"

"His appetite's been good, actually. Really, things are going okay. I wish you hadn't . . ." Iman trailed off, and Asma straightened, dropping a box on the top of the stack.

"Wish I hadn't what?"

"I really wish you hadn't taken up all this room in the garage with your stuff," Iman replied, sniffing. "I need it for my party supplies. And storage units aren't that expensive, you know."

Asma rolled her eyes and walked back to slam her trunk. Welcome home, indeed.

"UGH, THERE'S SO MUCH TRAFFIC!" ASMA TAPPED impatiently at the wheel, frustrated by the red brake lights ahead of her. Rehana's plane had landed a half hour ago, and even though Asma had left Sacramento exceptionally early to make it to San Francisco on time, she was still fifteen minutes away *without* traffic.

"Don't worry," said Fatima, her voice floating out of Asma's cell phone perched on the dashboard. "It'll take some time for her to get her luggage."

Fatima was still at her cousin's place and she wasn't budging. Her cousin had said she could stay as long as she wanted, and Fatima told Asma that she fully intended to take her up on that offer. Especially after Salman finally reappeared and reached out to her.

"You should've heard him, Asma. Sobbing on the phone—like *I* cheated on *him*."

"Crying out of guilt?"

"You'd think, right? But no, he's having this midlife crisis—he was blubbering on and on about how he's always done what's expected of him, how the pressure was too intense. I was trying to be understanding and part of me felt sorry for him. But another part of me was so angry. I thought, does he even realize who he's talking to? My entire life has been about doing what was expected of me and I didn't run off and have an affair."

"I was just thinking the other day about Columbia."

"Right? I'm sure that didn't even cross his mind, he's so busy wallowing in self-pity," said Fatima.

Asma hung up and exited the freeway for SFO. A car cut in front of her and Asma honked longer than necessary. Talking about Salman filled Asma with rage. She wanted nothing more than to drive to his house and throttle him. But Asma had been swallowing her anger, trying to listen without judgment as Fatima figured out her next steps. Fatima had her parents on one side telling her to forgive Salman and work things out and her cousin on the other side telling her to drop him. This was something Fatima needed to decide on her own.

By the time Asma made it through the airport traffic and pulled into the terminal, Rehana was already standing curbside with her bags.

Asma jumped out of the car and hugged her aunt. Rehana had cut her impromptu trip short after Mr. Ibrahim's heart attack, and though they had connected a few times over FaceTime throughout the summer,

Asma had longed to have longer conversations. With Asma's mother gone, Rehana seemed to be the key to Asma's understanding of her younger years and all the choices that had brought her to where she was.

Rehana settled into the front seat as Asma grabbed her bags from the curb. They were weighed down to the absolute max, and possibly even heavier than that. Likely filled with all the requests Iman and Mr. Ibrahim had sent her over the summer, including custom-tailored clothes and bespoke jewelry.

"Abu and Iman send their salaams and will see you at home." Asma closed the trunk and got back into the car. "Iman is coordinating a swimming pool housewarming—a pool warming, if you will," she said with a roll of her eyes. "And Abu was on the phone with his new best friend—Mrs. Dr. Aunty Gulnaz Dadabhoy." Asma used all of Mrs. Gulnaz's titles, a hat tip to her father.

Asma pulled away from the curb as the airport traffic police made their way menacingly toward her.

"MashAllah, it's good to have family in the area, especially during a time like this," Rehana said.

"Yes, especially such *distinguished* family." Asma said with a smile. "Did Abu tell you who else they've reconnected with?"

"Omar Khan?" Rehana asked, with a glance at Asma. "Yes, he mentioned it. I always liked Omar."

Asma stared at her aunt incredulously.

"You did?"

"He was a very nice boy. It's not his fault what happened with his father."

"Don't you think it's weird that he's interested in being friends with us again?"

"I think it's been good for your father and Iman."

"Because Omar is still single?"

"Because it's nice to be in touch with old friends."

"I don't know about that," Asma said. "Not when the old friend screwed you over."

"That's not a nice word, Asma," Rehana admonished. "And people make mistakes. We should be willing to forgive."

"Of course we should," Asma said, her mind no longer on Omar. The conversation had reminded her of her aunt's previous judgments of Farooq. "But only if the person admits that they were wrong and asks for forgiveness."

Asma didn't have to say it. Rehana knew exactly what she was talking about.

"You want to talk about this again?" Rehana asked. "I thought your graduation would have settled things. You wouldn't have become a doctor if you'd married Farooq Waheed."

"No, I don't want to talk about it," Asma said, immediately regretting that she had steered the conversation in this direction. Though she disagreed with her aunt. Who said Farooq would have kept her from becoming a doctor? He'd been nothing but supportive when they were together in college. Asma knew they could have made it work, somehow. But there was no point in imagining the life they could have had if they'd remained together in college—Farooq was with Lubna now. That life was an impossibility.

They rode for a few minutes in silence.

"You don't know I wouldn't have become a doctor," Asma said, changing her mind. She *did* want to talk about it. "Your concern was that he didn't have money. Look how everything turned out."

"MashAllah, he did well—but none of us knew that was what would happen."

"I knew that he was a good guy."

"He wouldn't have been able to support you."

"So now that he has money, he's suddenly marriage material?"

"Asma, it's all written. What is meant for you will not miss you."

"What does that mean?"

"If he is your naseeb, it will happen."

"It's too late. He and Lubna are practically engaged," Asma replied. Rehana didn't reply, she only clicked her tongue, watching the cars crisscross on the highway in front of them.

Asma stared at the road ahead of her, clenching the steering wheel so tightly that her knuckles turned white. A slow-burning anger bubbled up inside her, her excitement over seeing her aunt extinguished.

Rehana had torpedoed her relationship with Farooq all those years ago and, despite how everything had turned out, she still couldn't apologize or admit that she was wrong.

As Asma reached the freeway on-ramp, she pressed down on the accelerator, glad to find the freeway empty. At that moment, she would have rather been anywhere than in the car with her aunt.

TWENTY

O f course, as soon as Asma was settled into the house in Sacramento, her father insisted on yet another visit to Mrs. Gulnaz Dadabhoy. Despite Asma's protests—namely, that after her father's heart attack, the Dadabhoys should be visiting them, instead of the other way around—she, Iman, Rehana, and Mr. Ibrahim spent an entire afternoon in that same garish living room, sipping chai and listening to Mrs. Dadabhoy wax poetic about the virtues—and money—of her son Zubayr, while her granddaughter Shagufta sat silently scrolling on her phone. Asma managed to hold it together until they got in the car to go home.

"I can't believe you're trying to set me up with a man who has a daughter who is almost my age!"

"Oh no, you're mistaken," Mr. Ibrahim replied. "She's not trying to set you up with her son."

"Yeah, Asma, way to have a big head," said Iman. "He's a hundred-millionaire, why would Aunty try to set you up with him?"

"Aunty knows a lot of people," Rehana said. "It'll be good for her to have her eye out for you."

"Of course *you* were in on this too," Asma practically spat at her aunt.

For so long, she had thought Rehana had wanted what was best for her, but Asma now realized that wasn't the case. She wanted not what was best for Asma but what she *thought* was best for Asma—really what was in the best interest of the family.

She and her aunt spent the rest of the car ride in tense silence as her father went on his constant refrain about the beauty of the Dadabhoy house and how fortunate the Ibrahims were to have such wealthy and well-connected relatives so nearby. But Asma's anger grew, like the heat of a pressure cooker, until she was nearly bursting with it.

It all spilled out later that evening, at a family dinner to which Omar Khan had apparently been invited.

"You remember what she said about Hassan last time we were there?" Asma said, slamming her hand on the dining room table for emphasis. "That he's not a real doctor! You should've seen her face. Like Hassan's a quack practicing out of the trunk of his car."

Omar chuckled, seemingly enjoying Asma's recounting of the visit.

"Well, he's technically not a real doctor," Iman said.

"Like me?"

"Yeah, but I mean a doctor with a job."

Asma glared at her sister. "I had a job. I moved here and gave it up, remember?"

"Of course I remember, you won't let any of us forget."

"Omar found me a very good cardiologist," Mr. Ibrahim said. "I'm sure he can help you find something around here. In private practice?" He glanced at Omar, as if these were marching orders enough for the younger man.

"No, thanks," Asma said. "I can do it myself."

"Oh, come on, Asma," said Omar. "Let me help. My fund invests extensively in the medical field, and I would be happy to introduce you to some of my local contacts."

Despite her irritation with her family, Asma knew it would be foolish to pass up the opportunity for local contacts. While she hated the idea of leaving emergency medicine for private practice, it would give her the flexibility to take Mr. Ibrahim to his appointments and help out around the house more.

"Okay," Asma replied. "I would appreciate that."

"Definitely," said Omar. "Let's meet this weekend to discuss strategy."

OMAR CALLED ASMA THE DAY AFTER THAT DINNER and suggested they meet up for brunch. Asma assumed Omar would pick some pretentious, trendy restaurant filled with people taking their overpriced food too seriously—but when she googled the café that

Omar suggested, she was discomfited to see it reviewed as one of Sacramento's most romantic first-date locations.

Asma spotted Omar sitting on a bench outside the restaurant, wearing linen shorts, a polo, and sunglasses. He looked good, like a model in the diversity issue of a surf-and-sand magazine, if they had such a thing. Asma didn't realize how intently she was admiring the view until he turned and saw her. She felt herself flush, then waved, hoping he hadn't noticed her checking him out.

"There you are!" he said. "I put our names down for a table on the patio."

The waitress ushered them to a corner table with a riverside view before leaving them to peruse the menu. Asma zeroed in on it with intense focus, trying to ignore the other patrons dining on the patio—clearly all couples from the way they were seated. It was uncomfortably intimate.

Asma settled on the goat cheese frittata, before pulling out her notebook and pen from her purse. She was here for business. Only business.

"Thanks for meeting with me. I'll just be taking notes while you talk," said Asma in her most formal tone. "Any recs you can give me about who to contact for further information would be great."

But Omar was clearly not in the mood. He waved his hand toward her notebook.

"In a bit—we have more important matters to discuss first. Chocolate or apple beignets?"

"Uhh . . . let's go with apple."

"Now that that's settled," said Omar, "I need you to finish your rant from the other night. It was quite entertaining."

"What rant?"

"About the Dadabhoys. I couldn't stop laughing this week thinking about it."

"What's to know? They're snobs. And such poor manners. But everyone kisses up to them because they're rich. It's gross."

"And hilarious."

"I wish everyone would tell them to go you know where."

"That would signal the end of time. It wouldn't happen. It's the community we live in. There's a social order."

"You sound like Abu! There's only a social order because we allow it to continue."

Omar's smile became a bit wistful.

"The social order will persist whether you and I like it or not. Your father's a wise man who recognizes that."

"These material markers of status are BS. It's all so shallow and fake."

"Of course, we couldn't expect someone like you to understand the world of the shallow and fake."

Omar paused as he and Asma made eye contact. The intimacy of the look—and the realization that she had never before sat across the table from such a good-looking man—flustered Asma, and she laughed to break the tension.

Asma was grateful to see the waitress returning to take their order. But it was only a momentary interruption. Omar's attention was back on Asma the minute the waitress left the table.

"I spent the better part of my twenties rebelling," Omar continued. "But it got me nowhere. I realize now that it's easier to play by the community's rules. And use them to your advantage."

"Is that why you broke off contact with Iman?" Asma asked. "You were rebelling?"

Omar's smile faded, replaced by a look of remorse.

"I felt like I had to after what happened with my father. So many people were involved in his financial schemes, not just your family, there was so much bad blood. And so many secrets. I didn't even know where he had run off to initially. I needed to get my life in order."

"But no one blamed you."

"I know that now. I didn't know it at the time. I thought everyone was upset with me. Your father especially. But seeing my father in the condition he's in now?" Omar shook his head. "I knew it was time to make amends. I've had the chance to apologize to your father and your sister. And I should apologize to you too. I'm sorry."

Omar seemed so sincere and earnest that Asma felt her doubt over his intentions dissipate. Asma took his words in as their waitress returned to the table with their food.

"You don't need to apologize to me. But I appreciate it."

Asma looked up from her plate to find Omar smiling at her. And this time, she smiled right back.

TWENTY-ONE

A sma woke up early and stretched. She sat up in bed, feeling refreshed. Over a month in Sacramento, and she had finally finished unpacking the last of her boxes the previous day. Sacramento had not been that bad. Neither had living again with her father and Iman. Not that she would ever admit it to anyone. There was comfort in slipping right back into the role she knew so well, being the responsible one in the house.

True to his word, Omar had arranged for Asma to interview with the head of a local family practice, which promised flexible hours and ample one-on-one time with patients, none of the irregular shifts and breakneck pace that usually accompanied emergency medicine back in Palo Alto. Asma thought of how many patients she saw in the ER would have benefited from the standard of care a primary care physician could have afforded them. It was a tempting position, she had to admit. But there was a part of her that knew she'd miss the adrenaline of the ER, the feeling of "now or never" decision-making. And the sense that she was saving lives in real time, not just treating ear infections and migraines and type 2 diabetes.

Downstairs her father was sitting at the kitchen table, newspaper spread out in front of him, busy on a sudoku puzzle. This is how he'd spent every morning since returning to Sacramento after his heart attack. "It's important to keep your brain active," he kept saying.

Mr. Ibrahim looked up from the paper when Asma entered the kitchen, his forehead deeply creased in concentration. His look softened at the sight of his middle daughter.

"You're looking nice, beti."

Asma was stunned. She couldn't remember the last time her father had paid her a compliment on her physical appearance.

"Thanks, Abu. So are you," Asma said. "I'm glad I'm here to help."

"He was doing just fine before you got here," Iman said, coming into the kitchen.

"You mean, besides the heart attack?"

Iman rolled her eyes and perched her sunglasses on top of her head. She looked stunning. Her face was made up with precision and subtlety lost on most beauty influencers. She was wearing a soft black silk blouse paired with deep red capris and holding ridiculously expensive shoes.

"Where are you going?" Asma asked.

"Target. I have some stuff to pick up for a party."

"In that outfit?"

From the look on Iman's face, Asma had caught her in a lie. "Some of us don't wear chappals and a fleece when we go shopping, Asma."

Asma's eyes narrowed. What was Iman trying to hide?

"Which party?" Asma asked. There was no point in trying to get the truth out of Iman now, in front of their dad. "The soiree to celebrate reupholstered furniture? Or a puppy shower for a new dog?"

"Don't be a jerk. It's for Noreen's son's birthday party, I told you and Abu about it weeks ago."

"Dr. Sheikh's grandson," said Mr. Ibrahim. "Dr. Sheikh is an anesthesiologist. And the president of the masjid board. He just received a medal from the FBI's Sacramento Field Office."

"For being a native informant?" asked Asma.

"Native what?"

"She's being rude," said Iman. "He was just trying to be helpful. Their family is super rich and well-connected. They basically gave me a blank check for this party."

"Pick up something for tomorrow while you're out," said Mr. Ibrahim.

"What's tomorrow?" Asma asked.

"We're going for lunch at Mrs. Dr. Dadabhoy's house after jumma namaz."

"Not me," said Asma. "I don't need her matchmaking services. Plus, I have plans."

Iman looked incredulous. "You? Have plans?"

"Yes, Iman. I have plans. I'm going to Oakland to have lunch with Fatima."

Iman made a face and put on the oversized designer sunglasses that had been perched on her head. She headed out of the kitchen while Mr. Ibrahim looked at Asma with a confused look.

"Who are you having lunch with?"

"Fatima. Fatima Malik."

Mr. Ibrahim continued to stare at Asma as though he couldn't place the name.

"Abu, you can't be serious. Fatima, my best friend from Cal?"

Mr. Ibrahim shrugged. "Reschedule. The Ahmeds and Rafiques will be at lunch too."

Asma was annoyed that her father was pretending not to remember Fatima.

"No!" Asma said, louder than she intended. Mr. Ibrahim seemed more surprised than angry at her outburst. Asma lowered her voice. "We've been trying to get together since I got here. Tomorrow afternoon is the first day that worked."

"You'd rather see her than have lunch with three of Sacramento's most important families?"

"Abu, I'd rather have lunch at Taco Bell by myself than with the three most important families in Sacramento."

Mr. Ibrahim scoffed, but Asma knew he was hiding a smile.

ASMA SAT, INDICATOR ON, WAITING HER TURN to park in the lot of Al-Madinah, a former liquor store turned first halal meat market in Sacramento that sold a mishmash of halal groceries to the area's diverse Muslim population. She hated coming to Al-Madinah. The store was always packed and the parking lot a disaster—runaway shopping carts, double-parked cars, and people attempting U-turns in flagrant violation of the posted one-way signs.

A car pulled out from a spot near the front, but before Asma, who was next in line, could pull in, she was cut off by a battered minivan that U-turned into the open spot.

She slammed on the horn. "What the hell?"

Rehana, sitting in the passenger seat, put a hand on Asma's shoulder to calm her down and to direct her to an open spot near the back of the lot.

Asma was still annoyed by her father's feigned ignorance about Fatima. Rehana had dragged Asma out of the house to cool her off, saying she needed help picking up groceries.

"I do so much for Abu and he can't even be bothered to remember the important people in my life?" Asma remembered her father's complete amnesia about Farooq when he reappeared on the scene; one of the most formative relationships, and heartbreaks, of her life hadn't even registered.

Asma jostled a sticky shopping cart free from the stacks at the entrance to the store. She pushed it behind Rehana, who was already inside, walking toward the butcher at the back and stopping to pull tins and boxes from the shelves.

"You know your father, Asma. He doesn't mean any harm."

"It's just another example of how secondary my relationships are to him, especially if the person isn't *distinguished*," Asma said, trying not to be pointed about the meaning associated with her comment—she didn't want to bring Farooq up with her aunt again.

The line in front of the butcher spilled into the frozen foods aisle. Buying meat at Al-Madinah was not an organized affair—there were no little paper number tickets or digital number clocks. Things were even worse on the weekends. The butcher was truly survival of the fittest—the strongest among the customers managed to snag the freshest and choicest cuts of meat in a timely manner while the weak were left to loiter and scavenge at the leftovers.

Asma watched in awe as Rehana pushed past the crowd of waiting customers and jostled for position to grab the attention of one of the men behind the counter. There was something about Rehana's presence that commanded attention. Through all the yelling and grabbing, Asma saw one of the butchers head straight toward Rehana to take down her order. As Rehana rattled off how she wanted her chicken, beef, and goat cut and packed, something on the shelf next to Asma caught her eye: halal beef jerky.

Asma felt a pang of sadness at the sight of it, remembering her conversation with Farooq at the Qureishis' kitchen table. So much had happened in the months since that morning—it felt like a different time.

Asma shook her head to remind herself: she was moving forward, no looking back. She took a picture of the beef jerky and texted it to Omar: *How do you feel about beef jerky?* He definitely looked like someone who needed to keep up his protein intake, and she wondered how much he worked out to maintain his physique.

She was throwing the beef jerky into her cart when she felt her phone vibrate. She looked down, expecting to see a text from Omar, but instead she saw a notification for an email. It was from the private practice with which she'd interviewed:

> *Dear Dr. Ibrahim,*
> *We are pleased to offer you a staff position at Sierra Oaks Internal Medicine . . .*

Asma forgot for a minute that she was at Al-Madinah. She felt a bit dizzy as she read and reread the email, wondering if she should find somewhere to sit. Rehana returned to the shopping cart, arms loaded with wrapped packets of meat.

Asma held up her phone.

"I got the job," she said, her voice sounding far away as she spoke. Was this it? Was this how it happened? She'd give up emergency medicine and start dispensing antidepressants and albuterol?

"Mubarak!"

"Hold on a sec," Asma said. "I need to forward this email to Omar."

Rehana took control of the cart, navigating it toward the produce section on the side of the store as Asma trailed behind her, nose in her phone.

Rehana was bagging up eggplants when Asma finished her email.

"Looks like you've changed your mind about Omar."

"I might have been too harsh at first."

"That was nice of him to help set up the interview."

"Very nice. I basically leapfrogged the entire application process."

"He's a good boy. Very pleasant. And handsome."

"I see what you're trying to do, Aunty. We're just friends. Abu has his eyes on him for Iman."

"Iman isn't interested," Rehana said. Asma looked curiously at Rehana, wondering what she knew. She was grateful when a passing shopper accidentally rammed his cart into Asma's leg.

"I hate this place. I'll wait for you in the car."

As Asma walked outside, she wondered what Rehana meant by implying that something was going on between her and Omar. Was it because he really was interested and Rehana thought they would be compatible? Or because he fit into Rehana's preconceived expectations of what Asma needed? Her numbed surprise about the job offer faded, replaced by an irritation she couldn't quite place.

It was only when her phone buzzed with texts from Omar—*CONGRATS! So proud of you!* And then, *I feel strongly about beef jerky!!* with two thumbs-up emojis—that Asma felt like smiling.

TWENTY-TWO

A sma pulled up in front of a former warehouse converted into trendy lofts in Oakland where Fatima's cousin lived. She took off her sunglasses and checked her cell phone, which had been ringing nonstop since she left home. Five missed calls from Maryam, the last one just minutes ago. The calls would continue until Maryam managed to get her on the phone.

"What's wrong?" Asma asked her sister.

"Nothing, why?"

"You called me five times."

"I was just calling to say hi. I— Boys! Put that down!"

Asma could hear her nephews in the background. "Maryam, let me call you back later this afternoon."

Maryam was back on the phone. "I'll be busy. I have to take Aunty Bushra and Lubna to physical therapy. I'm like the family chauffeur. You know, Saba should be the one driving them but she's been busy doing God knows what with Tariq. I keep having to remind her to cool it, they're not yet married."

"How's Lubna?"

"Loving the attention. Aunty and Lubna got so used to Kamran cooking that he's still doing it! Naveed's here almost every day bringing us food and— Zaki! I said to put that down! You're going to ruin your lunch."

"Maryam, I really have—

"I wish someone would cook for me. This whole thing has been so hard. I don't know why Aunty turned down Farooq's offer to have a physical therapist come to the house for Lubna. She knows I have the children to look after. Zayd, I'm going to count to three. One—"

"Maryam—"

"Two—"

"Maryam!"

"Good. Now leave, I'm trying to talk to Asma Khala. Like I was saying, it would've been so much more convenient. I don't know why Aunty is being so formal with Farooq. He and Lubna are practically engaged, apparently he asked Saba for Lubna's ring size."

"Maryam, I need to go." Asma couldn't hear anymore. Her stomach was going sour with every word, and she didn't want to ruin her lunch with Fatima. "I'm late."

"For what?"

"Lunch with Fatima."

"Fatima? Fatima Malik?"

"Yes, Fatima Malik. Do I have any other friends named Fatima?"

"Jeez, Asma, what's with the attitude?"

"Sorry, it's just that Abu is acting like he can't remember her."

"Of course I remember her. Maybe you can find out what happened with her husband. I heard they split up because he was cheating on her with a law student. How cliché."

And with that, Asma hung up on her sister.

"THIS PLACE IS AMAZING!"

Asma took in Fatima's cousin's loft—floor-to-ceiling windows, exposed brick and pipes, and an open floor plan with stainless steel appliances. What appeared to be extremely expensive artwork adorned the walls.

"I know, I feel like I'm on a TV set. Some legal drama about a high-powered, kick-ass attorney with a great job, a fabulous apartment, and a fridge stocked with fancy Italian sodas. You want one?"

"Sure," said Asma gazing out the window.

"God, the way the aunties used to talk about my cousin," said Fatima, shaking her head as she opened the fridge. "Even my mom—her own aunt! You should've heard her when she bought this place. 'Now she'll never get married,' she said, 'she's too independent.' Yes, because what man in his right mind would want to be with a woman who makes good money and owns a home."

Asma settled on a barstool across the counter from Fatima, who popped open a drink.

"Fatima, I owe you an apology," Asma said.

Fatima looked surprised. "For what?"

"For not believing you when you had your suspicions about Salman."

"Asma, please—you're not responsible for him cheating."

"No, but I shouldn't have tried to convince you that everything was okay. I should've encouraged you to listen to your gut."

"I'd had the gut feeling for a while. But I was in denial."

"You were under a lot of pressure. You know, with your fertility journey."

Fatima was quiet for a second.

"The thing is," she said, then stopped. She drew in her breath before starting again. "The thing is that the cheating wasn't even what I was worried about. It was everything else. I was so mad at my parents—but they said exactly what I was thinking deep down. I knew people would talk—about me, about my family. You know what the aunties are saying—that it's my fault. I didn't give him what he needed so he was forced to get it elsewhere."

Asma remembered what the aunties said at the ameen.

"I keep thinking about what will happen if we break up," Fatima continued. "People will be trying to set him up again before the divorce papers are even signed. And I'll be an old divorced hag at twenty-seven."

"It's so unfair," said Asma.

"It is. But I keep telling myself that this happened for a reason. I mean, I agreed to marry him for my parents' sake. I did what they wanted me to do, and what did it bring me? At least now I'm free from my pathological need to make them happy. It's not possible."

Asma sat for a second to take things in, to process Fatima's words on the futility of living her life for the sake of pleasing others, even her own parents.

"Anyway, enough of this. I'm so sick of thinking about it," Fatima said. "What's new with you? What's this I hear about you and Omar Khan?"

"What did you hear?"

"You know he's the hot single guy on everyone's radar. My cousin heard that he's seeing someone."

"We're just friends."

"Okay." Fatima smiled.

"We are! I mean, I like spending time with him. He's fun, he's cute."

Fatima raised her eyebrows, amused.

It was the first time Asma had spoken to Fatima about a guy other than Farooq. She felt inexplicably embarrassed. She shook her head and made a face. "You know he had that whole thing with Iman. Even though Rehana Aunty said she's not interested anymore."

"So, what's the problem, then?"

"I don't know—he's so smooth and charming and has that whole finance-guy thing going on. He's not someone I imagined myself with."

"You mean, he's not Farooq."

"Definitely not Farooq. The complete opposite."

"You can change your mind, you know. Allow someone else in."

Asma gulped down her Italian soda to avoid saying out loud to Fatima what she felt confused about inside. That she was beginning to wonder if she already had.

WHEN HER PHONE RANG DURING THE DRIVE back to Sacramento, Asma assumed it would be Maryam again. But instead, she saw the number for her old hospital on her caller ID.

"Hello, Asma?" Dr. Saucedo's voice was instantly recognizable, though it sounded a bit more strained than Asma remembered.

"Dr. Saucedo, so good to hear from you," Asma replied. "How are things in the ER?"

"That's what I'm calling about, actually," Dr. Saucedo replied. "I had a patient come through who asked for you when he was admitted. One of the Green Meadows residents. A Mr. Shepard?"

"Again?" Asma asked. "Tell me it's not another case of Legionnaires'. Last time I spoke with the health department, they assured me that they were going to make sure all the air conditioners in the facility were replaced in the next six weeks."

"Well, apparently they didn't follow through on that," Dr. Saucedo replied. "Because I'm told we've had three more cases of bacterial pneumonia come through in the last month. And unfortunately none of the residents here were on the lookout for it. I only realized it myself when Mr. Shepard was admitted."

"How are his stats?" Asma asked. "If he gets testy, just ask him about his granddaughter, her name is Olivia."

"Asma," Dr. Saucedo said, her voice threaded through with emotion. "I'm so sorry. I called because Mr. Shephard didn't respond to this last course of antibiotics. He passed away this morning."

"No!" Asma said, feeling the barrier that usually kept her professional life separate from her personal life crumble. She pulled the car over to the side of the highway and punched the button for her hazard lights, her eyes already filled with tears.

"I'm so sorry nobody here caught it," Dr. Saucedo said. "I wish I'd followed up myself."

"I should have done it," Asma replied. "Even if I wasn't working at the hospital, I should have made sure Green Meadows was in compliance."

"That wasn't your job, Asma," Dr. Saucedo replied. "It was incredible work for you to identify the pattern in the first place. Nobody else here did. You've got a real gift."

Asma felt her face crumple into tears. For Mr. Shepard, but also for herself. It was why she hadn't yet accepted the job offer from Sierra Oaks. She missed the ER, missed relying on her instincts to make decisions when seconds counted and lives hung in the balance. It was what she'd wanted ever since Farooq broke his leg falling into that ravine. Or perhaps even before that. Maybe she'd wanted this ever since her mother died. She wanted to be the one in control, making the decisions. So maybe she could make a difference for people like Mr. Shephard. Maybe, if she'd taken the job at her old hospital and remained in the Bay, Mr. Shepard would still be alive.

NOT EVEN ASMA'S LINGERING MELANCHOLY over Mr. Shepard's death proved to be enough to get her out of the child's birthday party that Iman was coordinating that weekend in San Jose. Despite Asma's explanation that she simply wasn't up for it, Iman insisted. It was Mr. Ibrahim's first party since his heart attack, after all, and everyone who was anyone was going to be there.

Asma took her time getting ready for the party, hoping that by dragging her feet she could delay their arrival. And, indeed, they were already running a half hour late when she finished dressing and came downstairs. She plopped down in front of the TV as she waited another half an hour for Mr. Ibrahim to change his clothes after deciding that a sherwani was too formal for a child's backyard party.

After the two-and-a-half-hour drive, which would've

been shorter if her father hadn't insisted on driving, they were over an hour late. They walked into the backyard through the house's side entrance and Asma's mouth dropped open in amazement. Not because they were some of the first guests to arrive—besides, of course, the child's non-Desi friends from preschool who were already there—but rather, because of the party's décor. It was a frog-themed party Pinterest board come to life.

Frogs were everywhere. From the frog lanterns adorning the trees and bushes, to the frog plates and green utensils, to the frog-shaped cake pops and cookies on the dessert table, to the real-life aquarium set up in the corner. Asma couldn't find a place to rest her eyes where she wouldn't be assaulted by a frog.

Iman, chatting with a man wearing a frog costume, spotted her family from across the yard. Her smile was fixed in place while talking to the frog but disappeared as she marched over to her family.

"You guys didn't wear green?"

"Oh no!" Mr. Ibrahim said. "I knew you mentioned how I was supposed to dress. I just couldn't remember."

"You guys are going to throw everything off."

"It'll be okay, Iman," Asma said. "There's enough green at this party for all of us."

"That's true—it really came together."

"It's beautiful! Exceptional!" Mr. Ibrahim crowed.

"You've outdone yourself" was all Rehana could say.

"You know what else is going to be green?" Iman asked. "Alia Memon. She was dying to coordinate this party, but Noreen was adamant that I do it."

Iman looked around the backyard admiringly. "This is so much better than that sheep-themed aqeeqah Alia coordinated last month for her cousin's new baby. It's like, we get it—it's an aqeeqah. You don't need to inundate us with sheep to remind us that they're being slaughtered."

"Don't you think this is a bit much?" asked Asma.

"No way." Iman turned on her heel, gesturing for her family to follow. "This is a milestone birthday!"

And as Iman led them farther into the backyard to show off the rest of the décor—"I can't wait for you to see the party favors; you're never going to guess what they are!"—Asma took in the huge banner hanging over the frog cake: *Happy 3rd Birthday!*

TWO HOURS AFTER THE START TIME NOTED ON the invitation, the party was in full swing. Children jumped in the bouncy house frog while their parents huddled in little packs around the backyard.

Like tadpole schools, thought Asma.

Asma stood by herself on the side of the yard, the only woman at the party her age without a husband and a child. She ate a frog-shaped cupcake, mesmerized by the man in a frog costume making frog balloons for a group of children. She had spent the first hour of the party texting frog pictures to Omar and giggling over his snarky replies. She was about to find Iman and see when they were finally allowed to leave when she saw some party latecomers entering through the side gate: Sophia and Yusef.

She and Sophia had texted occasionally over the past few months, but Asma hadn't spoken to her since moving to Sacramento. Asma was so surprised to see them she nearly stumbled putting her cupcake down on the table to greet Sophia with a big hug.

"What a pleasant surprise!" said Asma. "I didn't know you two were coming."

"Of course! Uncle is my father's cousin," Sophia said, looking just as happy to see Asma as she was to see them.

So not only were the Waheeds now wealthy, Asma thought, it turns out they had rich and well-connected family members too.

Asma shook off the realization and turned to greet Yusef, who stood next to Sophia, silently marveling at the scene before him in the backyard.

"This place is a trip," he said.

"I've never seen anything like it," Sophia agreed.

"And let's hope we never have to again," added Asma.

"Oh!" Sophia said, her face lighting up. "You weren't planning a frog-themed bridal shower for Lubna?"

Asma felt a jolt at Sophia's words, like a fiery gust of wind. And then a wave of nausea quickly followed.

"What?"

"Farooq called us with the news on our way here. We're thrilled!"

Asma felt the blood drain from her face. Farooq had proposed. She suddenly felt dizzy and her legs threatened to give out from under her.

"Are you okay?" Sophia looked at Asma with alarm.

"I'm just . . . too warm. I need to sit down."

"Quick, sweetie, grab that chair." Sophia ushered Yusef toward the folding chairs on the side of the yard.

Asma sat down on the chair Yusef brought her and took the bottle of water that Sophia snagged from a table nearby.

"It must be the heat, I didn't realize it was going to be so hot today," said Yusef.

Asma put her head in her lap. She wanted nothing more than for Sophia and Yusef to stop talking and leave so she could process the news. She squeezed her head with her knees, hoping to simultaneously drown out their conversation and convey that she needed time to herself.

It did neither.

"Can't say this whole engagement didn't take me by surprise," Sophia said.

"Me too," said Yusef.

"Although I suppose we should've seen it coming."

"Really? It seems so fast to me."

"Me too, but I think that's how people do it these days."

"I guess. Perhaps I'm just too old, I don't get these millennials—or are they Gen Z? Are we millennials?"

Their voices sounded increasingly remote as Asma shut her eyes, willing everything away. She wanted nothing more than for the people around her to disappear so she could give in to the overriding emotion coursing through her in that moment—grief. Because it seemed no matter how hard she'd tried to convince herself that she was moving forward and had done the right thing in getting out of Lubna's way when it came to Farooq, that didn't mean she'd stopped loving him. She had been a fool to think otherwise. All she wanted to do was cry into her hands.

But instead, she was in the middle of this unhinged green frog nightmare of a birthday party being tended to by Farooq's sister of all people. She had to hold it together. She forced herself to remember when she was a baby intern just starting out in the ER, the first time a patient crashed right in front of her. The woman slumped over, and when Asma felt for a pulse, she had none. It was the moment she knew she could be a doctor—and a great one—right then, when she refused to give in to her own panic. She simply refused to feel it, and then she set to work saving the woman's life. That was what Asma decided to do now, with her grief. She shoved it down, knowing it could have her later, and stood up and smiled at Farooq's sister. Made small talk for a few minutes surrounded by manic frog paraphernalia and then told Iman she was catching a ride home. Finally, when she got back to the house in Sacramento after the most expensive Uber she'd ever taken, she locked herself in the upstairs bathroom of their house, turned on the shower, and sobbed into a hand towel.

TWENTY-THREE

A sma didn't have Farooq's number. She combed through her inbox in a panic, hoping to find it buried in an email, but she came up empty. She tried his old number shortly after the party—on a prayer that it would somehow, miraculously work. But the number had been assigned years earlier to another person. Unable to think of a way to get it from her family without having to contend with unwelcome questions, she even resorted to calling his company. After fifteen minutes of working her way through the company's prerecorded phone directory, only to be accidentally cut off, she gave up.

Not that she knew what she was going to say to him, if she could get hold of him. Something along the lines of *Marry me, not Lubna*, perhaps? Even thinking of it made her shudder with embarrassment and shame. But still, she needed to talk to him. To make sure he was certain about Lubna, even though Asma was the one who had pushed him toward her. She wanted to make sure this all wasn't some big mistake.

Her phone had been buzzing continuously all afternoon. Mostly Maryam and Iman, probably dying to be the first to share Lubna's good news. Asma ignored all the calls and texts, which she knew would be about the engagement or wedding plans, undoubtedly already underway. She knew how her family was, like a SWAT team at the ready. And at the word *engagement* they would spring into coordinated action, breaking down doors and badgering florists for better prices. She wondered, with another drop of her stomach, if Iman would oversee planning the wedding. That would be quite a coup for her business—wedding planner for the hottest Desi couple of the year. But Asma couldn't think of any of it now. She would deal with all of that later.

And there was no time, anyway. As soon as she got home, Asma remembered: Omar was taking her out to celebrate her job offer tonight. She had tried to get out of it—calling him to tell him that she was beat after the party and wanted to take a rain check. But when his phone went straight to voicemail, she hung up without leaving a message. So there she was, trying to care about her hair while the love of her life was probably already discussing wedding plans with her sister-in-law. She would have laughed, if she weren't perpetually on the edge of tears.

Omar was on the board of the Sacramento History

Museum and had invited Asma along for their annual friends-and-family party, promising her a night of glitz and good food.

When she arrived, wearing a simple but no doubt expensive green dress that she had helped herself to from Iman's closet, Asma made her way into the lobby of the museum, peering at the artwork in the hallway while looking around for Omar. She was already regretting her decision not to cancel, concerned that the makeup she had unartfully applied wouldn't adequately cover up her red, puffy eyes. She hated coming to these types of functions by herself—she knew no one and felt uncomfortable at the thought of having to make small talk with strangers.

Still, there was the food. She took a mini quiche off the tray of a passing waiter, then stood in a corner of the lobby, pretending to be engrossed in the bronze bust of an old white man she didn't recognize.

"Asma! So lovely to see you!"

Asma turned at the sound of her name and found Dr. Sandra Kim, the head of Sierra Oaks Internal Medicine, who had interviewed her for the job.

"Dr. Kim!"

"I was just thinking about you this morning. We're waiting eagerly for a response to our offer."

"I was honored to receive it. I'm just discussing the logistics with my family." Asma hoped she would be forgiven for her white lie. Apart from Rehana, she still hadn't told her family about the job offer.

"We would be lucky to have you. Omar can't stop singing your praises." Dr. Kim looked around. "Where did he go, by the way? I thought I just saw him on the patio."

"Oh, yes," Asma said, relieved to hear where she could find Omar. "I just came in to get one of these." Asma held up her mini quiche, then stepped outside.

Guests were milling about the back patio, drinks in hand. Asma spotted Omar in a corner, his back to her, deep in conversation with a woman dressed in a black cocktail dress and strappy stilettos. As Asma approached, she was surprised to see Shagufta Dadabhoy, Mrs. Dadabhoy's granddaughter. This didn't exactly seem like the compulsive texter's scene, and Omar hadn't let on that he knew the Dadabhoys.

Asma stopped walking, wondering if she should slip away unnoticed, but it was too late. Shagufta had seen her. She stopped talking so suddenly that Omar turned around, curious to see who had interrupted their conversation.

"Hey, salaam," Asma said, waving her hand awkwardly, still holding the mini quiche. "Sorry, I didn't mean to interrupt."

"No worries, Asma," Omar said with a warm smile. "I'm just wrapping up here. I'll come find you in a minute."

Shagufta barely acknowledged Asma. True to form, she pulled out her phone and stared at the screen to forgo any interaction.

Asma headed toward the bar set up on the other side of the veranda. She popped the mini quiche in her mouth as she waited for the bartender to make her mocktail. She wondered why Shagufta was at the reception in the first place. Probably a courtesy invite, Asma thought, no doubt suggested by her father.

Asma threw a few dollars into the bartender's tip jar, then made her way to the patio railing and looked out onto the museum's grounds, dimly lit by decorative lamps strung from the trees. Although in the middle of Sacramento, the museum had acres of land where the groundskeepers tended to a small orchard.

Asma walked down the patio's wooden staircase to the rows of orange trees, a calm oasis away from the bustle of the guests. She found a small path between the trees and walked down the aisle, taking in the sharp citrus scent of the air. She was picking up a fallen orange from the ground when Omar joined her.

"You know, they have a buffet table full of hors d'oeuvres if you're hungry."

"Nothing like fresh fruit." Asma held up the orange. She looked behind Omar, motioning toward the museum's main building.

"I didn't realize the Dadabhoys would be here."

"Yeah, me neither."

"Lovers of history?"

"It appears so."

"What happened to Shagufta?"

"She wandered off somewhere." Omar looked around

at the trees surrounding them. "Let's walk toward the back, they have lemon trees. Perhaps we'll find Mrs. Dadabhoy back there, sucking on one."

Asma giggled as she and Omar set down the path. She let her hands brush over the leaves of the trees they passed.

"This reminds me of our backyard in Palo Alto. We used to hand out bags of oranges and lemons from the trees my mom planted when we were young."

"I remember your mother's garden here in Sacramento. It seemed like your mom was always outside when I came over."

Asma immediately regretted bringing up her mother. She'd closely guarded memories of her over the years, hoarding them in her mind, afraid that if she shared too much or too often, they would slip away.

"She was such a wonderful woman," Omar said, reaching down to pick up an orange strewn across their path. "She was the only aunty who ever wanted to know how *I* was doing—not how I was doing in school."

It had been years since Asma had spoken with anyone at length about her mother. She rarely remembered her with her father and sisters, afraid that the emotions unearthed by their memories would shake the foundation of the life she had built after her death. When she had wanted to talk about her, she had done so only with the two people she knew who could emotionally support her: Fatima and Farooq.

She still remembered the first time she talked about

her mother to Farooq. They had been studying on the quad, Asma hunched over her biology textbook. Farooq had reached up and brushed the hair out of her eyes. It had triggered a memory so vivid—*"How can you see the world through that hair!"* her mother used to say while sweeping Asma's hair out of her face—that Asma had burst into tears. Farooq had wrapped his arms around her and held her as she wept. He didn't ask any questions, didn't try to fix things or make it better. But that was Farooq. He understood, somehow, when something was beyond his reach. Too big a feeling, or too painful a memory. He understood that simply sitting there, unflinching, was enough. Unlike her father, who would be overcome by his own emotions, or her sisters, who would, no doubt, make it about themselves.

Asma turned toward the trees to hide the tears that sprang into her eyes. She had to stop thinking about Farooq. Still, the pain was so fresh that she couldn't help wrapping her arms around herself for a moment, as if she needed to hold herself together. Omar glanced in her direction, then slipped off his suit jacket and draped it over her shoulders. And though she wasn't cold, Asma was grateful for it. It felt comforting, to be cared for, even in the smallest of ways.

"After my father's stroke, I started thinking a lot about my legacy—how will I be remembered and for what?" Omar continued.

Asma dabbed at the corner of her eye with her finger. "We're not responsible for our parents' actions."

"No, we're not. But who they are forms so much of who we become. I mean, look at you. You're the backbone of your family. You're a testament to your mother's life. I'm sure she would've been so proud."

Asma choked up, unable to hold back her tears. She didn't know if she was crying because of Farooq or because she desperately missed her mother. Or because of the realization that she'd inadvertently repeated her mother's choices—changing the course of her life for the benefit of her family. Was this really what her mother would've wanted?

"Oh no, I'm so sorry, I didn't mean to upset you."

"It's fine, I'm fine." Asma brushed her face with the back of her hand, then searched in vain for a Kleenex in her purse.

"Stupid clutch purses," she said. "Why am I even carrying this? I barely have room for my phone."

"They look good," Omar said. "Must be made by a man."

He patted his pants pockets. Finding nothing, he reached up to undo the knot in his tie.

"Here, use this."

"No, no, it's okay!"

"Please, take it. Seems like I'm the only guy here wearing one. I forgot I'm in Sacramento."

Asma took the tie from Omar's outstretched hand and hesitated before using it to wipe her cheeks.

"Thanks," she said. "I owe you."

"You owe me nothing," Omar replied.

Omar's comment coupled with the way he was looking at her made Asma shift with both discomfort and
desire. She thought back to her conversations with
Fatima and Rehana about Omar as a love interest, all
of a sudden confused.

Asma was busy folding up the tie and avoiding eye
contact when she saw Omar's hand approaching her
face. And then he reached out and swept the hair back
from her eyes.

TWENTY-FOUR

⸺✦⸺

Asma woke up late the next morning to her phone buzzing incessantly. Maryam again. When Asma looked, she found that fourteen missed calls and texts had amassed since the previous night. Begrudgingly, she picked up the phone.

"Maryam?"

"Where have you been?" Maryam nearly shouted over the line. "I've been trying to get you for the past twenty-four hours? What if I were sick, or one of the boys? What if there was an emergency?"

"Well, I assume you would have called Iman or Abu and they could have walked down the hall and woken me up," Asma replied, still groggy from sleeping so hard after the previous night out with Omar. "Anyway, I know about Lubna's engagement. Sophia told me at the party."

"What party?"

"A three-year-old's frog-themed birthday party,"

Asma said, a palm pressed to her forehead. Already exhausted by this conversation.

"Oh right, Iman told me about that," Maryam replied. "But how does Sophia know already?"

"Farooq told her, of course," Asma replied. She felt a catch in her throat as she said his name. Her desperate, unsuccessful attempts to reach him the previous day had left her feeling spent and resigned. Perhaps this was how it would have to be from now on, she thought through her exhaustion. She'd have to grow accustomed to his presence in her life, no matter how painful, as Lubna's husband. Or would she? Her thoughts were all over the place.

Maybe it wouldn't all be bad. There was the glimmer of something when she thought of the previous night with Omar. And her new job offer in Sacramento. Perhaps there was a life she could have here. Maybe not the one she'd wanted for so long with Farooq, but something worthwhile all the same.

"Licking his wounds, I imagine," Maryam said. "I mean, we all think it's very sudden. Almost nobody saw it coming. Though, not to blame the victim, but he should have been more careful. Those high-powered business types think they're immune. He was traveling so much for work, it's no wonder Lubna's attention was elsewhere."

"Maryam, I have no idea what you're talking about," Asma said, dragging herself out of bed and rubbing her eyes, some of yesterday's makeup smearing across her cheeks. She'd been so worn out over the emotional roller coaster of the previous day, she had just splashed some water on her skin and crawled into bed.

"I know, we were all totally confused too," Maryam continued. "Aunty Bushra is so upset, she thinks Lubna led him on. She's been trying to get hold of him, but he's not answering anyone's calls. It's like he just disappeared."

"Who?" Asma asked, trying to keep up with Maryam's manic pace as her brain was still turning on. "Who disappeared?"

"Farooq," Maryam replied, drawing out the name as if Asma wouldn't recognize it.

"What?" Asma repeated. "Wait, Farooq isn't answering anyone's calls?"

"Asma, am I not speaking English? Why is this so hard to follow?"

"Tell me again. From the beginning. Why can't anyone get hold of Farooq?"

"Oh, I don't know," Maryam said, her voice suddenly dripping with sarcasm. "Maybe because Lubna just got engaged to one of his friends? I mean, is that a good enough reason?"

The phone nearly slipped from Asma's grasp, and she fumbled to catch it.

"Maryam, Maryam," Asma said, interrupting Maryam's continuing tirade about how Asma really needed to pay better attention. "Who is Lubna engaged to?"

"*Naveed!*" Maryam replied, shouting the name at

Asma. "Honestly, where have you been? Lubna threw Farooq over for Naveed!"

"What?" Asma asked, suddenly breathless.

"Yeah, apparently Farooq asked Kamran to cook for Lubna while she was at the rehab center—you know, hospital food is garbage—and Naveed is still off from work and has all this free time, so he would drop the food off. So I guess all those weeks together . . . they just fell for each other!"

"I can't believe it," Asma said, sitting down hard on her bed. Farooq was not getting married. Asma felt so dizzy she put her head between her knees, as she had the day before with Sophia, still gripping the phone.

"And poor Farooq too," Maryam said, apparently not realizing Asma's shock over the phone. "Apparently this isn't the first time he's been dumped pretty hard. I guess there was some girl in college too. Still, I bet he never guessed he'd get dumped again after making all that money! But honestly, I give Lubna credit for her decision. Love over money. It's very mature. Something must have been knocked into place when she had that fall and hit her head."

"Right," Asma said, and her voice must have sounded vacant, because Maryam finally took notice.

"Asma, are you sure you're not sick? You sound a little . . . slow today."

"I'm fine," Asma said, clearing her throat. "Actually, Maryam, I have to go."

"Okay, well, act surprised when Lubna tells you, all right? You didn't hear any of this from me."

"Okay, Maryam," Asma said, hanging up the phone. She sat there, breathing hard for a few minutes, willing her heart rate to come back down. But it was all too much, the rush of relief she'd felt when Maryam had said the words. Lubna was engaged to Naveed. Not Farooq. The thoughts swirled around in Asma's head.

But the longer Asma sat on the bed, the lighter she felt. Soon a small smile crept over her face.

For the first time since Lubna's accident, she felt something toward Farooq that she never thought she'd feel again: hope.

THE SOUTH ASIAN ALLIANCE FOR LANGUAGE AND Reading's Literacy Gala was the *it* function of the year—an annual gathering of the who's who of Northern California's Pakistani elite. On this night, the Bay Area's richest and most exclusive Pakistani families paid thousands of dollars to put on their fanciest clothes and jewelry and gather in a swanky hotel, be treated to a gourmet five-course plated meal, drink alcohol surreptitiously from the hotel bar, and raise money for South Asia's most vulnerable of populations: poor girls deprived of basic life necessities like food and education.

For years, Mr. Ibrahim had been dying to attend, prior attempts thwarted by poor timing and a lack of business connections. But this year was his chance, and he wasn't going to let a lowly heart attack stop him. Omar's fund had purchased a table at the dinner months earlier, and Mr. Ibrahim had claimed seats for the Ibrahim family at the table almost before Omar could offer.

Asma had been planning to feign illness at the last minute. She couldn't think of a function more outside her comfort zone and she wasn't yet ready to see Omar. She had ignored his calls all week, unsure of how to reconcile whatever was going on between the two of them with her new information about Farooq's lack of a relationship with Lubna. Omar had texted her that he wanted to talk, but Asma decided she needed to figure out what she was feeling before they did.

She changed her mind about the gala after hearing about Lubna's engagement to Naveed. If Maryam was right, that Farooq had gone incommunicado, the gala might be her only opportunity to see him. She was desperate to talk to him, to figure out if they still had a chance. Yusef was the keynote speaker, so Farooq was sure to be there.

Asma kept her eyes peeled for Farooq from the minute she entered the hotel lobby with her father and Iman. They followed the signs to the pre-event reception in the grand ballroom's majestic foyer, decorated with huge, multicolored floral arrangements. Waiters in matching black-and-white uniforms carried trays of mango lassi shots to temper the spiciness of the appetizers from the buffet station that sat at the center of the room.

The first people Asma recognized were the last people she had any interest in seeing: the Dadabhoys. Mrs. Dadabhoy and Shagufta stood at a small cocktail table, the sour look on Mrs. Dadabhoy's face and Shagufta's preoccupation with her cell phone keeping other guests at bay. But not Mr. Ibrahim and Iman, who made a beeline for their table.

Asma held back and looked around the reception. Farooq was nowhere to be found. She moved in on the appetizers and piled up her plate, then stood in a corner trying to look natural while balancing her mound of mini kabobs. She gave up when the chutney began to drip off the side of her plate and joined her family and the Dadabhoys at the cocktail table.

Asma walked up in time to hear her father giving a running commentary on the other guests.

"There's Dr. Ali," said Mr. Ibrahim. "He just bought a new house in San Ramon. It was over three million dollars. Five baths, but only four bedrooms."

Mrs. Dadabhoy looked bored. She paid no attention as Mr. Ibrahim babbled on, instead scanning the crowd and checking out each person who crossed their path.

Someone entering the reception caught her eye and she cut off Mr. Ibrahim midsentence.

"Farooq Waheed?"

Asma's head jerked toward the entrance. Farooq

had entered the reception, alone. He was wearing a sharp black suit and stood by himself. He looked around the reception hall, tall and confident, smiling and nodding at those who passed, all of whom seemed to know exactly who he was. The sight of him took Asma's breath away.

"Do you know his company is worth hundreds of millions of dollars?" Mrs. Dadabhoy asked.

"Yes, indeed," Mr. Ibrahim beamed, proudly. "MashAllah, he did all that without even going to college!"

Asma almost spat out the kabob she was chewing and glared at her father. She knew he was a devoted social climber, but this hypocrisy and rewriting of history was too much for her to bear.

She was about to stalk off when Omar joined them at the table.

"Asma, there you are! I was hoping we could speak for a few moments."

Asma panicked as she saw Farooq heading, seemingly unaware, in their direction. The last thing she wanted was to be forced into making small talk with him in front of this crowd.

"Sure—I'm just going to run to the bathroom. We can chat when I get back."

But once again, she was too late. Farooq was just a few feet away. Her father called out.

"Farooq! Farooq Waheed!"

Farooq turned, looking shocked when he saw who

was beckoning him. He was too close to ignore Mr. Ibrahim. He walked to the table and gave his salaams, making steady eye contact with Asma as he greeted her.

"This is Farooq," Mr. Ibrahim said to Mrs. Dadabhoy, as if Farooq were an old golf buddy. "His sister stays in our Palo Alto home. And his brother—Dr. Waheed—is a professor in the Ivy League!" Mr. Ibrahim spoke as though he were bragging about his own children.

Asma noticed Farooq's back stiffen, but he kept a strained smile on his face. "How is your health, Uncle?"

Asma felt a rush of love so strong that she wanted to cry. Even though the man standing in front of Farooq had been the source of the greatest insult and heartbreak of his life, Farooq had the decency to inquire after his well-being.

"Much better, beta." Mr. Ibrahim smiled and patted Farooq on the shoulder.

"Farooq's brother-in-law Yusef Abdullah will be giving the keynote tonight," Asma said, a desperate attempt to get Farooq to look at her again. "He's a writer, so it'll be really interesting to hear him speak to the importance of literacy in development work."

"Indeed," Mr. Ibrahim agreed. "He's a very famous author. I am a big fan of his work."

Asma wanted to lunge across the table and strangle her father. He hadn't so much as read the back of one of Yusef's books.

"I've heard so much about his latest book," Omar

said. "I really need to pick it up. I just haven't had the time with work." Omar looked at Asma. "I'm sure you're going to miss reading for pleasure, too, once you start your new job."

"Her new what?" Farooq said, his eyes darting from Omar to Asma.

"Asma received an offer to join the top practice in Sacramento," Omar announced to the table.

"You did?" Mr. Ibrahim asked.

Asma stared at Omar, speechless, as he continued.

"It's an amazing opportunity and I know she'll be fantastic—they are very enthusiastic about having her on staff."

Asma felt light-headed. What was happening?

"Congratulations, that's wonderful news," Farooq said, though she could still tell, all these years later, when he was lying.

She opened her mouth to tell him that Omar was mistaken, that she hadn't yet accepted anything, but before she could, he nodded in the direction of the foyer's entrance.

"It was nice to see you all. My sister and Yusef just arrived. Please excuse me."

"WHAT WAS THAT ALL ABOUT?" ASMA HISSED, dragging Omar away from the table the minute Farooq was out of sight.

"What was what about?"

"You! Announcing my job offer to my family!"

"You hadn't told them yet?"

"No!"

Asma was almost shaking with frustration. She couldn't believe Omar—he had done everything wrong. Why had she tried to go against her gut and convince herself that he could be right for her? He was just like almost everyone else in her life—completely oblivious to what Asma wanted. Any feelings she had started to develop toward him were incinerated by anger. Their conversation was interrupted by the flashing of the foyer lights as the doors to the ballroom swung open. She and Omar were separated as they were swarmed by guests jostling toward the entrance. Asma found herself swept along with the crowd into the ballroom.

Elaborately decorated banquet tables—complete with centerpieces of cascading flowers—dotted the hall, positioned toward a raised stage at the front, flanked by both Pakistani and American flags. Attendees mingled as a small string ensemble played folk music in the corner, waiters mixing among guests and ushering them toward their tables.

Omar waved at Asma from a table near the front where his fund name was prominently displayed. She ignored him, looking around the hall for Farooq. She spotted him a few tables away from Omar's, greeting guests at his table. She made her way toward him, but as she did, the MC tapped the microphone asking everyone to take their seats. Asma hurried back over to

Omar's table, annoyed that he had saved her a seat right next to him.

"I'm so sorry," he said as she sat down, "I had no idea you hadn't yet told them, but I was a bit preoccupied. I need to talk to you about something."

Asma wasn't listening, her attention still on Farooq. She tried to catch his eye, but he wasn't looking her way. And, despite her best efforts to telepathically communicate with him, he didn't look her way for the duration of the dinner. By the time Yusef took the stage for his keynote, Asma was a mess. She tried to tune in to his remarks but kept losing focus until the very end:

"But what we can learn from these inspiring young women is the importance of perseverance, determination, and seizing opportunities even when it's difficult. It's never, ever too late. Thank you so much, it's been an honor."

The audience broke out into applause and cheers and stood up as Yusef left the stage. Asma didn't take her eyes off Farooq. He finally looked her way and met her gaze. They stood looking at each other for a second until Asma felt a light touch on her back. It was Omar, placing her dupatta on her shoulder. He leaned in and whispered in her ear.

"It fell on the floor."

Asma looked quickly back at Farooq, who was staring at his phone. He looked stricken when he glanced back up at Asma, and suddenly he was heading for the door.

"Be right back," Asma muttered to the table before taking off after him.

She rushed through the crowd, still standing and clapping. By the time she made her way into the lobby, Farooq was at the far end, striding toward the exit.

"Farooq! Farooq!"

He slowed down as Asma hurried toward him.

"I'm sorry we didn't get the chance to talk earlier. And I was so sorry to hear about Lubna."

"Yes, well. I've been thrown over again, it seems," Farooq said, his eyes averted. The strong, confident man she had been reacquainted with over the past few months was gone. He looked defeated, crumpled, and would not meet her gaze.

"I thought we could maybe take a walk outside and talk?" Asma persisted.

Now Farooq was looking behind her. She turned. Omar had followed her out of the ballroom.

"I'm sorry, I didn't mean to interrupt," Omar said, extending a hand to Farooq. "We haven't been formally introduced. I'm Omar Khan."

"Farooq Waheed," Farooq said brusquely, shaking his hand. "I don't mean to be rude, but I'm in a bit of a hurry. Some other time, Asma?" He said her name as if he were addressing a casual acquaintance. Someone he wanted to brush off. It stung enough that Asma took a step back and realized her arm was now brushing

Omar's. Omar raised a steadying hand to Asma's back—perhaps a reflex, or perhaps a possessive move, in the presence of another man. But it didn't matter, because Farooq obviously believed it was the latter.

"Have a good night, you two," Farooq said.

And before Asma could explain—to tell Farooq that he was wrong, that she only wanted him—Farooq left the building.

THE WOMEN'S PRAYER HALL AT THE MOSQUE was emptying out except for a group of ladies at the front hugging and crying. It was the funeral for one of their distantly related uncles; Asma didn't even remember him. Asma felt guilty for spending most of the janaza prayer going over the events from the Literacy Gala and figuring out how she could get in touch with Farooq. She'd just have to suck it up and ask Lubna for his number. As she stood with Iman near the back of the room, waiting for the crowd to clear so they could find their shoes jammed in the shoe racks outside the hall, she whispered some extra duas for the old man who had passed.

"He was ninety-one," Iman said. "Why is everyone acting like this was a big shock? He literally died of old age."

"You and Abu were the ones who wanted to come." Asma considered suggesting to Iman that she, too, offer up extra prayers.

Two ladies broke off from the group and made their way toward the exit. As Iman saw them approaching, she whispered, "These aunties are the worst. I'm out."

Iman left so quickly that Asma didn't have a chance to follow. She was forced to greet the women, whom she only vaguely recognized, with salaams and hugs. They were thrilled to see her.

"Ibrahim bhai's daughter, right? Mubarak, beti, so nice to hear your good news."

"Good news?"

"MashAllah, it's about time—you must be, what, thirty-eight?" the second aunty asked.

"I'm twenty-seven—"

The first aunty cut Asma off before she could finish.

"You know, these girls wait so long. They say, after I'm done with school, then after I'm done with this and that."

"Then they get so picky!" said the second aunty.

They spoke to each other as if Asma were not standing right in front of them. She tried to follow along, unsure what they were talking about.

"I just don't *feel* it, these girls say," said the first aunty. "What is this feeling?"

Asma was saved by a buzz in her pocket—a text from Fatima: *TELL ME WHAT'S HAPPENING!!!*

Asma looked up from her phone to excuse herself, but the aunties were busy talking. They didn't even notice when she slipped out of the prayer hall. But her aunty escape was thwarted when she encountered another group of them congregated outside the mosque. They greeted her with excitement.

"Finally! MashAllah!"

"Alhamdulillah, Alhamdulillah. Such wonderful news!" another one said, just as an old man walking by overheard and scowled.

"Inna lillahi wa inna illaihi rajioon. So sorry for your loss," said the aunty to the old man.

Asma wondered if the aunties had her mixed up with someone else. But then her phone was buzzing in her hand, and she stepped away from the aunties and the uncles to pick it up.

"You have to tell me everything," said Fatima.

"What?" Asma said. "I feel like I'm having an out-of-body experience right now. Why is everyone acting like I won the lottery and I'm the last to know?"

"Oh my God, you actually don't know, do you?" Fatima said.

"Fatima!" Asma replied. "What?"

"Okay, you have to get Instagram, I'm serious this time. Omar Khan posted a story of himself ring shopping at Tiffany's."

"Ring shopping?" Asma asked, her mouth suddenly dry. "Like . . ."

"Like an engagement ring. He's holding a small velvet ring box in the photo. And it says 'You all can keep a secret, right?' With a diamond ring and a heart emoji. Asma . . . is he about to ask you to marry him?"

"No," Asma replied. "Absolutely not. We've hung

out maybe two or three times? There's no way." But then a thought occurred to her. "Fatima, when did he post that photo?"

"Like, at seven last night, why?"

Asma thought back; he must have posted it right before arriving at the Literacy Gala. Her heart rate picked up. Was that why he kept trying to get her alone? And why he was so possessive around Farooq? Another thought occurred to her then—Farooq. Maybe that was what he saw on his phone. Maybe that was the reason he'd left in such a hurry and been so terse with her when he did. Did Farooq believe that Omar was going to ask Asma to marry him that same night?

"People have been congratulating me all morning," Asma said. "They must assume that Omar and I are engaged! And what about Iman? Rehana said she's not interested, but Iman has never said anything to me."

"Well . . ." Fatima said carefully, "have you considered what you'll say if he does ask you?"

"I'm going to throw up," Asma replied.

"Oh, honey," Fatima said, and Asma could hear the reassuring smile in her voice. "Whatever you do, don't do that."

TWENTY-FIVE

A sma needed to think things through before she
talked to anyone else—much less Omar. She called
a Lyft and silenced her phone in anticipation of Maryam
catching this gossip all the way in San Jose, but when
she glanced down a few minutes later, there was a missed
call from Omar. Her stomach did an uncomfortable
flip-flop, and she nearly asked the Lyft driver to pull
over so she could get some air.

When she finally got home, Asma walked into the
house to find Iman and Mr. Ibrahim sitting in the living
room with a man she'd never seen.

"Asma, beti, you're home. We have some wonderful
news about an engagement."

"I promise you, it's not true," Asma replied. "I'm
not engaged, nobody asked, it's not happening. Yet. Or
at all. Or yet."

"Asma," said Mr. Ibrahim patiently, "I'm not sure
what exactly you mean, but we're not talking about you."

"Oh." Asma was so confused. "Okay." She looked at the man, who smiled warmly at her.

"This is Mrs. Gulnaz Dadabhoy's son—and Shagufta's father, of course—Zubayr Dadabhoy. He has just come to ask for Iman's hand."

Asma felt faint. She looked at Iman, who sat on the love seat with a smug look on her face.

Iman was getting married to . . . Shagufta's father?

"COME, ZUBAYR, I WANT TO SHOW YOU OUR garden," Mr. Ibrahim said.

Asma breathed a sigh of relief when Mr. Ibrahim led Shagufta's father out of the room. She felt as though she was going to crawl out of her skin in his presence. Now Asma understood why Iman had seemed so secretive for the past few months. Why Rehana had been so certain that Iman had no interest in getting back together with Omar. But still. Zubayr Dadabhoy? Father of the incessant texter? Son of the sour old lady with the bad manners and the plantation-style house? Asma thought back to the afternoon she spent sitting in that living room, its furniture still covered in plastic, while Mrs. Dadabhoy wondered aloud what sort of match might be suitable for Asma. Only now did Asma realize why her father hadn't enlisted Mrs. Dadabhoy's help for Iman . . . because that match had already been made.

As soon as they were alone, Asma turned to Iman.

"Okay, tell me everything."

"Can you believe it?"

"Um, no, I can't," replied Asma. "What's going on?"

"I'm engaged," Iman replied. "To Zubayr."

"Why?" Asma asked.

"Because that's what you do when you want to marry someone." Iman spoke slowly, as if explaining the concept of an engagement to a child.

"Iman, you don't have to do this."

"Do what?"

"You don't have to marry some old guy just because you're about to turn thirty."

"He's not that old, Asma. He's in his midforties. I'm like Amal Clooney. I could never have married a man my own age."

"He's related to us!"

"Our third cousin, like, three times removed. It's fine. This is how royalty used to marry."

Asma could only shake her head.

"I want to do this, Asma," Iman said, reaching over and taking Asma's hand. "You're the only one who doesn't do what you want."

"What's that supposed to mean?" Asma asked, pulling her hand away.

"You sit around, waiting for things to work out for you, and when they don't, you blame everyone else."

"What are you talking about?"

"Where should I start? How about moving here? No

one asked you to. But you left your beloved hospital, then blamed all of us for your choice."

"I didn't blame anyone."

"You've been complaining since you moved. We all know you'd rather be in Palo Alto working in that dirty ER, no matter the opportunities you have here," Iman said. "And what about Farooq?"

"What about him?"

"You think I didn't know about that? Abu said no all those years ago and you just gave up—you didn't even fight for him."

"You don't know what you're talking about," Asma said, bristling at the implication that her breakup with Farooq was somehow a result of her own failing. Still, the comment stung.

"I don't?" Iman asked. "You don't think I heard you crying every night for months? I tried, Asma. I tried to talk to you but you didn't even notice."

Asma stared at Iman. She had known? Asma faintly remembered Iman knocking on her door during a few of her crying sessions; she had quickly composed herself before answering the door. It had never occurred to her that Iman was trying in her own way to provide an opening for them to talk.

"And then fine, you get a second chance because life has been good to you and then you're such a wimp with that too. You just sit back and let him hook up with Lubna."

"Shut up, Iman."

Iman stopped talking, perhaps realizing that she'd gone too far. The two of them sat in silence.

"Why can't you just be happy for me?" Iman asked finally.

"I *am* happy for you."

"No, you're not. You think you're better than me."

"I do not!"

"Of course you do. You think you're better than all of us. You're always making fun of my events. And you mock Maryam, the whiny stay-at-home mom. You're the busy and important doctor."

"I never said that."

"You didn't have to. You say it in the way you talk to us, the way you act, the way you look when we're talking."

"I'm not going to sit here and listen to this." Asma rose from the couch and started out of the living room.

"Then, go!" Iman stood up. "I'm the one who has been here all this time, taking care of Abu."

At this, Asma spun around. "You? Taking care of Abu? How? Spending his money?"

"See! That's what I'm talking about. Yes, I spend his money. But I'm also the one who has been living here with him, looking after him, making sure he's taken care of."

"Haven't I been living here too?"

"Not because you want to. It's out of guilt. And obligation. And you remind us of that every day," yelled

Iman. "You act like you're the only one who misses Ammi. Don't you think I do too? Don't you think it hurt that she turned to *you* to take care of everything? Even though I'm older? She didn't trust me! But I've been here. I never left his side!"

Iman was ugly crying, her face red and crumpled. She wiped her face with the back of her hand.

Asma was speechless. Iman always acted like she had it all together. Asma had fallen apart at her mother's funeral and Iman had been perfectly composed— she had remained that way throughout the mourning period and in the years that followed. This was the first time Asma had ever seen Iman cry.

Asma looked at her sister and saw her, perhaps for the first time. It had all been an act, a protective shield. A responsibility Iman felt, being the oldest daughter, to keep it together, a secret vow she had made to a woman she didn't think believed in her. Maybe it was a way for her to hide her pain and continue with her life, which, until now, Asma realized, had not gone according to her plan.

But as Asma stood there staring at her sister, the crack of vulnerability that had opened up on her face closed. Before Asma could say anything, Iman turned and ran out of the room.

ASMA REMEMBERED VERY LITTLE OF THE DAYS following her mother's death, the memories jumbled into one another. The house full of people, the unwanted hugs and kisses, the food—so much food. One day, unable to take the crying and Quran recitation that had been playing on loop nonstop, Asma left. She walked without a destination and eventually found herself in a park near the house where she sat for hours, thinking about nothing and everything at the same time.

After the confrontation with Iman, Asma also started walking, until she found herself in another park. The perfectly trimmed grass, carefully pruned flower bushes, and brick pathways looked eerily familiar, as if she'd rediscovered that same place from thirteen years ago.

Asma couldn't stop replaying the events of the day, especially Iman's accusations. She was overcome with shame and regret. Iman was right. Asma did think she was better than her sisters. Iman's events were frivolous and over-the-top and Maryam complained way too much about nothing.

But it was more than just that.

Asma realized her contempt for her sisters lay in how they'd chosen to live their lives: they had happily gone along with the status quo.

Iman had stayed at her father's side without complaint—over the years she had provided him company and an audience and had never even attempted to move out or live on her own. Maryam, too, had done what was expected of her. She had met a nice man ap-

proved by her father and had married young into a re-
spectable family.

And yet. Her sisters were both happy and doing
well. Iman was good at her job, her business was thriv-
ing, and she had just met a man who seemed to be
everything she'd been looking for. And, despite all of
Maryam's whining, Asma knew she was grateful for
her beautiful children, a stable and dependable partner,
and a loving extended family.

It was only Asma who was unhappy. She had convinced herself over the years that it was her mother's
dying wish and her responsibility to take care of her
family—managing her father's medical care, keeping
watch over their finances, and doing what was required behind the scenes to make sure things didn't
fall apart. She had played the martyr card and had
done it all without being asked, yet blamed her family. Asma didn't think this was what her mother intended. It certainly wasn't what Asma wanted. But her
chosen role in her family had given her an excuse to
stay stagnant in her life—to not have to make hard
choices or fight for what she wanted. Like her job. And
Farooq.

And here she was. Thirteen years after the death of
her mother and nothing had changed. She was still in
the same place, unable to make moves without being
paralyzed by the fear of what might happen if she had
to take responsibility for the decisions in her life. She

was like this garden in Sacramento with its stupid brick pathway headed absolutely nowhere.

No more.

Asma sat in the park until the sun set, her resolve strengthening, then picked up her phone.

TWENTY-SIX

Fatima called her as Asma was walking back to the house.

"So . . ." her best friend began. "That might have been a bit of a false alarm. About Omar. And the engagement ring."

"What do you mean?" Asma asked. Not that it mattered anymore. Asma was not going to marry Omar Khan even if he asked, of that much she was certain.

"Well, it turns out that ring was for someone else."

"Someone else?"

"He posted a photo of the two of them. He calls her 'Shaggy'? I don't know, she looks a little young."

"Shaggy?" Asma said. "I have no idea who that could be. But listen, Fatima, I honestly don't care. When I tell you that Omar is the last thing on my mind right now, you've got to believe me."

"Okay, so what is on your mind right now?" Fatima asked.

"Other than the fact that Iman is engaged out of

nowhere to an elderly cousin of ours, and we had a huge fight? Long story short, I realized that I have to find a way to finally stop making excuses and go after the life that I want," Asma replied. Shocked at how easily the words came out.

"I mean, those aren't bad things to be thinking about," Fatima said. "But wait, Iman is engaged? What is in the air over there in Sacramento?"

"No idea," Asma replied. "I'm just glad that I haven't caught it yet."

"So you're not the least bit disappointed about Omar?"

"Surprisingly not," Asma said. "I told you he wasn't my type. Never trust a man that smooth."

"Who is this cousin Iman is engaged to?"

"You're not going to believe it, Fatima," Asma said. "He's in his forties, and his mother is awful. His whole family, really. I mean, they're absolutely stinking rich, but the emphasis is really on the stinking part."

"Okay, but . . . is she happy?" Fatima asked.

"She says she is," Asma replied. "I guess she is. It's what she's wanted." Asma let out a long breath. "Okay, okay. I know I need to be less judgmental. Believe me, Iman just gave me that whole speech too. But really, this guy has a teenage daughter! And if you ever met her you'd know . . ."

Asma couldn't finish the sentence. A flash of revelation hit her like a lightning bolt, until something like a manic giggle was rising in her throat.

"Oh, Fatima," Asma said. "You're never going to believe this."

"What?" Fatima asked.

"I think I know who Omar is engaged to," Asma replied.

MR. IBRAHIM AND IMAN WERE BACK AT THE kitchen table when Asma returned home, hours after she had first left.

"Omar Khan is engaged to Shagufta Dadabhoy?" Asma asked by way of greeting. Her father looked up from his phone.

"Yes," Mr. Ibrahim replied. "We just found out ourselves."

"And it doesn't bother you that he basically used us to get close to their family? And marry a nineteen-year-old for her father's business connections and her money?"

Rehana, washing dishes at the sink, turned off the faucet.

"Beti," Rehana said, "it would only bother us if he were making a fool of you. Shagufta is an entirely different story."

Asma looked at Iman, who had not acknowledged her presence.

"That haramzada doesn't think I know he used us to get to the Dadabhoys?" Mr. Ibrahim said. "He's a bigger fool than I thought. After all, I'll be his new stepgrandfather. He will never make another move without my knowledge or permission."

"Checkmate, bitch," Iman said under her breath.

Asma was surprised at how shrewd Mr. Ibrahim seemed now. She had always thought her father a bit of a simpleton when it came to navigating their financial and social interactions—he was easily dazzled by money and status and seemed to have little insight into all the social politics and underlying complexities. But he was right, Omar would answer to Mr. Ibrahim in all things from now on. In this instance, her father had come out ahead. Revenge at last.

Rehana set down a stack of plates on the table. Asma grabbed her hand, still wet from washing dishes.

"Aunty, can you please sit down?" Asma asked. "I want to talk to all of you. You too, Iman."

Iman put her phone down.

Once Asma had her family's attention, she took a deep breath.

"I wanted to let you all know that I turned down the position at Dr. Kim's private practice."

"You did what?" Mr. Ibrahim asked.

"I know it's a good opportunity," Asma continued quickly. "But I don't want it. I want to move back to the Bay. I only moved here to take care of you, Abu. But it was out of obligation."

Mr. Ibrahim didn't respond.

"I called Dr. Saucedo. The job they had open has

been filled, but she said she'd help me—that she would do whatever I needed her to do to get a position in emergency medicine." Asma paused and gathered herself before continuing. "And there's still an apartment in my old building. I just put down a deposit."

During Asma's walk home from the park, she had imagined her father's possible reactions to her news and practiced her responses. She braced herself for his outburst.

But it didn't come.

Instead, he slumped down in his seat. He looked defeated. Rehana placed her hand on Asma's arm.

"Is this about Omar?"

"No, Aunty. I'd made my decision about Omar even before I knew about his engagement to Shagufta. This has nothing to do with anyone else. It's about me. I love emergency medicine. And I loved my old hospital from the moment I started residency. I worked hard to be valued there. I never wanted to move back here."

Asma looked at Iman.

"Iman, you were right. I'm sorry. I should have been more honest about how I felt from the beginning. I've been angry and I blamed you all."

Iman didn't say anything, but her eyes moistened.

"So you want to move back and live on your own and work as a doctor?"

"Yes, Abu."

Mr. Ibrahim sat quietly before looking at Asma.

"What will people say?"

Finally, a question that Asma was prepared for.

"They won't say anything if you stand by me, Abu. They'll say, there's a man who loves and supports his daughters."

"No, they won't." Iman broke her silence. "We're not some white family in an after-school special. They'll talk. They'll never stop talking. They'll say that Abu has no control over his daughters. And that you'll never get married because you're too independent and career-minded.

"But," Iman continued before Asma could respond. "Who cares? These aunties are *so* annoying. And most of them have their own skeletons. We can't live our lives based on the fear of what they might say—especially because you know they're talking about us anyway."

Asma smiled at her sister. She knew how much Iman's opinion mattered to their father. That she was dispensing it in Asma's favor made her grateful. Perhaps this marked a small shift in their relationship, one where Iman came into her role as the older sister looking out for Asma.

Mr. Ibrahim nodded as if considering what Iman had just said.

"I think it's a good idea too," Rehana said.

"Really, Aunty?" Once upon a time, Asma had seen Rehana as a friend and an ally. Now, however, she wondered if Rehana wasn't trying to make up for her mistakes.

"Yes, beti." When Rehana turned to her, it was clear from her face that this was her way of apologizing. "I've only wanted what was best for you. And I realize now that I haven't always been right."

"Well then," Mr. Ibrahim said with a sigh. "If all of you are fine with this, then I guess I am too."

Asma looked at her father, astonished. She hadn't been expecting to convince him so easily. Was that it? Asma searched her father's face to see if he was upset—if the anger and yelling would come later. He just looked tired.

"I'm going to wash for dinner." Mr. Ibrahim pushed his seat back from the table and stood up. But he didn't leave.

"You know, your mother wanted to be a doctor," Mr. Ibrahim said after a moment. He turned to Asma. "Sometimes it's hard for me. You remind me so much of her."

Asma's eyes filled with tears as her father bent down, brushed the hair out of her face, and kissed her on the forehead.

FOR THE FOURTH TIME THAT YEAR, ASMA PACKED all of her belongings into boxes and loaded them into the trunk of her car. It didn't seem like very much, this physical representation of her life on her own. A few boxes of clothes and books. Keepsakes and some kitchen stuff she'd never unpacked after she moved from the

Bay. The box of her mother's saris, which Iman had insisted Asma take with her.

"I'm going to need all new clothes of my own now," Iman said, giving a regretful little shrug that Asma knew covered her delight at the prospect of being the wife of a wealthy business tycoon. "I don't think I'll have room for these anymore."

Asma knew better, though. Iman loved their mother's clothes just as much as Asma did. But it was a signal from her sister, Asma understood. A sign of approval and forgiveness. That Asma should have their mother's clothes.

Asma embraced Iman and Rehana and her father in the driveway of their house before she set off for Palo Alto. It felt significant, though she'd only be two hours away. She'd never left home before without the intention of someday coming back.

She stopped at the post office before she got on the highway, dropping the package she'd wrapped that morning in the mailbox. Another piece of her past wrapped up in brown paper and sent off into the world, every move she made that day leaving her feeling lighter, untethered, ready to move forward with her life in spite of what anyone else might think. And then she was on the highway, chasing the afternoon sun toward the horizon, headed west. Headed home, she thought, the term popping unprompted into her head. Home. The idea made her smile.

———

BY THE TIME ASMA MADE IT TO THE QUREISHIS',
she was an hour late for Lubna's party. The house looked
like it was being transformed into a clothing store when
Asma stepped inside, with wire racks of beautiful gar-
ments in the entryway and on the landing above the
staircase. Boxes of shoes and jewelry were stacked
against the walls. It paid to be an Instagram influencer
getting married, it seemed. Desi designers and boutique
owners were sending over racks of their finest stock
nearly every day, Lubna reported to Maryam. They had
all decided to make a weekend of going through the
bounty and selecting what Lubna would actually keep.

She found Maryam standing outside Lubna's room,
with the door partially ajar.

"I'm sorry I'm so late. Did you get my text?"

"No, the boys are playing with my phone. Where's
Iman?"

"She'll be here in a bit." Asma lowered her voice.
"She's out with her boo."

"That's Uncle Boo to you," Maryam said with a giggle. Then, looking at Asma with concern: "You okay?"

"Yeah—why?"

"You've been all over the place recently. Like, literally," Maryam said. "Palo Alto to San Jose to Sacramento back to Palo Alto. I just wanted to check in."

Asma looked at her younger sister with affection—

this was the first time Maryam had ever really asked how she was doing. "This is the best I've felt in months."

"Good," said Maryam. "Just remember, even though you are now the only one in our entire family who is not married or coupled off—you're not alone."

Asma chuckled. "Thanks for the reminder."

"I'm serious, Asma," Maryam said. "You're always taking care of everyone. It's time to sit back and let us take care of you. I mean, I *am* a mother. I have the whole nurturing thing down, it comes with the job."

Asma reached for her sister, the one she'd been emotionally tending to for most of her life. She'd spent so much time taking care of Maryam that she hadn't stopped to let her grow into the woman, and mother, she could be. And here she was, with the emotional maturity to recognize that it was time for things to change.

"I am lucky to have you," Asma said, choking up.

"Asma, beti, is that you?" Bushra called out from inside the room. "Did you hear back from the restaurant?"

Asma gave Maryam a big hug and dried her eyes.

"Iman said she'll negotiate the contract, Aunty," she called back. "She can get you the price you want, no problem."

It was Maryam's turn to lower her voice.

"I told Aunty we should just postpone the engagement until Karachi Tandoori is available, I don't know why she's insisting on Lahore Kabob."

"The food at these restaurants all tastes the same."

"It's not about the food. It's about class."

"Oh, right. Of course."

"Speaking of class, did you see Shagufta's engagement ring?" Maryam rapped on the doorframe. "Saba, show Asma that picture of Shagufta's ring!"

"It's huge!" Saba appeared at the bedroom door, her phone open to Instagram.

"Tacky big, if you ask me," Lubna added from inside.

"Enough with this picture nonsense, hurry up and finish dressing!" said Bushra.

"We're hurrying, we're hurrying!"

Maryam grabbed the phone from Saba's hand as Lubna cried out, "*Ow!* Ammi!"

"Stop moving!"

Asma peered over Maryam's shoulder at the picture on Saba's phone.

"Wow, it *is* huge."

"You mean, wow, it *is* tacky."

"They're not that tacky!" said Hassan.

Hassan, Naveed, and Farooq were coming upstairs, all of them wearing matching turbans.

"Looking good!" Asma said with a laugh.

Farooq startled at the sight of her, then slipped the turban off his head, his cheeks reddening.

"Those things might be uglier than Shagufta's engagement ring," Maryam said, passing Saba's phone to Hassan.

"Who is the sucker who bought her this?" Hassan asked.

"Omar."

"Omar?"

"Omar Khan."

"Omar Khan?"

"Are you going to just repeat after me?"

Out of the corner of her eye, Asma saw Farooq—who had thus far avoided eye contact—look sharply at her. Had he not heard about Omar's engagement to someone who was most decidedly . . . not Asma?

"Good riddance," Maryam was saying. "I hear he's crooked. Plus, gross—what kind of man in his early thirties marries a nineteen-year-old?"

Maryam was so busy shaking her head in disgust that she didn't notice a look pass between the men that Asma could only interpret as "a lucky man." Asma made a face at them.

"Okay, she's ready!" announced Saba.

"Wait, hold on!" Asma said. "Naveed can't see the bride!"

"Oh, come on," said Naveed, "it's just her engagement outfit."

"Oh, yes!" Bushra said from inside the room. "These Americans say it's bad luck."

Hassan flipped the turban off Naveed's head. "Go check that Kamran has everything he needs in the kitchen. I'm getting hungry."

Naveed put up a minor protest as the others forced

him back downstairs. Once they were out of sight, Asma gave Saba the go-ahead.

The bedroom door opened as Saba announced, "Presenting . . . our beautiful bride!"

Lubna stepped out in a deep green lengha, the floor-length skirt covered in delicate, hand-stitched embroidery. She looked gorgeous. As Asma and Maryam crowded around her to admire the intricate work, Asma noticed that not everyone was focused on Lubna's outfit. Farooq stood back from the group, his eyes never leaving Asma.

KAMRAN HAD OUTDONE HIMSELF WITH THEIR dinner. They came back downstairs to find the table covered with a nearly overwhelming amount of food, which Lubna set to work photographing for Instagram, tagging Kamran's restaurant. As they began to sit down, Asma attempted to maneuver herself so that she could sit beside Farooq, but Kamran ended up sandwiched between the two of them. Naveed, sitting at the head of the table, cracked jokes that kept Lubna and Saba in stitches for the duration of the meal. Asma marveled over his transformation from the last time they had all been together. How far he'd come since she first met him in San Francisco, months ago.

"It's like he's a whole new person," Asma said to Kamran.

"I was just thinking the same thing. My sister's

engagement broke off before she met Naveed's father. It took her years to recover. Looks like Naveed is nothing like his mother."

"I'm not surprised," Asma said. "Men bounce back much quicker from these things."

Farooq choked on his water and began coughing violently. Asma peered around Kamran with concern as Kamran pounded him on the back. "You okay?"

"I'm fine," said Farooq, reddening once more.

"So you think it's easier for men to get over women than the other way around?" Kamran asked.

"I don't think men get as emotionally attached," Asma replied, not because she really believed it. More because she wanted to see Farooq's reaction. To bait him, even, into saying something.

"Maybe we move on faster to forget, to bury our pain," Kamran said. "Women talk about everything. Men talk about nothing."

"Maybe. Or maybe guys don't need to emotionally invest because they have so many more options."

"How so?" asked Kamran.

"Men can marry women from back home. Or non-Muslim women. Or women much younger than themselves."

"Women can too," Kamran said.

"Come on, you know that's not true," Asma said with a pointed look. "Imagine what would happen if your niece came home and said she wanted to marry her Latino, non-Muslim friend. Everyone would freak out. But that's exactly what happened with the imam at our mosque, and everyone celebrated. MashAllah, he found someone! A new Muslim!"

Kamran opened his mouth to respond, then closed it. The rest of their little party was leaning back from the table, complaining of being stuffed, though they hadn't made much of a dent in the food.

"I want to finish this conversation later," Kamran said. "But right now I need to go make chai."

"I'll start packing this up," said Asma, and started gathering the plates of uneaten food. Maryam helped her for a minute before being distracted by Saba and Lubna, who were debating whether to post sneak-peek snippets of her outfits to Instagram. But when Asma turned, Farooq had taken the platter Maryam had set down and was helping Asma clear the table. They carried what they could into the kitchen, setting the platters on the counter and beginning to wrap them up. Kamran, who was pouring out cups of chai, glanced at the two of them.

"Um," he said, blushing a bit. "Would you two mind taking over for a minute? I think I hear Naveed calling . . ." He hustled out of the kitchen before Asma could tell him that she was pretty sure Naveed was in the bathroom. She looked at Farooq, who appeared to be trying to keep from grinning as the two of them were left alone in the kitchen.

"Smooth," Farooq said, almost to himself. He motioned to the cups of chai. "Shall we try this again?"

"Sure," Asma replied, feeling her pulse pick up.

"Did you mean what you were saying in there? About how men aren't as hurt by heartbreak?" Farooq asked, as he held out the first empty cup.

"No," Asma said quickly. "I don't really know why I said that." They both fell silent then. She'd wanted so badly to talk to him alone, but now her mind was blank when it came to where she should start or what she should say. They were through filling four cups of chai before she rustled up the courage. "I sent you something," she blurted out finally. She wondered if the package had even reached him—she'd sent it to his office, after all, and who knew if it had finally made it to his desk.

Farooq nodded.

"Yeah. I got it," he replied. "And the note. But . . ." He paused. "I wasn't sure what it meant, exactly."

Asma considered what she'd written on the paper she'd tucked into the copy of *The Rumi Collection* that he'd given her all those years ago. She told him it was hard for her to part with the book, because it had meant so much to her, but that she felt like he should have it. She had loved it for so long that the only way she could move forward was to let it go, to give it to someone who might love it anew. At the time, Asma thought her message had been clear, that she wanted to let go of her past mistakes and start fresh, start over. But now she wondered if Farooq had thought she was closing the door on their past so she could pursue a future with

Omar. Thinking back, it was likely that it was *exactly* what Farooq was thinking.

"I meant it to be a gesture, I guess," Asma said, feeling a bit breathless. They'd had so many misdirects and false starts, so many mixed signals. All she wanted was to wipe all of it clean. "That I'm ready to let go of all our mistakes."

"Our mistakes?" Farooq asked.

"The fact that I hurt you. I listened to my family instead of doing what I wanted," Asma said. "That's a lesson I'm only starting to learn, I guess. And Lubna . . ."

"That was not my finest hour," Farooq said, shaking his head. "I was still so angry with you, when you reappeared in my life. I thought . . . here's a beautiful young woman. That she was your sister-in-law felt right, in a vindictive way. It was cruel and unfair to Lubna, and I'm sorry for it."

"Thank you," Asma replied. They'd finished filling the cups, but both were lingering. Asma began wrapping up the food, just to have something to do with her hands.

"I'm just relieved that she's found what she wanted," Farooq continued. "But I needed you and your family to see that I could offer more than money. Trying to prove a point and protecting my ego." He shook his head, a sheen of tears in his eyes. "It was a mistake."

"We both made them," Asma replied, stopping what she was doing and reaching over, clasping his hand in hers. She cleared her throat, blinking back her own tears. "So that's what I was trying to say, I guess. That I'm ready to forget the past, and only focus on what's ahead."

"I wish it were that easy," Farooq replied, pulling his hand away. Asma's heart dropped. Of course it wasn't that easy. They'd both done so much to hurt the other—how could they ever pretend as though none of it had happened? But Farooq was opening his wallet and pulling out a folded strip of paper. He held it out to Asma. "I can't let go of the past," Farooq said. "I carry it with me, always."

Asma took the paper from his outstretched hand and unfolded it. It was the same strip of photo booth photos she'd thrown away, all those months ago.

"You carried it with you, all this time?" Asma asked, suddenly out of breath.

Farooq nodded. "I couldn't let myself forget what it was like to be that happy."

Asma had been waiting for these words for so many years, but now that she had them she couldn't think—she couldn't move. The pain, the hope, the love—it was all too much. She burst into tears. She was about to tell him she still loved him, despite all their time apart, and despite all the ways they'd failed each other over the years, when Maryam and Bushra came into the kitchen.

"I don't know why we can't keep a babysitter. I mean—"

Bushra cut Maryam off when she saw Asma.

"Asma, beti! What's wrong?"

"Nothing...I just..." Asma began, but she couldn't find the words. Maryam elbowed past Farooq and considered her sister, frowning.

"It must be the haleem, I thought it tasted weird," said Maryam.

"It's okay, I'm okay," Asma said, wiping her eyes and trying to stop her tears.

"You need some rest," Maryam said with her newfound resolve to take care of Asma. "I'll have Hassan take you home, you look awful."

"It's fine, I can go myself." She glanced back at Farooq, who met her gaze. A moment of understanding.

"Yeah, I bet it was the haleem. My stomach's starting to feel weird too," Maryam said, already clutching her belly.

"The haleem was great, don't you dare say anything to Kamran," Asma ordered Maryam as she headed out of the kitchen and toward the front door. She opened the door and waited, holding her breath. But when the sound of approaching footsteps made her turn, she was disappointed to see Hassan there instead of Farooq.

"Maryam said you're not feeling well?" Hassan said.

"It's okay, really," Asma replied, glancing over Hassan's shoulder as Farooq appeared behind him. "I probably just need some fresh air."

"Are you sure you don't want me to take you home?" he asked, jingling his car keys. "I wouldn't mind heading home and taking a nap while everyone is occupied here."

"I'm fine," Asma replied. "I'll just sit outside for a few minutes, see if I feel better."

Hassan nodded, then glanced behind him.

"Farooq, you mind taking Asma home if she doesn't feel better in a few? I swear, doctors make the worst patients."

Farooq hesitated and looked from Asma to Hassan and back to Asma again, unsure.

Asma nodded. "Yes, please—that would be perfect."

Hassan left Asma and Farooq standing face-to-face on the Qureishis' doorstep. They stood smiling at each other for a few moments—completely oblivious to the vendors streaming in and out of the house and Maryam calling after Hassan from inside—before Farooq reached over to sweep the hair out of Asma's face and take her hand.

TWENTY-SEVEN

A sma hit her phone to check the time. 4:15.

"I'm running late," Asma said to Fatima. "Farooq will be here any minute!"

Asma's shift at the hospital ended at three, but by the time she explained her patient's chart to the chief resident and made it to her car, it was three thirty. She raced to her apartment and jumped in the shower, patting herself on the back for having the foresight to iron her sari early that morning before she went into work.

She'd been back at the hospital for several months; the only reminder that she'd ever left was the new class of residents whose uncertainty reminded Asma so much of her own journey. Dr. Saucedo had managed to secure Asma a moonlighting position upon her return and for weeks they had strategized how to restructure the ER's budget to secure the funds for an additional position. Their scheming had paid off. Asma was now a bona fide ER doctor. And working right alongside her old friend Jackson, who had applied for the open ER position when Asma left for Sacramento.

"I'm Dr. S's sloppy seconds," he'd said with a smile. *"She's so relieved you're back."*

Asma pleated her sari and tucked it into her matching petticoat as Fatima peered at her through FaceTime.

"Am I doing this right?" she asked.

"Straighten it out a little and then fasten the pleats with a pin."

The rest of Lubna's bridal party had planned to meet at the hotel in downtown San Jose at noon for hair and makeup, and to have their matching bridesmaid saris professionally wrapped. Asma had assured everyone that she could do it herself—then spent her lunch breaks for the past week watching YouTube tutorials and enlisting Fatima's help over FaceTime.

Fatima had served Salman with divorce papers the month before. Despite the pleas of their families to try to reconcile, they had mutually agreed to part ways. Salman went back to life as a boring corporate lawyer—now on thin ice with his firm because of his poor judgment in hooking up with a summer associate. Fatima had packed up her things and moved to New York, ready for a fresh start and maybe a chance of once again making it into Columbia's School of Architecture. *"As a wise woman once told me, it's never too late,"* she'd said to Asma at the airport, both of them in tears.

Asma's phone buzzed, a text appearing over Fatima's face: *I'm here.*

Asma threw the sari's pallu over her shoulder and posed for Fatima, who gave her one final thumbs-up. She glanced at her makeup bag on the corner of her dresser, then shook her head. No time. She'd get Maryam to do her makeup at the hotel.

Asma brushed her hair with one hand while typing on her cell phone with the other: *Be down in a sec.*

Asma and Farooq's moment at the Qureishis' had been the start of a beautiful new phase in their relationship. They had ditched the rest of the group that afternoon, driven to Santa Cruz, and spoken for hours— starting with an apology from Asma.

"I was scared, I know that now. I felt like I would lose something either way. My family or you. And after everything with my mom . . ." Asma trailed off, realizing that she finally had the opportunity to tell Farooq the truth. "I didn't realize that losing you would be the biggest regret of my life."

Farooq's response to Asma's apology was a reminder of why she had fallen in love with him in the first place.

"When my company was bought, all I could think about was you. I was still so angry and wanted to show you that I made it. But the more time I spent around you, the more difficult it was for me to be angry. You had done it. You had become this amazing doctor. I was so proud of you. I thought . . . maybe my heart-break was worth that, in the end. You, being able to do so much good."

Mr. Ibrahim was unable to hide his surprise when

Farooq paid him a visit to ask for Asma's hand in marriage. It was Rehana who reminded him that Asma and Farooq had been engaged many years earlier, and that they had opposed the match. Asma had to bite her tongue as Mr. Ibrahim insisted that he would have remembered a man as handsome as Farooq from a family as distinguished as the Waheeds. Even so, Mr. Ibrahim—quick to assure Asma that he was a humble man, not above admitting that he may have been wrong—had given them his most sincere of blessings.

Another couple hadn't been so lucky. When word reached Mrs. Gulnaz Dadabhoy about Omar's father's financial schemes, she had been appalled. She had refused to agree to Omar and Shagufta's engagement until Omar had repaid some of his father's debt. First on his list: his father's onetime friend and client, Mr. Muhammad Ibrahim. The sum was so substantial that Mr. Ibrahim was able to pay off his debts and could afford to move back into the family's McMansion at the end of the Abdullahs' lease if he wanted, although he was quite content in Sacramento surrounded by his distinguished relatives.

But that was not the end of Omar Khan's troubles. The insider gossip from the aunties—as well as Asma's direct line to the family through Iman—was that neither Mrs. Dadabhoy nor Zubayr was pleased with Omar. Word was that his soon-to-be in-laws planned to severely limit his access to the family money. The prenup, according to Iman, had been described as "medieval" by Omar's lawyers, but Omar had no choice but to sign it.

Asma almost felt sorry for him. Not only did he have to contend with the Dadabhoys' disapproval, but he was also now permanently in her father's and Iman's social orbit. His comeuppance seemed to have dissolved their anger toward him, his new place at the bottom rung of the family hierarchy bringing them nothing but glee. Asma witnessed this new social order during Iman's engagement party, where Omar was banished to the periphery of the festivities, given the cold shoulder by most. He redeemed himself only marginally when he attempted to apologize to Asma for stringing her along. "You're amazing, Asma," he had said with a level of familiarity totally inappropriate for someone who was engaged to another. "I have nothing but the utmost respect for you."

Asma grabbed her purse—a clutch—from her nightstand and raced out of her bedroom. She smiled as she passed through her apartment, her walls adorned with pictures and mementos that captured the loves of her life—her photo booth picture with Farooq, the Halloween morning picture of her and her mom, and the beautiful red silk sari her mother had worn to the grand opening of her parents' showroom, carefully framed in a shadow box. And there was her dining room table, fully assembled—still IKEA, but put together with Farooq's help and now covered with boxes of his stuff. Her sisters had rolled their eyes when they heard that

Farooq would move into Asma's apartment after their wedding. But Asma wasn't about to break her lease for a second time.

Asma was almost at the front door when she noticed that she had forgotten to pin her pallu, which kept slipping off her shoulder. She rummaged through her console table drawer for an extra safety pin and stuck it clumsily in her shoulder, poking herself in the process. She made a mental note to ask Iman to fix it at the hotel. It would be good to see her sister. Asma had left her family in Sacramento confident for the first time ever that they would be just fine without her—although she did persuade them to hire a gardener for her mother's poor, neglected garden. They wouldn't have time to tend to it anyway. Iman was booked solid for as far as her calendar would go, with most of her events related to all their family's upcoming weddings—Lubna and Saba Qureishi's, in addition to Asma's and her own.

With a last look around her apartment, Asma swung open the front door and startled at the sight of Farooq on her front stoop. He was wearing a dark gray suit with a purple tie and pocket square that matched Asma's sari. He seemed amused.

"I look crazy, right?" she said, patting her hair. "I probably should've given myself a bit more time to get ready."

"I was wondering what you were doing in there."

"Sorry, I was rushing. My shift ended late and then I had to wrap this thing," she said, gesturing toward her sari pleats, which had come unraveled. "I didn't mean to keep you waiting."

Farooq smiled, then pulled a bouquet of purple peonies out from behind his back.

"I waited eight years—what's another fifteen minutes?"

Asma laughed as Farooq entered her apartment, scooped her into his arms, and closed the door behind them.

They were home, together. At last.

ACKNOWLEDGMENTS

I am so grateful to so many—

My wonderful agent, Ayesha Pande: I so appreciate your patience and encouragement over the many years it took me to learn how to write a book!

My dear friend Jessica Chiarella: If not for you, this book would've lived as a draft on my computer until the end of time. Thank you for helping me over the finish line.

My lovely editor, Maya Ziv: Thank you for your support, enthusiasm, and brilliant insights into deepening this story.

All the friends and editors who read my manuscript in various states over the years and helped me shape this book: Christine Sowder, Su'ad Abdul-Khabeer, Khalid Maznavi, Arielle Eckstut, Julie Mosow, Christine Pride, Ella Kurki.

My writing soulmate, Ayesha Mattu: I'm so blessed to have started on my book journey with you.

My extraordinary writing community: Camille Acker, Tanya Lane, VONA, VoCL, and the brave and inspiring writers of *Love, InshAllah* and *Salaam, Love*.

My hive mind: Clique, Green Mile to Silk Road, Trip to Sequoia Country.

The village that helped me carve out time to write while juggling life with small children: Feroza Maznavi, Muhammad Maznavi, Glenn Evans, Carolyn Evans, Sahana Ward, Hadiyah Muhammad, Hannah El-Amin.

My beautiful family: David, Layla, Maliha, and Idris. I love you so much!

ABOUT THE AUTHOR

Nura Maznavi is a writer, a lawyer, and the coeditor of the groundbreaking anthologies *Love, InshAllah: The Secret Love Lives of American Muslim Women* and *Salaam, Love: American Muslim Men on Love, Sex and Intimacy*. She lives in Southern California with her husband and three children.